CHEERS *To*
The DUKE

CHEERS To The DUKE

SALLY MacKENZIE

ZEBRA BOOKS
KENSINGTON PUBLISHING CORP.
www.kensingtonbooks.com

ZEBRA BOOKS are published by

Kensington Publishing Corp.
119 West 40th Street
New York, NY 10018

All Kensington titles, imprints, and distributed lines are available at special quantity discounts for bulk purchases for sales promotion, premiums, fund-raising, educational, or institutional use.

Special book excerpts or customized printings can also be created to fit specific needs. For details, write or phone the office of the Kensington Sales Manager: Attn.: Sales Department. Kensington Publishing Corp., 119 West 40th Street, New York, NY 10018. Phone: 1-800-221-2647.

Zebra and the Z logo Reg. U.S. Pat. & TM Off.

First Printing: October 2021
ISBN-13: 978-1-4201-4673-8
ISBN-13: 978-1-4201-4676-9 (eBook)

10 9 8 7 6 5 4 3 2 1

Printed in the United States of America

For my amazing, brilliant, clear-eyed, patient editor,
Esi Sogah who, as always,
has worked her magic on this book.

For my agent, Jessica Faust,
who talked me down off the ledge.

For Katharine—welcome to the clan!

For Ian—I hope by the time this book is out in the world,
we have been able to come see you.

For Kevin—as always.

And for my readers—thank you so much
for welcoming my characters into your lives.

Chapter One

End of June, Puddledon Manor

The widowed Lady Havenridge—Jo to her friends—strode up the path from the hopyard, Freddie, her brown and white spaniel, at her heels.

"The plants looked healthy, didn't they, Freddie?"

Freddie tented his brows over his warm brown eyes and whined low in his throat.

Oh, hell. He was right, of course. He remembered as well as she did what Pen said every year at this time: *It doesn't matter how the plants look. Blight or bugs can destroy the entire crop overnight.*

And if *that* happened . . .

No hops meant no ale. No ale, no income. No income, no Home. No Home, no place for her and all the other women and children to live.

Anxiety churned in the pit of her stomach. She worried about the hops every year, but this year was far, far worse. This year Pen wasn't here to keep a close eye on things. Pen *and* Caro, their former brewer.

Now the crop—and the Home's survival—rested solely on Jo's shoulders.

Her anxiety boiled over.

"Ten years, Freddie! *Over* ten years. The three of us built the Home from nothing, and then"—she snapped her fingers—"just like that, they *both* marry and go off to live on their husbands' estates, *deserting* me."

Pen had wed the Earl of Darrow last summer; Caro, Viscount Oakland just after Christmas.

"I understand Pen. Her daughter must come first, and the earl *is* Harriet's father. But Caro? You know how *she* feels about men."

Freddie growled. He shared Caro's low opinion of that breed.

"Oh, I'm happy for them." And she was—when she wasn't feeling abandoned and overwhelmed. "And I *am* thankful they got their husbands to contribute to the Home's coffers, but . . ." She shook her head. "You know the old saying—out of sight, out of mind. They'll get busy with their new lives—their new *families*—and all too soon the donations will stop, and *then* where will we be? We already rely far too much on the whims of the nobility."

Freddie raised his brows.

Well, yes. He was right. The noble on whose whims the Home most relied—the Duke of Grainger, the man who owned the Manor and provided the bulk of their funds—*had* proven to be a dependable sort.

Thank *God*.

"I imagine it's because he wasn't born to the nobility, Freddie. You'll remember that until a little over a year ago the man was just a London solicitor."

That had been another stressful time. The influenza had

swept through the Duke of Grainger's principal seat when the old duke, his heir, *and* the spare had all been in residence. They, as well as a large part of the household, had taken ill and died in a matter of days, muddying the succession so much it wasn't clear for *months* who was next in line. She'd combed the London papers daily, looking for any clue, dissecting every rumor. The Home's future depended on the man. If he was a callous sort, if he decided he wanted Puddledon Manor for his own use . . .

Freddie bumped against Jo's leg, and she reached down to scratch his ears.

"But he didn't toss us all out into the hedgerows, did he, Freddie?" Things had turned out well, *far* better than she'd hoped. "You have to admit the duke's been very supportive"—she smiled—"once he learned what the Home was, that is."

Apparently, the estate books had been as muddied as the succession. The new duke had sent his friend, the Earl of Darrow, down to Little Puddledon last August to discover what or who was behind one cryptic entry.

And that was how the earl found Pen once more and learned he had a daughter.

Freddie barked his agreement; though, being a dog, he likely didn't fully understand how much Jo had come to rely on the duke. The man was an excellent source of common—and not so common—sense. *And* he was a father himself, so he understood children's needs.

She'd been corresponding with him since shortly after Pen married. Once Caro left her, too, she'd become even more dependent on his advice. She had no one else to consult.

Well, no one I trust.

A squirrel dashed across their path at that moment. Freddie gave a delighted—and perhaps relieved—bark and bounded after it.

For one mad moment Jo wished *she* could forget her worries so easily and hie off across a field—a *figurative* field—chasing any new thing that caught her fancy. That she could escape—

Escape?!

She blinked, staring at Freddie but no longer seeing him.

People escape from traps. *I don't feel trapped, do I?*

No, of course she didn't. The Home—the Benevolent Home for the Maintenance and Support of Spinsters, Widows, and Abandoned Women and their Unfortunate Children—wasn't a trap. On the contrary, it had *freed* her. It had given her a purpose when she'd most needed one.

When Freddie—her *husband* Freddie, the handsome, charming, irresponsible rogue she'd married when she'd been hardly more than a girl—had lost everything on the turn of a card, put a pistol to his head, and made her a widow, she'd been . . .

Not shocked. Freddie had lived recklessly. She'd half expected him to come to such an end. Nor sad, really, beyond the feeling of regret anyone would have for a life ended too soon. No, the emotion she most remembered feeling was dread, a horrible, paralyzing, *sinking* fear that she'd be sent home, back to her father's house and her father's control.

I didn't stay paralyzed for long.

No. Within minutes, she'd stiffened her spine and vowed she'd not submit to a man—*any* man—ever again.

She was still a bit in awe of how she'd gathered her courage and asked the old Duke of Grainger, the man who'd won the game Freddie had lost, to let her come here to Little Puddledon. And then, once her mourning period was over, she'd persuaded him to let her turn Puddledon Manor into the Home, a place where women could live their lives free of male interference.

She took a deep breath and then blew it out slowly.

I managed then, when I was young and on my own for the first time. I can manage now.

The squirrel had scampered up a tree and out onto a branch high above Freddie's head. Now it chattered down at him while the dog jumped and spun below, barking wildly.

"Give up, Freddie. You don't want that squirrel. What would you do with it if you caught it?"

Freddie stopped, looked at her, and then looked back at the furry rodent. He must have concluded she had the right of it, because he gave one last bark, lifted his leg to water the tree, and trotted back to her.

I do sometimes wish I could just piss on my problems and walk away, though.

Jo frowned. *No, of course, I don't. What is the matter with me?*

She shook her head. It was past time to stop this foolish fretting and get back to her office. She needed to go over the books once more, looking for yet another way—or several ways—to economize.

Economizing isn't going to solve your biggest problem.

She sighed. All right, yes. It wasn't pounds and pence that kept her awake at night.

"To be honest, Freddie, it's—"

Something moved in the bushes, and Freddie darted off again to investigate.

Jo heaved another sigh and adjusted her bonnet. Perhaps

it was just as well she'd been interrupted. She'd not broached this subject with Freddie before, but it had been getting harder and harder to keep her tongue between her teeth.

When Caro had written to say she was marrying Viscount Oakland, she'd not sent the letter via the post. No, she'd had it delivered by the three London lightskirts she'd met at the viscount's estate and who, she wrote, now wished to live at the Home.

There was the problem.

Oh, the lightskirt part was fine. Many of the Home's residents had been in that trade. And while Fanny and Polly didn't have any experience in what was needed here—agriculture and brewing—they were learning. Livy, however . . .

Lud!

It was Livy—Olivia Williams—who really bedeviled Jo.

Well, *threatened* might be a better word.

Which was silly. In many ways, Livy understood Jo's concerns as none of the other women did. She'd been an independent businesswoman herself.

Except her business had been matching Cyprians with randy noblemen.

Which she could *not* do here. Jo had made that quite, *quite* clear.

Fortunately, there were no noblemen in the area. Livy wouldn't make much money from the local farmers. Still, Jo had taken the precaution of putting a lock on the door to the estate's folly, the gothic cottage that occasionally served as guest accommodations and where, she felt certain, Pen had conceived Harriet's brother.

The baby whose christening Jo had declined to attend.

Regret brushed her heart. It would have been nice to see Pen and Harriet again—and the baby, of course. And Pen had written that Caro would be there, too, with her new husband. Jo would like to meet him. *And* Pen had asked Jo to be the baby's godmother.

If only . . .

I can't be away from the Home now. I have to keep an eye on the hop plants.

More to the point, she had to keep an eye on Livy.

Freddie trotted back to her, and she stooped down, cupping his face in her hands, looking deep into his understanding eyes. She couldn't keep her worries to herself a moment longer.

"What is the matter with me, Freddie? I *know* I need help running the Home. I should be *happy* Livy is here. But . . ." She shook her head. "I don't trust her. Yet when I try to puzzle out why—what I think she'd do that would harm the Home—I draw a blank. Her ideas aren't bad. I just don't like them."

Be honest. Freddie will keep your confidence.

She leaned closer. Dropped her voice.

"I think she wants to push me aside and take over. She's got Fanny's and Polly's allegiance already, of course, and I suspect she's trying to persuade some of the other women to favor her as well."

Power struggles among the Home's residents were nothing new, but being sucked into them herself was. She *settled* disputes. She was the calm one. Rational. Cleareyed. Able to see both sides of any issue.

She was none of those things now.

"The Home was *my* idea, Freddie. Mine. Pen and Caro helped, but I was the one who came up with the notion. I was the one who got it started."

The Home was her *life*. It had given her a purpose all

those years ago, but, more importantly, it gave her a purpose *now*. If it was taken from her—

Freddie licked her nose, and she laughed, dropping her hold on him and standing up. He always knew how to make her feel better.

"You're right. I just need to give myself time to adjust. There have been a lot of changes. Once we get through the next few months, once the hops are harvested, I'm sure I'll feel better."

Freddie gave her what might have been a doubtful look, but she let it go without comment and started walking again, up the path, past the brewhouse, across the crushed stone yard toward her—

"Jo!"

Jo's stomach sank. That was Rosamund Lewis.

She looked over to see Rosamund hurrying toward her from the front of the house, Winifred Williams striding along behind.

"Livy sent me to get you."

Jo's stomach sank lower. Rosamund had that sparkle in her eyes that suggested she was gleefully awaiting some emotional fireworks.

But there was a sparkle in *Winifred's* eyes, too. That was very odd. Winifred was in charge of their stables—their very *small* stables, Jo's aging horse, Bumblebee, being the sole occupant. The only time Jo could remember seeing Winifred this excited was last August when the Earl of Darrow had left his Arabian with her for a few hours.

The earl wasn't here now, of course. He was at his estate with Pen, getting ready to welcome a houseful of guests to celebrate the christening of their son, his heir, Philip Arthur Edward Graham, Viscount Hurley.

This time regret plopped its heavy hindquarters smack down on her heart.

She shoved it away. "Is there a problem?"

Rosamund smiled slyly. "Not yet."

Jo frowned at her, but then her attention was claimed by Winifred, who was now close enough to grab Jo's arm.

"You have to see them, Jo." Winifred squeezed and gave her arm a little shake.

Jo winced. Winifred might be getting on in years, her hair gone quite gray, but she was still very strong.

"Ah." Jo stepped back, and, thankfully, Winifred let her go. She did hope she wouldn't find bruises later. "Them?"

"The horses. Four beautiful chestnuts. Not as beautiful as the earl's Arabian—or, at least, not beautiful in the same way. But still, beautiful." Winifred sighed with pleasure.

Before Winifred could continue her paean, Jo turned to Rosamund—who was smirking.

This was very bad. "Horses?"

Rosamund's smirk grew more pronounced. "The earl sent his traveling coach for you. It's very fine."

Jo's jaw dropped. Her eyes might have goggled. "Earl? T-traveling coach?"

"It must have caused quite a stir when it came through the village," Winifred said. "I'm surprised Tom didn't follow behind."

Winifred's tone was a little gloating. Winifred and Tom, the ostler at the Dancing Duck, had a bit of a friendly rivalry, not that either of them often got to tend to any horse worth gloating over.

"You'll have a lovely journey to Darrow, Jo," Winifred said. "I wish I could go along."

"I am not going to Darrow. I sent my regrets."

Winifred frowned at her. "But the coach is here."

Jo looked at Rosamund. "I wonder why."

Rosamund shrugged. "Maybe the earl wouldn't take no for an answer."

Jo did not think that was the case, but she also thought that, while Rosamund might have a good guess as to what had occurred, she wasn't the one who had meddled.

This had Livy's fingerprints all over it.

"Come on, Jo. You don't want to keep the horses standing." As always Winifred kept her priorities straight.

True. The sooner Jo had a word with Livy, the sooner the coach could be on its way—without her.

"Very well." She headed for the front of the house, Freddie loping along beside her, leaving the other women to keep up as best they could. She turned the corner—

Lud! She'd half hoped Rosamund and Winifred had been telling her a tall tale, but no. There was indeed a carriage in the drive—and a footman in what she supposed was Darrow livery loading a large trunk onto it.

And Livy, directing the man.

"Livy!" Jo strode toward her.

Livy didn't bat an eyelid. Oh, no. The witch *smiled* as if nothing was the least bit amiss.

"I'm glad Rosamund and Winifred found you so quickly, Jo. All's ready here. The coachman says if you set off within the hour, you can reach the Horse and Pelican— which he assures me is a very comfortable inn—in time for supper. You'll stop there overnight and then arrive at Darrow midmorning."

White-hot fury exploded through her. No one—*no one*— made decisions for her anymore, and certainly not someone who was scheming to take control of her charity whilst her back was turned—or, more to the point, whilst her back was miles away.

"I am *not* going to Darrow," Jo hissed through clenched teeth.

Livy smiled at the coachman, whose eyes had gone round as saucers. "Give us a moment."

She grabbed Jo's arm—fortunately not the one Winifred had mauled.

Jo shook her off. "Livy—"

"Hear me out, Jo." Livy walked a few yards away, just out of the coachman's earshot, and looked back.

The coachman cleared his throat. "Pardon me, madam, but the horses . . ."

Winifred and Rosamund had caught up, and Winifred added her appeal to his. "You don't want to keep the horses standing, Jo."

Indeed. What she *wanted* was to send the man and his bloody horses away at once, but it would likely be tidier to deal with Livy first.

"Yes, yes. I'll just be a minute."

Jo—with Freddie—stepped over to Livy, opened her mouth to tell the woman precisely what she thought about her shocking meddl—

"I know you weren't planning to go to the christening, Jo," Livy said softly before Jo could get a word out. "I saw your note. I freely admit I tore it up and sent a letter of acceptance instead." Her lips curved into what looked like an apologetic smile.

Livy's words made Jo's fingers twitch, eager to wrap around the woman's neck, but her tone . . .

Was that *compassion* she heard in Livy's voice? Understanding?

It couldn't be, and yet—

"You need a break, Jo. A holiday."

She remembered how she'd felt watching Freddie chase that squirrel across the field.

"You are driving yourself mad"—Livy shrugged—"and everyone else mad as well."

"W-what?" Livy was wrong. She must be. Yes, Jo might have been feeling a bit tense lately. Who wouldn't be tense after losing two longtime partners? But she had herself under control.

Most of the time.

It was just that she felt she had to do *everything* now. Or at least supervise everything. Fanny and Polly were so new at their jobs. If they failed, the Home would fail and all the women and children living there would be, well, *homeless*. What would become of them?

What would become of me?

Her chest tightened.

She felt a light touch on her arm, pulling her away from the edge of the dark abyss she was teetering on and bringing her attention back to the present and Livy.

"Fanny is in a constant fidget, Jo. She's worried that something will happen to the hops and you'll throw her out on her ear."

"*What?!*"

Winifred, Rosamund, and the coachman all looked Jo's way.

Jo lowered her voice. "Where did Fanny get that daft idea? I've *never* thrown anyone out of the Home." Even when Rosamund's daughter had been torturing Harriet last summer, Jo hadn't threatened Rosamund with eviction.

Livy was shaking her head. "Fanny's not stupid, Jo. She knows you're constantly going down to the hopyard to inspect the plants. She sees how you look at her."

Had the world turned topsy-turvy? Jo felt as if she needed to put out a hand to steady herself.

She put both hands on her hips instead. "How I *look* at her? What do you mean by that?"

Was that *pity* on Livy's face? Perhaps she would wrap her hands around the woman's neck—

She took a deep, steadying breath. *Good Lord! Maybe I have lost a bit of perspective.*

"You wrinkle your brows like this," Livy said, scrunching up her face in a comical—and sadly familiar—way. "And you stare, though it's clear you aren't really seeing the person you're staring at."

"Oh."

"It upsets Fanny. She's come to me in tears on more than one occasion."

"Ah." *How could I not have known that? Caro always said I was the tenderhearted one.*

"You do it to Polly, too, but Polly just gets angry. So far, she's only complained to me, but I'm afraid if matters don't improve, she'll soon start venting her spleen to anyone who will listen."

That's not good.

Livy might well have heard Jo's thought. "I'm not saying anyone will take her side, but just having sides is a bad business. I've always found it best to nip such things in the bud the moment I become aware of them."

Jo nodded. Livy was right. "I'll have a word with Polly—and with Fanny, too."

Livy raised a skeptical brow. "Oh? And what will you say?"

Jo opened her mouth—and stopped. What *would* she say?

Livy was shaking her head. "You're worried about

what *might* happen, Jo. You've got no complaint with either Fanny's or Polly's *actual* work, do you?"

"N-no."

"Madam." Urgency and deference battled in the coachman's voice. "The *horses*."

"You've had a rough time of it, Jo. Everyone knows that. You depended on Caro—and Pen—and now they're gone. But you can't bring them back by frowning and glowering."

Livy's voice was warm and soothing. Jo felt comforted—*No! Livy just wants to get rid of me so she can take over.*

Was that true? Or had she let stress and anxiety twist her thinking?

Jo looked down at Freddie to see if he could advise her.

He was too busy scratching his ear to offer her any thoughts.

"*Madam*." The coachman's voice had a touch of panic now. "*Please*."

"Yes, Jo." That was Winifred. "Think of the horses."

"You really do need a break, Jo. A fortnight away will give you a fresh outlook. It will be good for you"—Livy grinned—"and for us."

"But . . ." But what? Jo felt the tide of everyone else's opinion—and, yes, perhaps her own desire—pulling her toward the coach and Darrow. She made one last attempt to resist.

"But Freddie—"

Livy snorted. "Freddie will be fine. Does he look at all concerned?"

He did not. If anything, he was the picture of nonchalance, sprawled on the grass, tongue hanging out.

"I should take him with me."

Livy snorted louder. "Right. And have him growl at all

the gentlemen? That would make for *such* a comfortable gathering."

Livy had a point.

"And you should talk to *people*, Jo."

Jo flushed. Livy might have a point there, too. It was possible she'd been . . . well, you couldn't call it *conversing* with Freddie, but she might have been sharing her thoughts with him a little too frequently.

"You won't be gone *that* long. Only a fortnight. I can manage things for two weeks."

True. And if Jo were honest with herself, she'd admit it was unlikely Livy would stage a coup while she was gone. Livy might be ambitious, but she was also smart. She must recognize that while she knew a lot about running a business, she knew very little about running *this* business.

It would *be nice to see Pen again. And Caro.*

She could find some time to talk to them about the Home, get their insights, their advice. That would make the trip worthwhile. And yet . . .

"The hop plants—"

Livy waved that concern away. "Fanny will keep a close eye on them"—she gave Jo a very pointed look—"just as she's been doing all along."

"Oh." Jo felt her resistance give way. "Oh, all right. I'll go."

She heard the coachman emit a deep sigh of relief.

"Excellent." Livy grinned with what looked very much like relief, too.

Have I really been so difficult to live with?

Her gut told her that perhaps she had.

Jo turned toward the coach—the coachman had already let down the steps.

"Your trunk is loaded, madam." He held out a hand to

help her in—not that she needed any help. "If you please. We *must* consider the horses."

"Yes." Winifred nodded. "The horses."

Jo put her foot on the first step—and stopped.

She could almost hear the coachman's teeth grinding.

"Go on." Livy came over to shoo her into the vehicle. "I packed everything you'll need." She laughed. "You didn't have many dresses to choose from."

It was no surprise that a London courtesan would think Jo's plain, serviceable wardrobe lacking.

"The Home will be here when you get back, won't it, Freddie?"

Freddie had bestirred himself to walk over with Livy. He looked at Jo and barked his agreement, wagging his tail in an encouraging fashion.

Is he looking forward to getting a break from me, too? Me and my constant yammering?

"Don't worry." Livy looked at Rosamund and Winifred. "You can trust us to keep everything running smoothly. Isn't that right, ladies?"

"Yes, Jo." Winifred nodded earnestly. Rosamund—

Oh, what the hell did it matter? She probably *did* need to get away for a while. As Livy said, she'd only be gone a fortnight. What could go wrong in a mere fourteen days?

She climbed into the coach—and the coachman folded up the steps the moment her foot cleared the last tread.

"And who knows," Livy said as Jo settled herself on the squabs. "Maybe you'll find love—and a new husband—at Darrow."

Jo's mouth dropped open as the door slammed shut.

Chapter Two

The Duke of Grainger—or, as he still thought of himself, Edward Russell—stood in yet another London ballroom and listened to yet another young woman talk.

Or tried to listen. His mind kept wandering.

The Earl of Darrow, whom he'd counted on last year to provide some sensible conversation at these insipid affairs, was now happily married. Today, he'd begun welcoming guests to his country estate for the christening of his heir. He'd invited Edward to serve as the baby's godfather, and Edward had agreed, but with the stipulation that he'd come down the day before the christening so he could attend a few more balls and soirees here in Town.

He was rethinking that plan.

"Oh!" The young woman—Lady Iris Wood—looked out the window, rather theatrically, he thought. "It's a lovely night, isn't it, Your Grace?" She batted her lashes at him.

"Indeed." He wished to remarry and have more children. He'd thought that almost any well-bred young woman would do.

He'd been mistaken. Lady Iris, for example, would *not* do. She was too . . .

Annoying? Self-centered?

Desperate?

"I've heard Lord Windom's gardens are quite impressive." Lady Iris gave him what she must think was a coy look, clearly hoping he'd ask her to stroll among the greenery.

Yes, desperate. The poor girl veritably *reeked* of desperation.

He should have realized it the moment they'd been introduced—well, even before that. It wasn't as if he'd not heard her story. She was the eldest of the "flower sisters," as the *ton* called them. The next sister, Lady Rose, had just snared a marquess, and the youngest flower, Lady Violet, was making her bows with the next crop of debutantes. If Lady Iris didn't harvest a peer before the Season ended, she'd find herself planted firmly on the matrimonial shelf.

Desperate women did desperate things, especially in dark gardens. He'd saved Darrow from precisely such an ill-advised excursion into the shrubbery last August.

"I imagine they are," he said. "However, I'm afraid I'm not much interested in plants."

He *did* feel for her. Unmarried daughters of the *ton* were all rather like flowers, cultivated in hothouses, watered and fed, protected from sun and wind and blight until they bloomed. And then their parents displayed them on the Marriage Mart, hoping they'd catch the eye of a wealthy peer who would marry them and take over their care. They had no power, beyond their powers of seduction, nor any real control over their own lives.

To be honest, most women had no control over their lives, which was one reason he was happy to support that charity in Little Puddledon—the Benevolent Home for the Maintenance and Support of Spinsters, Widows, and Abandoned Women and their Unfortunate Children. He'd been corresponding with the foundress, Lady Havenridge, since August and had been quite impressed by her. She seemed to be a very sensible female, levelheaded and yet, at the same time, intensely passionate about her cause.

And now he would finally get to meet her in person. Darrow had written she was to be the baby's godmother.

If I go down to Darrow sooner, I'll have more time to discuss the Home with Lady Havenridge.

"But do you have any interest in what can happen in a leafy corner?" Lady Iris said archly, bringing his attention back to her.

Good God!

"No."

She frowned at his abrupt answer and appeared— blessedly—at a loss for words.

His conscience prodded him. If his wife were still alive, she'd tell him he shouldn't be so blunt. It wasn't Lady Iris's fault that Society was constructed the way it was.

If Helen were still alive, I wouldn't be standing here.

True. Still, Helen would expect better of him, so he tried to soften his rejection. "Lady Iris, I know you wish to find a husband, but I am—" *Don't say* not interested. "I am too old for you."

The moment the words were out he wished he could recall them. He *was* too old for her, but, if rumors were true, he was a good fifteen years younger than any of the other fellows she was pursuing.

He tried again. "My wife was just about your age when we married. We—"

Lady Iris finally regained her powers of speech.

Unfortunately.

"And now you need a new wife. A young wife who can

give you more children. You may have your heir, Your Grace, but you still need your spare."

True. Which was one reason he'd been forcing himself to haunt Society's ballrooms.

Clearly, he would need to haunt them a while longer. But, equally clearly, he needed a break. He should have known Lady Iris wouldn't do for him and taken pains not to get caught with her in such a public tête-à-tête.

Well, time to put an end to this as politely as he could.

He pinned a smile to his lips and bowed. "Lady Iris, I'm sorry, but I believe it would be best if I returned you to your chaperone."

Zeus! You'd think he'd spat on her and called her a blood-sucking, wart-ridden, snaggletoothed witch. Her brows snapped down. Her eyes narrowed. Her nostrils flared.

"Why?" The word came out in a hiss, a rather impressive enunciative trick.

Did she expect an answer? What should he say?

Because I find you repulsive? Because the thought of spending one more second in your presence makes me want to curse, loudly?

No, of course he shouldn't—couldn't—say any of that. He—

He wasn't given the option to try diplomacy. After only a brief pause, she swept on.

Lady Iris might not be a witch, but this Society flower had definitely turned into a stinging nettle.

"What is the *matter* with you? I'm well-bred. Beautiful."

And becoming less beautiful with each ugly word.

He noticed how everyone within hearing range had paused their own conversations and cocked their ears in

Lady Iris's direction, likely salivating at the thought of the delicious helping of gossip she was about to dish up.

The woman was too angry to notice. He should try to bring it to her attention.

"Lady Iris, you might want to—"

She did *not* want to listen to him. She rushed on.

"You should be *happy* that I'm willing to consider you. In case it has escaped your attention, you are not thought to be much of a marital prize. Yes, you may be a duke now, but you were just a *solicitor* a short while ago. You had to *work* for your bread."

The disdain dripping from her words sent a cold rage howling through him, scattering all his kinder impulses.

And then his years of working as a solicitor—years of keeping his tongue between his teeth when what he'd really wanted to do was share a few home truths—took over. Instead of telling Lady Iris precisely what he thought of her, he pressed his lips together. Tightly.

I'm a duke. She's a defenseless woman. I cannot—should not—berate her, and especially not here in a society ballroom.

And *she is not my problem, thank God.*

But he *was* a duke now. He no longer had to listen to this abuse. He could turn on his heel and leave.

Which is precisely what he did. Without a word of farewell—he couldn't have managed a polite word—he showed her his back and strode across the ballroom, leaving raised eyebrows and whispers in his wake.

He felt a brief—a *very* brief—twinge of pity for her, but he brushed it away. Lady Iris would find plenty of sympathetic ears into which she could unburden herself. She'd had the right of it. To the *ton*'s fastidious nostrils, he *did* still stink of the shop.

Suddenly, he wanted—*desperately* wanted—out of this hot, stifling ballroom that reeked of perfume and candle-wax and sweat. He wanted to be far, far away from the false smiles and nasty whispers, the scornful looks. He was sick of the haughty *ton*, and he was especially sick of them treating him like some jumped-up shopkeeper while simultaneously fawning over his title.

The bloody toadeaters. He was done with them.

The footman lounging by the front door straightened the moment he saw Edward approaching and jumped to pull the door open, as if he were afraid Edward might kick it down if he didn't move fast enough.

Edward might have done so. He was angry enough to try.

He nodded at the man—no need to be rude to the fellow—stepped out into the night, took a deep breath—

And started coughing.

Damn London air. It was thick with smoke and the fetid smell of the streets and the Thames.

And the noise! Even at this late hour, carriages and carts rattled over the cobblestones, street vendors hawked their wares, dogs barked, and inebriated men sang bawdy ditties at the top of their lungs.

He jumped back to avoid one drunken lout, who weaved past him and then grabbed a lamppost and emptied his stomach into the gutter, contributing to the ambient stench.

Edward's stomach roiled, threatening to add *its* contents to the mess. *Blech!*

He turned and headed toward his townhouse. He needed to get back to the country with its clean air, open fields, and quiet. He'd known the Season was wearing on him, but he'd been trying to push through. He'd kept telling himself that the next event or the one after that would be the one where he'd find a woman to marry. That if he skipped this ball or that soiree, he'd miss his chance.

Zeus, when had he turned into such a bloody cabbage-head?

Well, to be fair, it wasn't as if he'd ever done any wife-hunting before. He'd worked with Helen's father. He'd got to know Helen—and to fall in love with her—gradually, naturally.

He sure as hell hadn't had to prance around under the eyes of the annoying nobility, being looked over as if he were a horse up for auction at Tattersalls. It was a wonder no one had yet asked to see his teeth.

Remember, you don't need *to marry again. You have your heir.*

Right. He scowled down at some unidentifiable muck on the pavement as he stepped over it. And why did he care about the succession at all? *He* hadn't been in line for the title until Fate had intervened. If worse came to worst, they could just shake the family tree again.

It's not the succession I care about. I want *more children. I want a mother for Thomas.*

Yes. And he'd met any number of perfectly pleasant women who would do both those things perfectly pleasantly. They just didn't make his heart beat faster.

Or his less noble organ stir with interest.

He stopped in front of his townhouse. He was thirty-five years old, blast it. He wasn't a lad any longer, but he sure as hell wasn't dead. And yet he might as well be.

He hadn't been with a woman in over a *year*, since he'd been plucked from his former life and thrust into his new, very public position.

He climbed the steps to his front door and stared morosely at the pineapple-shaped knocker.

He could, if he wished, pay for physical release. He'd paid for it in the past. But now that he was the Duke of Grainger—the *solicitor* duke . . .

Nothing was secret in London, especially nothing that involved him. People would talk. His servants would talk. Thomas would hear. The boy was old enough to get the general drift of the gossip, and, well, perhaps there was a touch of the puritan in him, but he didn't want his son listening to accounts of his father's assignations.

And simple physical release isn't what you really want, is it?

He could satisfy *that* in the privacy of his room with just his hand for company.

Hell and damnation! He hadn't thought to find love again, but he *had* hoped to find friendship. Companionship. Respect.

And now . . .

Now he was beginning to fear he'd never find a woman who could look past his title to see *him*, Edward Russell. Who would find his past career a *good* thing, not something to be despised, whispered about, wished away.

He let out the breath he hadn't realized he'd been holding. The last year had been difficult. The christening party might be the perfect time to relax and reassess his goals. Perhaps he would decide to give up looking for a wife, at least for now.

Jakes, his butler, must have been watching for him because he swung the door open just as Edward pulled his key out of his pocket.

"Your Grace," Jakes said, a faint note of reproach shading his voice, "you know I—or one of the footmen—am always on duty."

Jakes had come with the title and was very good at his

job, which was why Edward hadn't replaced him. At least one of them should have some notion of how a duke—and a duke's household—should go on.

To be honest, Edward's upbringing had probably been more like a butler's than a duke's. He, too, had had to find a trade to support himself.

"I'm quite capable of letting myself in, you know, Jakes," he grumbled as he stepped over the threshold—and felt like an imposter again. A proper duke would probably quell the butler with one haughty sniff or a cocked eyebrow. He must just sound peevish.

All right, he'd admit it. He *did* sound peevish, even to himself.

"Of course, you are, Your Grace," Jakes said soothingly, in a tone Edward recognized. It was not unlike the one he used when he wished to mollify Thomas.

He glared at Jakes.

Jakes looked blandly back at him. Zeus, the man was good.

Edward handed the fellow his hat. "I'm off to Darrow in the morning."

Jakes's eyes widened.

Ha! He'd finally managed to shake the bloody fellow's composure.

"So soon, Your Grace? I'd been given to understand that you weren't leaving until next week."

"I changed my mind."

Jakes recovered at once, of course, and bowed slightly. "Very good, Your Grace. I will let the staff know." He cleared his throat. "I assume you've already informed Ambrose?"

Ambrose was Edward's valet—also inherited with the

title—and, no, he hadn't told the man. He'd just made the decision, as Jakes likely knew all too well.

"No. I'll tell him when I see him that he has a bit of a holiday coming."

Jakes's brows shot up before he quickly schooled his features.

"It will be just Thomas and I going. And John Coachman, of course." Edward was not going to drive his own carriage. He knew his limitations. He had very little— some would say no—skill with the ribbons, not having grown up the pampered son of a nobleman.

Another strike against him in the eyes of the *ton*.

Jakes nodded, apparently speechless at the thought of the Duke of Grainger undertaking a journey without his valet.

Edward smiled—ducally, he hoped—and headed for the stairs. He doubted Ambrose would be surprised to be left behind. The valet had grown resigned to being little more than a male laundress.

Oh, Ambrose did *try* to be a proper valet. He'd been pleading with Edward from the moment Edward had first donned the ducal coronet to let him take over his dressing—and Edward had flatly refused. He'd been putting on his own clothes since he was a lad. He wasn't about to let anyone treat him like a life-sized doll now.

He'd even refused to let the man shave him. Poor Ambrose had been reduced to moaning and sending him baleful looks, predicting that Edward's hand would slip and he'd slit his own throat.

Getting free of the dour fellow for a fortnight was another benefit of his decision to leave for Darrow in the morning.

Edward bounded up the stairs, feeling lighter than he

had in months. Then he walked down the corridor and quietly pushed open the door to the schoolroom—he'd had the hinges oiled so he could come in and check on Thomas without waking him.

He woke Bear, though. The big dog appeared at the door to Thomas's bedroom and then came over to have his ears scratched.

"Good boy, Bear," Edward whispered.

A small voice came through the darkness. "Papa?"

Oh, blast. He *had* woken Thomas.

He stepped into the bedroom and saw Thomas sitting up in bed.

"You should be asleep." He took a spill from the mantel and lit a candle. "Not a bad dream, I hope?"

Thomas shook his head. "N-no. I-I just heard you come in."

God, how I love this boy.

Edward sat on the edge of the bed—and his heart clenched. Even in the uncertain light, he could see Thomas's young face was twisted with worry, his eyes wide as they looked up at him.

"D-did you find a w-wife tonight, Papa?"

Zeus!

"Oh, Thomas." He swept his son up in his arms and hugged him tightly. How he wished he could protect the boy from all pain and every disappointment. He would give anything—give his very life—for his son.

And now there were tears leaking from his eyes.

I've not really thought about how my search for a wife is affecting Thomas, have I?

If he hadn't already decided to go to Darrow in the morning, this would have persuaded him. He and Thomas *both* needed a break. Darrow's daughter, Harriet—the child the earl had had with Lady Darrow long before they were married—would be there, as would Darrow's nieces. They were girls, yes, and, he thought, older than Thomas, but they *were* children. And Darrow's daughter had lived most of her life with only one parent. She might understand and feel some sympathy for Thomas.

And *he* would be there. He'd not be spending hours and hours at some deadly dull Society event.

"No, I didn't find a wife." He held the boy away from him and smiled. "I say, how would you like to go off to the country tomorrow?"

A stricken look came over Thomas's face. "Back to G-Grainger?"

He thinks I'm sending him away. Dear God, I have some work to do.

"No. No, of course not. To the christening party at Darrow with me."

"Really?" Thomas's sudden grin lit the room like another candle—or at least it lit Edward's heart. The boy gave a happy little bounce. "Yes! And can we bring Bear?"

Ah. A large, shaggy mongrel hadn't been part of the invitation, but . . .

It *was* the country. Darrow must have dogs of his own, and Bear was well-behaved.

Most of the time.

Darrow does owe me a favor.

Hell, Darrow owed him his current happiness. If Edward hadn't sent him to Little Puddledon last summer to discover what a mysterious entry in the old duke's books meant, Darrow wouldn't have found his now-wife and discovered they'd had a daughter together.

And there would be no baby to christen.

"Yes, we can bring Bear."

Thomas's grin widened and he flung his arms around Edward's neck. "Oh, thank you, Papa."

There are the bloody tears again.

Edward squeezed his eyes shut, willing the dampness away, and hugged Thomas until he found his composure. Then he gently disentangled himself and drew back, resting his hands on his son's shoulders.

"Now go to sleep." He was relieved to hear his voice was steady. "We leave early in the morning."

"Yes, Papa." Thomas bounced on the bed again—and then stopped, frowning. "Will you be shopping for a wife at the party?"

"No."

Wait, was that true? He wouldn't be shopping—that part was right—but if some suitable, unattached female miraculously appeared? What then?

"Or, I don't think so. I expect this will be mostly a family gathering, Thomas—children and old grannies and happily married couples. But if there *are* any unattached ladies, I won't turn my back on them. That would be rude, wouldn't it?"

Thomas nodded tentatively.

And this could work to his advantage. What better way to take the measure of a woman than to see her with his son? "And you'll be there, so can give me your advice on the matter."

He'd said that half in jest, but Thomas nodded seriously.

"I promise I will, Papa. And I can tell you what the servants say, too."

Oh, hell. If he could stop the servants from gossiping around Thomas, he would.

"Mr. Ambrose told Mr. Jakes yesterday that you'd be married by now if you'd just let him see to your clothes."

The boy's brows slanted down. "I think you look fine as you are."

If that was the worst Thomas heard, he must be thankful.

And he was doubly glad they were leaving Ambrose behind.

"Ah. Well, thank you." He stood. "Now, do lie down. I was serious about getting an early start."

Thomas nodded and stretched out again on the bed. "I hope you find someone nice, Papa. I'd like a mother, I think." He frowned. "Though not an evil one like in fairy tales."

Edward tucked the coverlet around his son. "Definitely not." He smiled. "And remember, you've promised to advise me. I'm sure you'll keep me from making such a mistake."

Thomas didn't smile in return. "But what if we're both fooled? What if she only *seems* nice? Or what if she changes once you're married?"

Thomas was right. There were no guarantees in life—if there were, Helen would not have died. Edward hoped he'd not make a foolish choice—he would certainly try not to. But he'd seen more than one otherwise sensible man allow his cock, or simple loneliness, to lead him to disaster.

"It's true no one can know the future, Thomas, but I promise to do my best to choose wisely." Then he bent down so he could look Thomas in the eyes—and so that Thomas could look *him* in the eyes. "But no matter what happens, Thomas, I will always look out for you. You come first, so you must come to me at once if you ever have a problem with—with anything. I will sort things out. I will take care of you."

"But if your new wife doesn't like me . . ." Thomas's voice trailed off. He looked so small and defenseless.

"Then I will send her off to one of our remote estates."

Thomas looked reassured, but still uncertain.

Of *course*, he was uncertain. Life was uncertain, so bloody, bloody uncertain.

When he'd married, he'd assumed he and Helen would have several children—sons *and* daughters. They hadn't. It had taken them five years to conceive, and then Helen had died shortly after giving birth to Thomas.

Zeus! There was a hole in his life where Helen had been, where he'd thought a family would be. It *ached* to be filled.

Enough. He would take this holiday from London— from its ballrooms full of desperate women—and enjoy being with Thomas in the country. And if something else developed . . .

He would neither hope for nor look for anything beyond a pleasant fortnight away from Town.

"Let's not worry. Let's just have some fun for the next two weeks, shall we?"

Thomas grinned, and if there was a touch of wistfulness in his eyes—well, that could just be the wavering light.

Edward blew out the candle and made his way by the fire's glow past Bear, out of the schoolroom, and down the corridor to his bedchamber. Yes, a break from London and his hunt for a wife was likely just what he needed. Distance often made things come into better focus. He liked Darrow and had liked what little he'd seen of Lady Darrow.

And remember, you'll be able to speak to Lady Havenridge about the Home. That will be good.

Very true. He should have gone down to Little Puddledon a while ago to see the Home himself, but he hadn't felt any urgency. Darrow had said the place was well run, and Lady Havenridge's letters had given him confidence in her abilities. Still, it would be good to finally meet her. Letters were fine, but even the best-written ones left themselves open to misinterpretation.

He closed the door to his room and started to loosen his cravat. He'd always found it much better to speak face-to-face with someone so he could see the person's reactions and ask questions to clarify points.

And there *was* one thing he'd like to discuss with her. Darrow had said the Home didn't take in mothers with sons. Perhaps they could find a way to—

"Your Grace!" Ambrose came hurrying into the room from wherever he'd been hiding. "I didn't expect you to be home so early."

"I didn't expect to be home so early, but here I am." Edward untied his cravat—and swore Ambrose's fingers twitched. It must take all of the valet's self-control not to push Edward's hands away and do it himself.

Ambrose nodded, his eyes still on Edward's cravat. "I did look in earlier after Jakes told me you'd come back, Your Grace, but I didn't see you."

And it would be bloody wonderful not to feel like he had someone watching him all the time. "I stopped to check on my son." He started to drop his cravat on the floor.

Ambrose dove and caught it midair. "I see, Your Grace. Of course, Your Grace."

Edward shrugged out of his coat—a coat Ambrose told him at least once a day was too loosely cut to set off his figure.

And Ambrose didn't disappoint this time, either. "I do wish you'd allow your tailor to fit you properly, Your Grace."

Edward tried to muffle his laugh, but failed—and then felt guilty when he saw Ambrose's hurt expression.

Oh, what the hell. He was going to get free of the fellow tomorrow. He might as well be generous now and throw him a sop.

"Do you suppose you could help me off with my boots, Ambrose?"

Chapter Three

Jo strode across the broad lawn, trying to walk off her anger and find some measure of serenity. She'd arrived at the Earl of Darrow's estate a little earlier, been shown up to her room, opened her trunk—

And discovered Livy hadn't packed a single suitable garment.

Dear *Lord*, where had the woman got those things? A few dresses looked familiar—until Jo held one up and saw someone had removed most of its bodice. Other dresses were new—and even *more* scandalous. And the scrap of cloth Livy had packed for Jo to sleep in was far too diaphanous to wear at all—even with all the candles snuffed and the coverlet pulled up to her chin.

Well, Livy *had* operated a business matching men with lightskirts. Still, she should have known a house party to celebrate a baby's christening would require a different wardrobe than, say, a Christmas orgy at a viscount's country estate.

Livy should have known that *Jo* would require a different wardrobe.

Jo snorted. Of *course* the evil woman had known it. The

altered dresses must be part of her plan to take over the Home. Hadn't she all but admitted she had some sort of scheme in mind just before the coach door closed? Love and husbands, indeed! Jo had been surprised by her words, but had chalked them up to wishful thinking.

Ha! Now the matter was crystal clear. It wasn't wishful thinking—it was a carefully laid plot. The jade must be hoping that, wrapped in a more . . . *alluring* package, Jo would entice a titled gentleman into offering for her and taking her off to his estate—just as Pen and Caro had gone off.

Giving Livy exactly what she wanted—control of the Home.

It was a rather far-fetched fantasy, though. Why would Livy think that Jo would encounter a single man in search of a wife at a family christening party? And perhaps even more to the point, why in the world would she imagine *any* fellow would wish to ally himself with a widow who thought it appropriate to attend such a gathering dressed as a lightskirt?

If there *was* an unattached male here, it was far more likely he'd think Jo was available for a bit of bedroom frolicking. Many widows *were* accommodating in that regard. But a waltz between the sheets wouldn't achieve Livy's goal . . .

Oh! Unless Livy thought such activity would result in a child nine months hence. That *might* be her plan. However, one would think an experienced madam would conclude that if Jo hadn't conceived in three years of marriage, she was not going to do so after just a few nights of, er, passion, especially given her advanced age.

And all that completely ignored the fact that Jo was most definitely *not* in the market for a husband. Livy didn't honestly think she'd be swept away by a handsome face, did she? She'd made that mistake before—she wasn't going to make it again, especially when it would take her away from the life she'd worked so hard to build.

Still, it was the only explanation Jo could come up with for those, those . . .

They hardly qualified as dresses, there was so little to them.

I should have unpacked at that inn. Then I would have discovered Livy's mischief and could have told the coachman to turn back to Little Puddledon.

Livy had likely—and correctly—assumed Jo would be too exhausted when they'd stopped overnight at the Horse and Pelican to do more than take off her dress and fall into bed in her shift—and then put the same dress back on in the morning.

Well, it was too late now. She couldn't ask to leave—she'd just arrived. How could she explain that to Pen?

She snorted again. She wouldn't have to explain anything once Pen caught sight of her in one of those dresses. Pen would call up the coach herself to take her back to the Home.

Particularly if I wear that red dress—

Her cheeks burned as the shocking dress of red satin and lace flashed before her mind's eye.

I need to discuss the matter with Freddie.

But she couldn't. Freddie wasn't here. She would have to hope the simple action of putting one foot in front of the other would calm her enough that she could come up with a sensible course of action on her own.

She continued on across the lawn toward a line of trees, careful to keep an eye out for mole holes and cow piles.

I'll ask Pen if she has a shawl of some sort I can borrow. Or . . . There must be a seamstress on the premises.

Though adding fabric was a bit trickier than taking it away. And there was a *lot* of fabric that needed to be added. The red dress might be the skimpiest, but none of them— with the exception of the dress she had on right now— were suitable for anything but a brothel.

I'll just have to hide in the curtains.

Now *there* was an idea. She could imagine what everyone would say to tha—

"Bear!"

What?! A bear *in* England*?*

She spun around. For an instant, she thought the shaggy creature bounding toward her was indeed a bear, escaped from a traveling menagerie perhaps.

And then she realized it was just a large, enthusiastic dog with a young boy in pursuit.

She did not wish to be bowled over by the exuberant animal and thus dirty the one modest dress in her possession, so when the dog came close enough—and hoping that it was an obedient creature—she gave it a firm command: "Sit!"

The dog sat. Fortunately. He looked like the slobbery sort—the friendly, slobbery sort, which would also spell disaster for her dress.

They both waited for the boy to catch up.

"I'm. Sorry. Madam," the boy said between pants when he reached them.

She'd guess the lad was about seven or eight years old. He was thin, all arms and legs, with a mop of reddish-brown hair and a scattering of freckles across his nose.

"It's quite all right. Take a moment to catch your breath, and then you can introduce me to this fine fellow."

The boy's large, hazel eyes had been shadowed when he'd first reached her, his brows tented, but at her words, he flashed a grin, revealing a large gap where his two front teeth should be.

He took a deep breath and then said seriously, a note of pride in his voice, "This is Bear. He can do tricks. I taught him."

"Did you? How very clever. What can he do?"

He flashed his gap-toothed grin again and then turned to his dog. "Shake hands with the lady, Bear."

Bear offered a paw.

Jo took it. "Pleased to make your acquaintance, Bear."

That made the boy giggle. "Good boy, Bear." He gave the dog a hug.

He was a charming child, bright-eyed and energetic. He must live on the estate, though he seemed too well-spoken and direct to be a tenant's child. Perhaps his father was the local vicar.

"And you are, sir?"

The boy glanced at her before turning back to his dog as if suddenly shy. "Thomas, madam."

Perhaps he *was* a tenant's child, one that had benefited from charity schooling. She would have to ask Pen about that. In Jo's opinion, every estate should have a thriving school. Some peers thought education would make their tenants dissatisfied with their lot and lead to unrest, but Jo did not agree with that position.

"I'm pleased to make your acquaintance as well, Thomas." She extended her hand. "I'm . . ."

Lady Havenridge felt too formal for the situation. She didn't want to risk cutting the nascent bond she felt forming between them. And she'd never really liked the title. It recalled Freddie and her less than successful marriage.

She would introduce herself by what the children at the Home called her. "I'm Miss Jo."

The boy took her hand. He had a good strong hand-shake, especially for a youngster.

"I am sorry Bear ran at you like that," he said, looking her in the eye. "We spent the morning in the carriage—"

So not a tenant's child nor the vicar's son. He must have come with one of the other guests.

"—and, well, when we got out, Bear saw a squirrel."

Jo knew all about dogs and squirrels.

"I hope he didn't frighten you, Miss Jo."

Jo smiled. "No, he didn't frighten me, though I suppose he might have if I were afraid of dogs. Some people are, you know."

The boy nodded earnestly, and then looked down at Bear, who'd flopped onto the grass, tongue lolling out, looking about as frightening as a fur coat.

"I know. And Bear's so big, he scares even people who don't usually mind dogs. I should have put him on a lead."

His parents had raised him well. He didn't try to bluff or bluster or scoff that anyone would be so poor-spirited as to be alarmed by his pet, but accepted responsibility for his mistake.

Not that she would call this a mistake. Even the best-trained animal—and Bear seemed very well trained—had a mind of its own and sometimes used it to the surprise and consternation of its owner. And, given the disparity in size, she would wager that even if Bear had been on a leash, he would have easily pulled free of the boy's hold.

"Well, no harm done," she said. "And I *do* understand. I have a dog myself."

"You do?" Thomas's eyes brightened and he looked around eagerly. "Where is he?"

"I didn't bring him." She felt a sharp pang of regret. If other guests—

No. Other dogs didn't react to men the way Freddie did.

The boy was frowning. "Why didn't you?"

"Freddie doesn't, ah . . ." No point in beating about the bush. "He doesn't like men."

Thomas's eyes widened. "How do you know?"

"He growls whenever one comes close."

The boy didn't leave it there, of course. Children, unlike adults, always asked questions.

"Why?"

"Erm, I think because the man who had Freddie before me wasn't very nice to him."

She wouldn't tell Thomas the details—it was not a happy story. Harvey Miller, who owned a small, dilapidated farm abutting the Home's property and who was one of Jo's least favorite people, had been on the verge of drowning poor Freddie for the common puppy sin of chewing his boots when Jo had happened upon him. She'd persuaded him—with the help of a large stick and a lot of shouting—to give Freddie to her.

"Does Freddie like boys?"

Jo blinked. *Did* Freddie like boys?

"I don't know. We have only girls at the Home."

Thomas wrinkled his nose in what looked very much like disgust at the mention of girls.

Well, he *was* a young boy. He likely—

"Does he growl at your husband?"

How had the conversation taken *this* turn? "Husband? I don't have a husband."

"Oh." Thomas suddenly looked sad and oddly understanding. "He died. I'm sorry."

Freddie, her husband, *had* died, of course, but . . . ah! She thought she saw the problem.

"The girls aren't *my* daughters, Thomas. I run a *Benevolent* Home for women and children—" She stopped. That wasn't quite accurate, was it? "That is, for women and girls."

Thomas looked even sadder, his narrow shoulders drooping. "Do *you* not like boys, then?"

Oh, dear. Perhaps it *had* sounded that way. "No, it's not that. The Home is too small to have both boys *and* girls. We had to choose."

"And you chose girls."

She suddenly felt very guilty.

Nonsense! There was no guilt involved. The Home *was* too small for both genders.

"Circumstances chose, Thomas. It just so happened that the first mothers who came to the Home had daughters."

Well, and from her observations, women with boys had no trouble finding husbands. They were proven breeders. Men wanted sons who could carry on their names, work their fields.

Not that she was going to say *that* to a child.

And what if mothers of sons also wanted the opportunity to live their lives free of men?

She hadn't considered the matter from that perspective.

But it didn't change things. The Home *was* too small to accommodate everyone.

Thomas frowned, opened his mouth as if to argue—

And then Bear gave a great woof, sprang to his feet, and took off, loping back toward the house—and a masculine figure.

"That's Papa," Thomas said. "He went in to see to our bags and greet the earl. I was supposed to stay close to the house with Bear."

The man now walking over the lawn toward them, a satchel slung over one shoulder, looked large, even at a distance, with broad shoulders and an athletic stride that spoke of strength.

Jo frowned. Thomas didn't seem worried, but she couldn't take anything for granted, especially not with a child involved. Men could be quick to anger when their orders weren't followed to a T.

"He won't cut up rusty with you, will he?" she asked, watching carefully for the boy's reaction.

Thomas shrugged and smiled. Clearly, he wasn't the least bit concerned.

"Oh, no. Papa only gets angry when he thinks I've done something dangerous and could have got hurt."

Well, that was good. It sounded as if the man was a reasonable fellow.

Who must now be wondering exactly who was talking to his son. At least she wasn't in one of Livy's horrid dresses. Any of those would have given him the entirely wrong impression of her character.

Still, a cautious father would not wish his young son striking up a conversation with a stranger. She should follow Bear's example and go—

"Papa's looking for a wife."

Her eyes snapped back to Thomas. She could not have heard him correctly.

Lud! Was that *hope* she saw in the boy's eyes?

No. He's only just met me.

She looked back at his father. The dog was dancing around him, barking with canine joy while the man laughed.

Her idiotic heart did an odd little dance of its own.

Stupid! You are not a young girl to be swayed by a handsome face and figure again.

"You said you don't have a husband."

Oh, Lord, it *had* been hope she'd seen in the boy's eyes—and now heard in his voice.

"Would you like to marry Papa?"

She looked down at him. She should tell him no, of course, but gently. She didn't want to hurt him.

"I'd like a mother." Thomas smiled wistfully. "I never knew mine. She died when I was born."

Jo's heart twisted. "Oh. I'm so sor—"

"I think I'd like to have *you* as a mother."

And now her heart stopped. She . . .

She mustn't encourage him, but she needn't make a great deal of the matter, either. This notion was certain to pass quickly.

And if it didn't, his father should be the one to explain things. Not her.

"You *talk* to me," Thomas was saying. "You *look* at me. You don't ignore me the way most grown-ups do."

Clearly, the boy was wise beyond his years—but he *was* still young, too young to understand that you couldn't simply hope what you wanted into existence.

Young children didn't think the same way as adults or even older children did. They believed wishes could be granted, dreams made real—

No. The boy lost his mother. He must understand all too well that life isn't a fairy tale.

Thomas wrinkled his nose. "The ladies who want to marry Papa *pretend* to like me, but I can tell they just wish I would go away." He looked over at his father and his voice wavered. "For-forever."

Oh! Her arms ached to wrap themselves around his slight form, but she forced them to stay at her sides. She wanted to tell him everything would be all right, but he must have learned, as she had, that life offered no guarantees.

And, to be blunt, it didn't matter what Thomas wished for. She was sorry to disappoint him, but she wasn't interested in acquiring a husband. She did not want to leave the Home, no matter how much Livy might scheme to get her to do so. She couldn't. It was her life's work—her child, if you will. She could not abandon it, and especially not now. Livy was too new to the place to know how to keep it afloat.

I shouldn't have come. I shouldn't have left Livy in charge even for just a fortnight.

"You smile with your eyes," Thomas said. "Not just your mouth. The ladies . . . When they smile, their eyes are hard and mean."

This boy was *far* too old for his years—and too bright to be comforted by platitudes, even though that was all she had to offer him. "I hope your father is wise and marries a kind woman."

But men didn't look for kindness in a wife, did they? They looked for wealth and breeding and beauty, none of which had anything to do with kindness.

This man would surely look for all that. He was close enough now that she could see just how strikingly handsome he was. He was an adult version of the boy, tall, with auburn hair and eyes—

Eyes that were focused on her, assessing her. *Warning* her.

A small spark of vanity flared to life, offended by the total absence of admir—

Stop! This man should *be thinking solely of his son's welfare. And, Freddie's courtship aside, when have you ever given a fig for male admiration?*

Now, apparently. She was definitely—and irrationally—miffed. She—

Good God! Revelation hit her like a thunderbolt. *This* must be the man Livy had had in mind when she'd altered all those dresses.

Who is he? How did Livy know he'd be here?

Livy corresponded with Caro, but then so did Jo. Caro hadn't said anything to Jo about the party, let alone who might be attending.

Jo frowned. Though it *had* been several weeks since she'd heard from Caro.

Well, more like a month.

Or, maybe two.

She'd put off answering Caro's last letter because she'd not wanted to treat her to a long list of worries and complaints—or to give her the impression she couldn't manage on her own.

"Papa, this is Miss Jo." Thomas's words tumbled out as soon as his father was within earshot. "I've just met her. Well, Bear met her first. He got away from me—he went after a squirrel. I tried to catch him but he was too fast. But Miss Jo didn't mind. She wasn't afraid at all. She told Bear to sit and he did."

"Ah." The man's expression relaxed a little.

Jo knew she should say something, but she was suddenly, unaccountably nervous. It felt as if a kaleidoscope of butterflies had taken wing in her stomach.

Fortunately, Thomas kept talking.

"Miss Jo has a dog named Freddie, Papa, but she didn't bring him to the house party because he doesn't like men."

"Oh?"

She heard the humor in Thomas's father's voice. He arched an eyebrow at her.

The fluttering grew—

This is ridiculous. You are an independent widow of thirty-four, not a seventeen-year-old ninny. Get control of yourself!

She ordered the butterflies to disperse and forced a smile.

"Freddie is generally very well-behaved, sir. He's never bitten anyone. But he *does* growl, and he's not used to strangers, especially men, so I wasn't completely certain how he would acquit himself here."

One corner of the man's lips quirked up.

For some reason that she preferred not to examine, she did not care to have Thomas's father laughing at her. Well, perhaps not *laughing*, at least not outright, but . . . on the verge of laughter. Did he think her a country bumpkin?

I am dressed in an old, travel-stained gown, and this bonnet must be . . .

Lud, could it be almost ten years old? And it had never been fashionable. She wasn't going to seduce anyone in *this* outfit—

Seduce?! Where in God's name had that *come from?*

From that trunkful of scandalous dresses, of course. From that red scrap of lace and satin. She looked down at Bear to hide her flush.

And perhaps the thought had come from the man himself. There was something very seductive about him. He was tall, handsome, dressed in what were clearly Town-tailored clothes—

Just like Freddie when first you saw him. You don't need to have another charming rogue pass through your life.

True, but she thought this man was *not* like Freddie in the ways that mattered. Freddie had never had this presence about him, this feeling of intensity, of intelligence. And Freddie had never been a father.

She couldn't fault Freddie for that, but she also couldn't in her wildest dreams imagine he'd be this protective and concerned for a child's well-being.

Freddie had been, at heart, deeply irresponsible. He'd lived in the moment, with little—with *no*—thought of past or future. It had given him an aura of fun and danger and had been captivating when she'd been seventeen.

It had been less appealing to live with.

This man, however . . .

She met his eyes—

And felt a definite pull of attraction.

She repressed it—mostly.

Focus!

She should introduce herself since the oaf hadn't bothered to make himself known to her. She hadn't used her title with the boy, but it might be wise to use it now. Being even just a minor member of the *ton* usually elicited a certain measure of deference that she felt very much in need of at the moment.

Well, it did in the country. In London . . .

In London, her connection to Freddie—and to the indelible mark of his suicide—would likely elicit disgust. The *ton* had a long memory.

And Freddie had been considered a bit of a dirty dish even before he'd killed himself.

This man might well wrinkle his nose at her. So be it. Best to find out now. It wasn't as if they could avoid each other for the next two weeks.

She raised her chin. "I told Thomas I'm Miss Jo, sir. It is what the children call me at the Home I run—the Benevolent Home for the Maintenance and Support of Spinsters,

Widows, and Abandoned Women and their Unfortunate Children." She recited the full name in a strong voice. With pride.

The man's eyes widened—well, it *was* a mouthful. But . . . Did the corners of his mouth twitch, too?

"But I'm more properly known as Lady Havenridge, widow of the former Baron Havenridge." *There. Let's see what the fellow makes of that!*

It appeared her title only amused him more. She could tell he was fighting valiantly to swallow a laugh.

She was not used to *this* reaction when she revealed her identity. It was rather disconcerting.

"And you are?" she prompted.

"I'm . . ." His voice wavered. He pressed his lips together, but that didn't prevent a snort from escaping his nose. "I'm—oh, oh, argh."

He doubled over and howled.

She looked at Thomas.

"Papa is the Duke of Grainger," he said.

Good Lord!

She gaped in horror at the man whose predecessor had won Puddledon Manor from Freddie in that ill-fated card game; the man who had sent their current host, the Earl of Darrow, to Little Puddledon to investigate the Home; the man she'd been corresponding with for months in the hopes he would continue his financial support. The man whose good sense she'd come to depend on, whose letters she'd looked forward to, with whom she'd felt she was forming a bond, if only of the epistolary sort.

The man who was far younger and handsomer and, well, *male* than she'd imagined.

The man who was now laughing so hard he had tears in his eyes.

* * *

"P-Pardon me," Edward gasped. He shouldn't be laughing. The woman must think him a Bedlamite—a Bedlamite on whom her charity relied—but the situation did have all the markings of a farce.

He managed to swallow his mirth and bow. "It's a pleasure to meet you finally, Lady Havenridge. I knew you'd be here—Darrow mentioned you were to be the baby's godmother—but I hadn't expected—"

Fortunately, his years as a solicitor took control of his tongue.

"—to meet you in a field with Thomas and Bear."

What he'd almost said was he hadn't expected her to be so attractive.

He'd been concerned when he'd seen a woman with Thomas. Not alarmed—not quite that. It *was* the country, and Bear would not have left Thomas's side if the female had been at all threatening. But Thomas was a child—mature for his age, yes, perceptive, but still only a young boy. Edward wished to evaluate any adult who interacted with him.

Thoroughly evaluate.

Zounds, where had that *thought come from?*

He pushed it away.

Or tried to. He was dealing with a bit of mental vertigo at the moment.

Lady Havenridge did not match the picture he'd formed of her from Darrow's report and his own reading of her letters. She looked younger, for one. Not young—he knew she was close to his own age—but she was most certainly not the matronly, colorless female Darrow had described.

Well, the dress *was* matronly. The bonnet, too. But the woman . . .

The woman was bright red with mortification.

"The pleasure is mine, Your Grace," she told his cravat. The bodice of the matronly gown rose and fell rapidly.

She wasn't cowed by his title, was she? Or, worse, discomfited by her reliance on his charity?

Or overcome with lust and longing?

He almost laughed again. Apparently, today was his day for wildly inappropriate thoughts.

Though I would like it if she did *lust after me.*

Everything inside him stilled.

Is that true?

Perhaps. He certainly felt far more . . . *interest* in Lady Havenridge than he had in any woman in London. And not just physical interest—though there was nothing "just" about *that* these days. Hell, *any* physical stirring was cause for celebration.

But he was also interested in her thoughts. He wanted to discuss her charity—its daily operations and her plans for the future. And he wanted to learn more about *her*, what had caused her to found the Home and what kept her so dedicated to the endeavor. It had been in operation for over a decade. She must have been quite young when she'd conceived the idea and put it into practice. That was really quite impressive.

Well, they had a fortnight to become better acquainted.

Much better acquainted.

Careful. There are many, many reasons why anything more than a simple friendship here would be a bad idea.

True. There was no getting around the fact that Lady Havenridge was beholden to him. Besides contributing funds, the dukedom owned the very building she lived in.

He had the power to evict her and her entire charity on a whim.

He would never do that, of course, but she had no way of knowing it. And he certainly didn't want any . . . connection they might develop to be colored by worry on her part that if she put a foot wrong, she'd risk retaliation.

"I should have realized you'd be here, Your Grace," she was saying. She had a clear, calm voice, though her color was still high. "I suppose I would have, if I'd given it more consideration."

Well, *that* was a leveler. Here he'd been looking forward to discussing her charity with her even before he'd met her and discovered he'd like to discuss much more, and she hadn't wasted a moment's thought on him.

"I *am* friends with Darrow." The words escaped before he could bite them back.

She glanced up at him and then back to his cravat, her color deepening again as she bit her lovely lower lip—

Stop that!

He looked over at Thomas. The boy had got bored with their talk and was romping nearby with Bear.

"Well, yes. Of course," she said. "I know that. I should, um, confess that I, er, hadn't actually planned to come. My decision was rather, ah, last minute."

His solicitor instincts alerted. She was hiding something. What?

He would find out eventually. He'd had years of experience ferreting out matters people preferred to keep to themselves. Often just holding one's tongue and waiting did the trick. There was something about silence that prompted people—especially people with secrets—to talk.

Her cheeks were still flushed, but now she met his gaze. "I suppose if I *had* given the matter any thought—"

She really did know how to take a man's vanity down several notches.

"—I'd have concluded that you would come later."

Which is exactly what he'd intended to do.

"I knew you were busy looking for—" She stopped, cleared her throat. "I mean I knew you were busy in London. You're a duke, after all. You have . . . business."

Hmm. It sounded as if she'd been reading the gossip columns. The bloody things breathlessly recounted every time he even looked at a female.

"But I didn't expect—well, I'll admit the thought never occurred to me—that your son and dog"—she smiled over at where Thomas and Bear were playing—"would be attending as well." She laughed. "Though I suppose Bear isn't precisely *attending*."

The laugh went straight to his heart and firmed his resolve—and something else which hadn't been firm in far too long—to get to know her better.

Well, he hoped they already *had* a friendship based on their months of correspondence. This fortnight together would let them build on that. If he remembered what Darrow had said about the expected guests, he and Lady Havenridge were the only two unattached adults. Odds were good they would be thrown together often.

He would see what, if anything developed.

You are *looking for a wife.*

Right. And Lady Havenridge has her charity to run.

He wasn't such a coxcomb that he thought she'd drop everything and jump at the opportunity to become his duchess, but he also wasn't going to assume she would dismiss the notion out of hand if they found they got along. It wasn't even as if she'd be giving up her charity. She'd merely be moving to another position, albeit at a distance. She—they—could certainly visit to see how things went on—

Don't get ahead of yourself.

"Yes, well, I'm afraid Bear wasn't invited, but I assumed Darrow wouldn't mind." He was happy he managed to keep his voice even.

Talk of Bear and invitations had got Thomas's attention. The boy frowned and came over.

"Did you ask Lord Darrow about Bear, Papa? *Does* he mind?"

Edward smiled and put a steadying hand on his son's shoulder. "I didn't see the earl, Thomas. He was out riding. But I doubt he'll have any objections. This is a large estate. And, if need be, Bear can sleep in the stables."

Thomas's frown deepened.

Blast. The boy was used to having Bear nearby. They'd got the dog when they'd first arrived at Grainger, just after their comfortable life had been changed forever by Edward's succession to the title. Bear had been little more than a puppy then—a fluffy ball with enormous paws—and he and Thomas had quickly become inseparable.

"Bear *is* a very well-behaved dog," Lady Havenridge said, smiling at Thomas. "I will be happy to vouch for his good manners if Lord Darrow needs a character reference."

Edward felt the tension drain out of Thomas's shoulder. The boy grinned at Lady Havenridge.

He might be grinning at her, too. She'd said exactly the right thing to calm Thomas's nerves.

Zounds, I'm more than half in love with the woman already. I—

I need to slow down.

He had to think like a solicitor. Focus on facts. He could *not* let his half-resurrected cock have any say in matters.

Yet.

He was hopeful that the time might come when he *could* consult that organ.

Bear was now sniffing Edward's satchel—which got Thomas's attention.

"What's in the bag, Papa?"

"I'm not entirely certain. I asked Lord Darrow's butler if I might have something for a picnic, and this is what came up from the kitchen. I haven't had a look inside yet."

"Oh! Let's look now!"

Edward laughed and held the bag away from Thomas—and Bear. "Patience."

Then he smiled at Lady Havenridge. "Thomas and I—and Bear—spent the morning cooped up in my traveling carriage, so I thought we'd go exploring and find a nice spot for our picnic. We'd be delighted if you'd care to join us." He hefted the satchel. "It feels like there's enough here to feed an army."

Thomas became his enthusiastic, if unwitting, coconspirator. "Yes, do come, Miss Jo!" He gave a little hop and then stopped, worry creasing his brow. "I mean, Lady Ha-Havenridge."

The woman laughed again.

Edward could get addicted to that sound.

"I'd be delighted to join you, but please, call me Miss Jo, Thomas. I'm sure that's what Harriet, Pen's—I mean Lady Darrow's—daughter will do. She's called me Miss Jo since she learned to talk."

Thomas grinned again, making Edward's heart cramp. Zeus, how he wished he could keep him safe from all life's disappointments and sorrows.

An impossible task, of course, especially as Thomas had already suffered the great sorrow of losing his mother. Not that Thomas missed *her*—missed Helen. He'd never known her.

Which was tragic in and of itself.

"And if you were to call me Lady Havenridge, I would have to call you by your title."

Thomas pulled a face. "I just want to be Thomas."

"Very well. Then I must be Miss Jo."

Thomas grinned. "Yes, Miss Jo!" And then he looked at Edward. "Where are we going to picnic, Papa?"

Edward gestured to the line of trees at the edge of the lawn. "The butler said there's a path through the woods that will take us to a nice spot by a stream. There's even a bench there to sit on while we eat. Does that sound good?"

"Yes! May Bear and I go look for the path?"

Edward nodded. "But stop when you find it. I don't want you going into the woods and getting too far ahead of us."

"Yes, Papa. We will, Papa. Come on, Bear!"

And then Thomas took off, Bear at his heels—or sometimes ahead.

Ah, to be a boy again, with no worries.

If only that were truly the case. Thomas seemed to have worries aplenty.

He turned to Lady Havenridge and offered her his arm. "Shall we follow, but at a more sedate pace?"

She laughed up at him. "Yes, but not at a *sedate* pace. We don't want to keep Thomas waiting—that would be torture."

Zeus, she understands the boy so well already.

Then she ignored his arm and started off across the lawn.

He watched her for a moment, admiring how straight

her back was, how determined and confident her stride. Clearly, she was used to charting her own course.

But traveling life by yourself could be lonely. There was joy in sharing the ups and downs of the journey with someone else.

Would Lady Havenridge agree? More to the point, would she be willing to adjust her path to run alongside his and Thomas's?

Did he want her to?

He had a fortnight to discover the answers to those questions.

Chapter Four

Lady Havenridge paused and looked back at him. "*Are* you coming?"

He grinned. She sounded so impatient.

"Yes." He caught up to her, but this time had the sense not to bother offering his arm. "I do hope we aren't keeping you from something?"

Why *was* she out walking alone? Darrow and the men had gone riding, but he'd got the impression the women were all still inside, gathered in one of the drawing rooms.

Her eyes slid away from his. "Oh, no. I . . . er. I was just stretching my legs. I, too, arrived this morning, a little before you."

And why were her cheeks suddenly flushed? It couldn't be from exertion. They were not walking that quickly. Was she uncomfortable being alone with him?

No. He'd given her the chance to decline his offer to join the picnic, but she hadn't taken it. And while it *was* true that Thomas and Bear weren't right by their sides to chaperone them, that problem—if it *was* a problem—would be remedied in a moment.

She wasn't a young girl, unused to male companionship.

She was a widow, but, perhaps more to the point, she'd run her charity for years. She must be used to dealing directly with men on business matters. She'd certainly been forthright in her letters, more so than many men, who were all too often intimidated by his title.

Blech! Intimidated by my title whilst turning up their noses at me.

Perhaps her heightened color had a more promising cause. Perhaps this brief moment together had unleashed her passions, making her lust—

That's not your reason talking.

Time to move the conversation along.

"Thomas and I—and Bear—" He smiled, hoping she'd smile back.

She kept her eyes trained in front of her, so he shrugged mentally and continued.

"We were able to leave London early this morning, but I believe Little Puddledon is quite a bit farther away, is it not?"

And now her cheeks were even redder. What in the world was going on?

"Y-yes. It is. I had to stay at an inn o-overnight."

She did not elaborate.

Had something happened at the inn? While a man might encounter problems on the road, a woman traveling alone, even a mature, independent one like Lady Havenridge, was at far greater risk for unpleasantness, if not actual physical harm. Was that what had happened?

He didn't think so. Lady Havenridge seemed more embarrassed than frightened or upset.

But what could she be embarrassed about?

"Oh?" He waited, giving her the opportunity to say more. She didn't.

This conversation was like pulling teeth. Perhaps he should bring up the Home. That would likely loosen her tongue. Was it what she was hoping for? But then why didn't she broach the topic herself?

He hoped she didn't. Yes, he wanted to discuss her charity, but not right now. Now he just wanted to enjoy being out in the country on a pleasant summer day with Thomas and Bear.

And Lady Havenridge.

Yes. Despite the current awkwardness, he felt . . . happy to have her walking at his side.

I must be daft.

And speaking of his son . . .

He looked around. Thomas and Bear had disappeared. "Thomas!"

Thomas's—and Bear's—heads popped out from between two trees. "Over here, Papa," Thomas called back. "We found the path!"

"Excellent!" He adjusted course, lengthening his stride.

No. Wait. He wasn't alone. He should—

Lady Havenridge passed him. Of course she did.

By the time they reached Thomas, the boy was hopping from foot to foot with eagerness to be off, and Bear was whining and wiggling.

"Now, Papa? Can we go *now*?"

Edward looked down the path. It was broad and straight. "Yes. But no going off on any side trails. I don't want to lose you."

"You won't lose me, Papa. I've got Bear. He'll find his way, won't you, Bear?"

Bear barked, wagging his tail vigorously.

"Perhaps he will, but I would prefer not to rely on him,

if you please." Edward hefted the satchel. "And I imagine you want your picnic, don't you? You must be hungry."

Thomas was always hungry.

Well, Thomas had always been hungry when last Edward had had the freedom to spend much time with him. *Bloody London Season.*

"Yes, Papa. I *am* hungry! We'll go find the bench now. Come on, Bear!"

Bear gave a joyous woof, and the two took off running.

Edward managed to keep from calling after them to take care. He sighed instead. "I need to learn to let go."

He'd said the words to himself, but of course Lady Havenridge heard them.

"It's hard to do, isn't it?"

He raised his brows before he could stop himself, and she flushed.

Hell. He hadn't meant to question her observation. He opened his mouth to try to mend matters, but she was already talking.

"Oh, I know. I don't have a child of my own, but I have counseled many mothers over the years." She smiled. "Mothers of girls, yes, but, more to the point, mothers who don't have the luxury of holding on to their children for long. Mothers who have no power in the face of a world that does not value them or their daughters."

Right. And here he was a man—and a duke now. He had enormous power compared to the women of the Home.

Worldly power. Wealth and political influence. But that wasn't the power that mattered to him.

He had no power over death. He'd learned that lesson all too well.

"It's just that I have to make all the decisions by myself.

My wife—Thomas's mother—died from childbirth. It's been just the two of us, just Thomas and I, his entire life."

That was no excuse, though, was it? The women of the Home had to raise their daughters alone, too, and, worse, they were alone not by fate, but by choice—the children's fathers' choice.

Though even that might be giving the men too much credit. It was just as likely they'd not spared a thought as to whether their few moments of fun had created a new life.

He felt Lady Havenridge's comforting touch on his arm.

"You seem to have done a good job raising Thomas, Your Grace. I was very impressed with the way he handled himself when I first met him. He was polite and well-spoken, direct but respectful. But, more importantly, he took responsibility for Bear's actions and seemed sincerely concerned about how they might have affected me. That is extremely mature behavior in anyone, but I think it's quite rare in such a young child."

His heart swelled with . . . pride, yes, but also some other emotion. Some rare, expansive happiness he wasn't certain he'd felt before. No one had ever praised Thomas to him this way.

Of course, they hadn't. He'd never discussed Thomas with another adult. Whom would he talk to? He could list his close friends on one hand and have fingers left over. Darrow. Livy Williams, a Cyprian he used to visit after Helen died and before he succeeded to the title. And . . .

Hell, is that it?

It might be. Helen had been his best friend—his only friend while she was alive. He hadn't felt the need for other close relationships. When she died, he'd focused solely on work and on Thomas.

And then, once he became duke . . . Bah! Everyone wanted something from him. He'd learned to view each new acquaintance with suspicion.

So why do I trust Lady Havenridge? I've just met her. In person.

He'd been corresponding with her for almost a year. He'd shared more thoughts with her than he'd shared with any other woman save Helen and Livy. And yes, the thoughts had been about her business, but when one's business was a charity for women and children, it was impossible to keep matters to simply pounds and pence. Topics spilled over into values of the non-monetary sort.

And it was impossible not to form an opinion about the woman's character, her determination, her passion—

Enough about passion.

He started down the path. He—they—should catch up to Thomas. Chances were the boy had found the bench and was wondering what had become of them.

"It must have been very hard having sole charge of a newborn," Lady Havenridge said as they stepped in under the trees. "Well, of course it was hard—*and* you'd just suffered a terrible loss with the death of your wife."

She looked up at him. Did he see compassion in her eyes? In the dappled forest light, it was hard to be certain. But he definitely heard compassion in her voice. It loosened a knot in his chest he'd not until that moment realized was there.

"I *thought* it was hard. Well, it was—all the feeding and changing and comforting." He smiled. "And all the sleep lost. But looking back, dealing with an infant was easy. In many ways, I just had to *be* there. Now I have to *think*. I can't just *tell* Thomas not to do something, I have to tell him *why*—and sometimes I don't know why myself."

Lady Havenridge nodded. She really was an excellent listener.

But that doesn't mean you have to spill all your private thoughts, all your worries, all the times you feel you've fallen short into her ears.

True. However, that seemed to be what he was going to do.

Perhaps it was the quiet of the woods, the soaring trees. It gave one the illusion of privacy, the feeling of a church confessional.

Or perhaps it was simply the chance to unburden himself to someone who seemed sympathetic and had far more experience with children than he had.

He'd been a solicitor. He knew the benefit of an expert opinion.

"When Thomas was little, keeping him safe was merely a matter of blocking off the stairs and putting the cutlery out of his reach. Now he is growing more and more independent. He can think for himself—he *needs* to think for himself. I know that. But I also know he doesn't have the experience to make good, informed decisions."

He looked down at her, willing her to understand. "Sometimes I want to order him to do something just because I say so, but that seems wrong."

"I quite agree," Lady Havenridge said with a decisive nod. "Oh, yes, once in a rare while, that sort of command has its place, but from what I've observed at the Home, in the general way of things, issuing orders only makes a child resentful. It doesn't teach her—or him—how to make good choices."

That was the heart of the problem, wasn't it?

"But how do you teach that skill? And, perhaps more to the point, how can I keep from worrying all the time?" He searched her face, hoping she had an answer for him. "Some decisions are easy. The consequence of a poor choice is minimal. If you don't finish your dinner, you're hungry later. If you don't wear your galoshes, your feet get wet. But others . . ."

He took a deep breath.

She smiled at him. "I don't think that you can ever stop worrying completely, but as you see Thomas make more and more decisions, starting with the easy ones like eating his dinner or wearing his galoshes, you'll see he gets better at it and you'll likely worry less. He'll learn to trust himself, and you'll learn to trust him"—her smile grew—"most of the time."

That made sense, but it didn't mean it would be easy.

The alternative, however, was unacceptable.

"I don't want to stifle Thomas's spirit. My father let me and my brothers roam the countryside at will. He didn't worry about us the way I worry about Thomas."

Lady Havenridge smiled. "You don't *know* that your father didn't worry. He might have managed to hide it."

He frowned. "I suppose that's possible."

She laughed, apparently recognizing his skepticism. "Or perhaps your father left all the worrying to your mother. Remember, you are both father and mother to Thomas."

"Right." Zeus, he wished he didn't have to go it alone, that he had someone like Lady Havenridge at his side to help him raise his son.

He looked down at her. *Perhaps someone* exactly *like Lady Havenridge.*

"From what I've seen," she was saying, "children who do best, who seem most able to weather life's slings and arrows, are those who are loved but not coddled. You love Thomas. Now you need to try not to coddle him. Let him make his own mistakes—within reason, of course. It's how he'll learn." She smiled. "I think you've done a better job of that than you seem to give yourself credit for. As I said before, I was very impressed with Thomas when I met him. I thought him quite charming, neither cocky nor timid. Very bright and self-possessed for a child his age."

His heart swelled with happiness again and his lips stretched into a broad and perhaps slightly demented grin. "Thank you. I don't often hear . . . That is, most women . . ."

He looked into her understanding, sympathetic eyes, and all of a sudden, an overwhelming need washed through him. Not a sexual need—this had nothing to do with his cock. No, it was more the need—the *desperate* need—a drowning man must feel for a life buoy he sees thrown within his reach. Or what a cold, lost man must feel when, after stumbling for days on end in the wilderness, he comes upon a house, smoke curling up from its chimney, candles flickering in the windows.

Words tumbled out before his brain had fully engaged. "I wish . . . Would you—"

Zeus! Bite your tongue, man!

He did, just in time. He looked away, down the dirt path flanked by the tall trunks of pine trees. He couldn't risk letting this all-too-perceptive woman glimpse his tangled thoughts. She'd be certain to see that he'd been on the verge of asking her to marry him, and then she'd think him a Bedlamite in truth.

What the hell is the matter with me?

It must be just that Lady Havenridge was the first sensible woman he'd conversed with since, well, Livy. She wasn't a London debutante, eager to wed and become a duchess. Oh, no. She was older. Wiser.

And she had a charity to run—one she would not want to leave. If he pressed her—if he even raised the topic of marriage—he'd risk ruining the comfortable business relationship they had.

You just met her in person a few minutes ago. How can you know you want to marry her? You might just want to hire her as Thomas's governess. Don't be an idiot.

All valid points but, apparently, he *was* an idiot because he was not persuaded.

But he did have self-control—he'd had years of training in that. He knew how to keep his own counsel.

He looked down at Lady Havenridge again, attired in her matronly dress and bonnet. She wasn't as young or as beautiful as the women who'd been pursuing him in London, but she was far more interesting. Her smile was warm, her gaze direct, her conversation intelligent. And . . .

His eyes dropped lower. He'd be willing to bet that under her rather plain dress, she was very lovely indeed.

There was no rush. They had a fortnight together. He would see what, if anything, developed between them.

When the duke broke eye contact, Jo looked off into the woods. She could tell he needed time to sort out his feelings.

She needed time to sort out hers, too.

Why do I feel so . . . disoriented?

Because I'm used to counseling mothers, *I suppose.*

She felt a thread of doubt at that explanation, but she pushed it aside.

Of course, that must be what it was. She'd never counseled fathers. With the exception of the Earl of Darrow, she'd never *met* the fathers whose daughters lived at the Home.

From what the mothers told her, the daughters hadn't met them, either.

Talking to the duke now made her realize how deeply she'd come to believe most men didn't care about their offspring—or even if they had offspring. She'd told herself the male of the species blithely scattered his seed hither and thither and never looked back to see if anything sprouted. Freddie had certainly never given her to think he cared if he'd gifted any of his lovers with a child.

Not that she and Freddie had ever had a real conversation about the matter—or about any matter.

Oh, she'd observed the families in Little Puddledon, of course. Obviously, those fathers accepted their children and likely loved them. Her own father—

She closed her eyes briefly as pain lanced through her.

When she'd chosen to go to Puddledon Manor, to strike out on her own instead of going back to her father's house, he had cut their connection. Neither he nor her mother had put pen to paper to write her in all the years she'd run the Home.

She clenched her jaw. Swallowed. She was fine with that. She didn't need them. But it still hurt.

She could not imagine the duke ever cutting ties to Thomas—or, as Freddie's father had done to Jo's sorrow, one day pressuring him to marry.

She glanced up to find he was now looking down at her. His eyes—

His eyes sent butterflies fluttering wildly through her stomach again. Suddenly, she was intensely aware of walking alone with a man—with *this* man. Aware, not threatened—not that. Just . . . alert and . . .

Excited?

Apparently so. Parts of her that had been asleep for over a decade awoke and stirred. *Need* stirred.

She'd not been with a man since well before Freddie died. He'd stopped coming to her bed once he'd realized she couldn't give him what he wanted—an heir. For carnal satisfaction, he far preferred frolicking in someone else's bed. *Many* someone elses. Professional someone elses.

She hadn't missed his . . . attentions. The physical side of marriage had been tolerable in the beginning, but she'd been just as happy when Freddie had decided to take his needs elsewhere. She certainly didn't crave bedroom activity the way many of the women at the Home did.

The experience might be different with this *man . . .*

Stop! What a shockingly inappropriate thought.

She was just feeling . . . odd now because she was used to dealing with women.

Well, yes, she did do business with some of the village men, but that was different. This was . . .

Business! Remember, this man is the Home's main benefactor!

The duke grinned. He suddenly looked as young and boyish as his son. As carefree.

Though, to be honest, Thomas had not seemed an especially carefree child.

"Zeus, it's good to be out in the country. I knew London's dirt and noise were wearing on me, but I hadn't realized how much until now." He snorted. "Well, dirt, noise, *and* the *ton*. London ballrooms can be dreadful places."

"Yes, indeed." She had too many memories of hot, crowded, *vicious* ballrooms—and the many sad, potted palms she'd hidden behind.

She must have put a bit too much emotion into those two words, because there was a pause and then the duke said, "Oh?"

Lud! She could *feel* him looking at her, but she kept her eyes on the path in front of them as if she were afraid some rogue tree root might leap up to trip her.

She must remember this man was far more perceptive than Freddie had ever been.

Well, what she was about to say could not come as a surprise to him. Freddie had been only a very minor actor in the *ton's* dramas, but no player was too small for the gossips. And he *had* killed himself. That guaranteed his memory—and her connection to him—would never be allowed to sink into oblivion.

"As you must know, my husband was not, ah, held in high esteem by polite society." She snorted loudly enough to cause a squirrel, one paw on the path in front of them, to reconsider and dart back into the underbrush. "Much of the *ton* gave him—and thus me—the cut direct. So, no, I do not miss London, and I *especially* do not miss London ballrooms with all the ladies and gentlemen staring and whispering and sniggering."

Oh, blast. She'd not meant to speak quite so forcefully.

"Right." Grainger's voice was forceful, too, tight with suppressed . . . anger?

She looked over and saw his face was tight, as well.

"I understand far better than you might realize, Lady Havenridge. Yes, I'm the Duke of Grainger now, but before that I was just a London solicitor." His lip curled. "To the lords and ladies of the *ton*, I still stink of the shop. They tolerate me only because they want me to make one of their daughters a duchess."

Yes, she *had* noted the disdain—sometimes faint, sometimes all too obvious—in the way the gossip columnists wrote about him.

"That must be . . ." She searched for the proper word, but came up only with a woefully inadequate, if safe, one. "Unpleasant."

This time it was the duke's snort that caused a squirrel to change direction.

She'd thought when she'd read the story of his being plucked from obscurity to great wealth and prestige, that he must have been delighted at his astounding good fortune. It was just like a fairy tale.

But real life rarely had tidy happily-ever-afters, did it?

"I suppose it must have been a shock to ascend so suddenly to the top of the peerage."

The duke gave a sharp nod. "It was. Who thinks an entire branch will be lopped off the family tree"—he snapped his fingers—"just like that? I grew up knowing I was related to the duke—distantly related. But I also knew I had to make my own way in the world." He looked down at her. "And I did. I worked hard, built a good life, a good career." He shook his head. "And then everything changed." He sighed. "Again."

They walked several steps in silence. Death had changed Jo's life in the snap of fingers, too—or more, in the pull of a trigger. It had changed the duke's life twice, first taking his wife and then the old duke and his family.

She would never have said hers and the duke's situations were similar, but perhaps they were, at least in this regard. They both knew how fragile life was.

She heard a jay screech high in the branches above them, a squirrel complain about their intrusion—and Thomas call to Bear somewhere farther up the path.

The duke heard Thomas as well and grinned down at her. "I do hope I won't have to fish him out of the water."

His smile did odd things to her breathing—but his words quickly pushed the fluttering aside. "He can swim, can't he?"

Grainger frowned. "Well enough to get to the bank if he did fall in. I'm not really worried, but—"

"Papa! Miss Jo!"

Thomas and a suspiciously wet-looking Bear came running back down the path toward them.

"We found the stream. Come see!"

Chapter Five

Well, that *was embarrassing.*

Except, oddly enough, it wasn't embarrassment Edward felt. It was . . .

Peace?

He walked along the path, watching Thomas hop and skip next to Lady Havenridge—they were now a few paces ahead of him with Bear in the lead—and listened to the boy's chatter and Lady Havenridge's replies.

"Does your dog like water, Miss Jo?"

"Oh, yes. I think all dogs must, don't you?"

His surroundings were certainly peaceful—if you discounted a young boy and a large dog. He'd always found the woods calming. The trees blocked out the sights and sounds—and worries—of the world and allowed him to focus on the present moment.

On Thomas.

And on Lady Havenridge.

He watched her smile down at his son. She was a very easy woman to talk to.

Too easy, as you've already discovered. A confidence shared cannot be unshared. You'd best be more cautious.

He was sick of being cautious. Since his elevation to the peerage, he'd felt he'd had to be on his guard every moment.

His instincts told him he could trust Lady Havenridge, and his instincts had always steered him right in the past. She wasn't a stranger. He'd been corresponding with her for months. Her letters had shown her to be intelligent. Thoughtful.

And now, to his pleasant surprise, he discovered she was also a good listener.

And kind. No other woman of his acquaintance would engage this way with his son.

And attractive. Don't forget attractive.

Yes. Not conventionally beautiful, perhaps. She would not be the first woman most men's eyes would find in a ballroom. To be honest, perhaps *his* eyes wouldn't have picked her out of a crowd of young—of young*er*—women.

Which just went to show how silly ballrooms were for meeting a prospective wife—

Whoa. Pull up. Remember—don't rush matters.

He wouldn't. He had a fortnight. He would see what, if anything, developed. If, by the end of the house party, things still looked promising, he would finally make that trip down to Little Puddledon to visit the Home and see Lady Havenridge at her charity. They could continue to explore their acquaintance and see if they might have a future together.

"Yes." Thomas hopped on one foot. "Bear likes water a lot!"

Lady Havenridge smiled knowingly. "And you have to be careful, don't you, when he comes *out* of the water?"

Thomas laughed—and the sound went straight to Edward's heart. Zeus, he'd not heard his son laugh enough of late.

"Yes! He shakes and sends water everywhere!"

They rounded a bend in the path and saw the stream— and a small clearing with the promised bench.

Bear took off for the water, Thomas following. "Come look at the fish, Miss Jo," he called over his shoulder.

"Are there a lot of them?" Lady Havenridge hurried after the boy with every appearance of enthusiasm.

Edward was left holding the bag.

Literally.

He walked over to the bench, put the satchel down, and then made his way to the stream. Thomas and Lady Havenridge were already crouched on the bank, their heads almost touching, both looking at something in the water.

"There's one!" Thomas's voice was bright with excitement.

"And there's another. Oh! Look over there, Thomas— there's a newt!"

"Where? Oh, yes, I see."

Bear came over to investigate as well, and the newt, wisely, darted under some leaves.

"Don't eat it, Bear!" Thomas looked up at Edward. "Papa, you missed the newt!"

Lady Havenridge looked up at him, too, her eyes laughing. "Come down here with us, Your Grace. If you are lucky, we'll see another." She directed her eyes at Bear and said, with mock sternness, "That is if *someone* doesn't frighten them all away."

Bear barked, but it was unclear whether he meant to argue his case or to encourage Edward to join the fun.

Edward smiled, a sudden lump in his throat making it

impossible to speak. Had he ever seen another adult—one that he didn't employ—engage with his son this way?

No.

You can't marry someone because she is good with Thomas.

True, but he was feeling more and more confident Lady Havenridge would be good with *him*. He was definitely looking forward to exploring the question, even if he had to squat on a muddy stream bank to do so.

But he would not be clambering around in the mud now. "May I suggest we eat before we get too dirty?"

Thomas frowned. "But, Papa, what if we miss some newts?"

"I think there will still be newts available for viewing after we eat."

Lady Havenridge nodded and stood, shaking out her skirts. "Yes, indeed. And it will be pleasanter to eat with clean hands, Thomas, don't you think?"

Thomas looked unpersuaded.

Edward opened his mouth to order the boy to come up, but stopped when Lady Havenridge laughed.

"Well, no matter," she said. "*I* prefer clean hands—and I'm quite hungry. It's been hours since I had breakfast." She smiled at Thomas. "Aren't you hungry?"

Thomas jumped up as if his stomach had just that moment spoken to him. "Yes, Miss Jo. I *am* hungry. I'm *starving*. It's been *hours* since I had breakfast, too."

Thomas said "hours" as if he meant days.

Edward led the way to the bench and took his seat at one end. Lady Havenridge sat at the other, and Thomas bounced up and down between them.

Bear sprawled at their feet and looked hopeful.

"What's in the bag, Papa?" Thomas leaned forward.

"Patience, Thomas," Edward said. "I have to open it first."

"Yes, Papa." Thomas sat back a few inches, still bouncing with excitement.

Edward smiled, and then opened the satchel and looked in. "Let's see. Ah. There's bread, cheese, apples—and some gingerbread for after."

Thomas leaned closer. "Gingerbread?"

"For after." Edward smiled and then turned to Bear. "And a nice beef bone for you."

Bear barked his approval and beat his tail on the ground.

Edward parceled out the provisions, and the next few minutes were spent happily chewing.

"Do you have any brothers, Miss Jo?" Thomas asked around a mouthful of bread and cheese.

Edward considered correcting his manners—besides talking with food in his mouth, it wasn't quite the thing to ask such personal questions—but he was interested in the answer, too, and Lady Havenridge was already speaking.

"No. Only sisters—three older and three younger."

Thomas wrinkled his nose, clearly not impressed by an all-female household. "Jasper says girls don't like bugs and frogs and things, but you do. I thought you must have a brother."

Edward frowned at Thomas. "Jasper?" Thomas's tutor's name was Henry. "Who's Jasper?"

"Mr. Green's son—the one who's two years older than I am."

Edward must have been staring blankly because Thomas added helpfully, "You know, Papa. Mr. *Green*. He has the farm next to Mr. Fisher's—the one with the white spot on the barn and a cow named Daisy."

"Right." He had no idea who Mr. Fisher was either. Clearly, he needed to pay more attention to a number of matters.

"Well, I'm afraid Jasper is misinformed," Lady Havenridge said. "Girls can like anything they want."

Thomas did not look completely convinced, but wisely chose not to argue the matter. "Papa has only brothers."

Lady Havenridge looked at him.

"It's true. I've three younger brothers—two in the army and one in the navy. I'm the only one still here in England."

He'd always thought he'd have a family like the one he'd grown up in, rough and tumble and happy. That's what he and Helen had wanted, but it hadn't happened.

"I'd like to have brothers," Thomas was telling Lady Havenridge. "Jasper has six." Thomas shrugged. "*Maybe* I'd like a sister. I don't know."

Lady Havenridge was not going to give him six children—

Of course, she isn't, you idiot. Suggest it and she'll give you a swift kick that will end your hopes of fathering even one more child. You'd better—

"Do you want children, Miss Jo?"

Good Lord! This time he *would* intervene.

"Thomas, that is *not* something you ask a lady."

Thomas was still looking at Lady Havenridge. "I'm sorry, Miss Jo. I didn't mean to make you sad."

And she *did* look sad, didn't she?

"But if you had a new husband, you might be able to have children." Thomas smiled brightly. "It's like getting lambs or foals or calves. You need a husband to make a baby."

Edward closed his eyes. He now understood what it felt like to die of embarrassment. And if he tried to say anything, he suspected he'd only make it worse. Clearly, it was time for a distraction.

"I say, is anyone ready for gingerbread?"

Chapter Six

Jo stood in her bedroom and looked out the window at the intricate hedge maze some previous Earl of Darrow had planted. Her focus, however, was on a different, less orderly maze—her tangled feelings.

She was so . . . unsettled. It was not like her. She usually knew her own mind. Yes, she'd been on edge since Caro had left the Home and Livy had moved in, but this was different. This was . . .

To be honest, she hardly recognized herself.

Instead of seeking out Pen or Caro when she'd got back from her informal picnic with the duke and his son, she'd come up here. She'd told herself she needed to wash her hands and face and change her clothes after being out in the mud, hunting fish and newts and skipping stones—which she did.

And which she had done, quite a while ago. And yet, here she was, still in her room.

Hiding? Is that *what I'm doing?*

No. She just needed some privacy, some time to sort out her thoughts before she was around other people, particularly her sharp-eyed former partners.

And the duke.

An odd frisson of excitement danced through her.

It's just that I'm eager to discuss the Home with him.

Ha! She didn't usually lie to herself, either. She *did* want to talk about her charity, of course, but that didn't explain the butterflies that were back in her stomach.

The hours she'd spent with Grainger and Thomas had been unlike anything she could remember. She'd felt free and light and, well, *playful.*

The duke had said he was happy because he'd left the dirt and noise of London behind, but she couldn't claim that as the explanation for her high spirits. She'd spent the last decade in the country.

But always working. Always worrying. Always alone—

She frowned. No. She might always be working and worrying, but she was never alone. The Home was far too crowded.

It's possible to be alone in the middle of a crowd.

True. And it was also true that her friendship with Pen and Caro, a friendship that had sustained her all these years, had changed. It wasn't just that they didn't live at the Home any longer. They had different priorities now. They had husbands. Families . . .

Maybe that was it. Today's activities had given Jo the illusion of being part of a family.

She'd spent years surrounded by children—well, *girls.* But the girls' mothers had been there, too. Jo had never had to *be* a mother—to *act* as a mother. And no child had ever asked her to do so.

No child had ever looked at her the way Thomas had looked at her. It had been . . . nice.

That didn't mean she could agree to what he'd asked. Of course not. She knew better than that. But it had made her feel . . . different. Connected. Happy. She had enjoyed being with him.

And you enjoyed being with his father.

The butterfly population in her stomach exploded. Some fluttered up into her chest—and others ventured down to her feminine bits.

Oh, Lord. She closed her eyes and groaned, resting her forehead against the window. *Why* did the man have to be so handsome?

And so kind and so—

She straightened and glared at the maze.

Stop! You are being foolish beyond permission. You are here for a fortnight. You are not looking for a husband, especially not a husband who will take you away from the Home.

Right. That was Livy's plan, not hers. And, more to the point, the duke would not want a wife who couldn't give him children. He might have his heir, but he would want his spare.

Well, she suspected he would like several spares as well as a few daughters.

And he *should* have more children. It would be a shame if he didn't. He was so good with Thomas.

She heard voices in the corridor. Everyone must be going down to the drawing room to assemble before dinner. She should go down, too. She couldn't spend the entire fortnight hiding in this room.

If I don't go down soon, Pen will send someone to fetch me.

She turned away from the window. It was time to stop cowering and—

She caught another look at herself in the glass and her courage deserted her. She'd chosen this dress because it seemed to have a little more of a bodice than the others, but it was still barely—with the emphasis on *bare*—decent. What was she going to do?

She looked around the room. She couldn't pull down the curtains or wrap herself in the coverlet—

Aha! She spotted a lace cloth draped over a table by the fire, protecting the wood from nicks and water stains. Well, now it could protect her from embarrassment, at least until she could ask Pen to lend her a proper shawl or a fichu.

She plucked it up, threw it around her shoulders, and sallied forth before her courage deserted her again.

Jo paused outside the door to the drawing room to adjust her makeshift shawl and exhort her resident butter-flies to settle down.

"May I get the door for you, madam?"

"Oh!" She hadn't heard the butler come up. He was standing next to her now, likely wondering why she'd been rooted to the spot like a gawk.

She would pretend she expected doors to be opened for her. "Er, yes. Thank you."

He looked relieved. "And shall I announce you?"

"Oh, no. No need of that." She would prefer to slink in and find some nice curtains to hide behind.

I'm being silly. It's just a little skin, no more than the vast majority of women show. It's not like I'm mother-naked.

She took a deep breath—and then a quick glance down to confirm she hadn't inadvertently exposed more of herself—and stepped over the threshold. She saw Lord Darrow's mother—now Lady Muddlegate—and her new husband, Lord Muddlegate, talking to Darrow's widowed sister, Letitia, and a man who must be Letitia's new husband,

Mr. Adam Marsh. Not far from them were some lovely, thick, concealing curtains—

"Jo!"

That was Caro's voice! Jo's head snapped around—

Oh! There was the Duke of Grainger, tall and handsome in his snowy cravat and dark superfine coat. Though he'd been equally handsome earlier when he'd been a bit wind-blown and rumpled—

Don't stare!

Her eyes veered off to the man he was talking to—a stranger—and then on to . . .

"Caro!" Seeing her former partner—her very *pregnant* former partner—hurrying toward her swept away all her feelings of awkwardness and self-consciousness. "It is *so* good to see you."

She gave Caro a hug.

There was rather a lot of Caro to hug.

Jo stepped back and smiled. "You look very well."

It was true. Until this moment, she'd not really believed Caro was happy. Yes, Caro's letters had been cheerful, but paper and pen could conceal as much as—or more than—they revealed. However, now that she could *see* her friend . . .

Caro glowed.

Though Jo thought her happiness was dimmed just slightly by a hint of fatigue.

"How do you feel?"

Caro grimaced. "Enormous. I can't believe I have almost two more months left." She sighed and put her hand on her belly. "And this little fellow seems to think it's time to jump and kick the minute I lie down to sleep." She snorted. "Or, rather, *try* to sleep."

Jo smiled as she always did when expectant mothers

unburdened themselves to her. "An active baby means a healthy baby. He—or she—will be out in the world soon."

"Not soon enough."

Caro grumbled, but it was clear she wasn't seriously complaining. She was just tired of being large and awkward—a reasonable reaction.

It was rather amazing what the female body could do.

Well, *some* female bodies.

Freddie had wanted Jo to have children—or, rather, he'd wanted her to have *a* child—his heir. It had been his sole reason for marrying her—a fact that, unfortunately, she'd learned only after the vows had been said.

She sometimes wondered if things would have been different between them . . . if she and Freddie might have got on better . . . if she'd been able to conceive.

She shrugged mentally. She'd never know, and it no longer mattered. She'd built a satisfying life. If she'd had children, she wouldn't have gone to Little Puddledon and established the Home—and helped many, many children and their mothers.

Things had worked out for the best.

"I hope the viscount treats you well?" Jo asked, though she already knew the answer. Caro would never put up with any man treating her less than well.

"Oh, yes. Nick is nothing like—" Caro pressed her lips together. "He's nothing like the peers I met in London." She dropped her voice, leaned closer. "I never dreamed I could be this happy, Jo. I wish you could find someone to love as much as I love Nick. Someone to marry and live happily ever after with."

Jo kept smiling. She'd long ago discovered that the newly wed all too often became marital missionaries, fervently trying to convert any spinster in their vicinity to the wonders of wedded bliss.

I'm not a spinster. I'm a widow. That's a very different breed.

Not to women like Caro, blinded as they were by matrimonial zeal.

"But, here, you must meet him, Jo." Caro took her arm and brought her over to the man who'd been talking to the Duke of Grainger and who was now, along with the duke, looking at them.

Jo ordered the blush she could feel rising to her cheeks to disperse—and hoped the light was too dim for anyone, especially the duke, to detect any heightened color.

"Nick, this is Jo—Lady Havenridge—whom I've told you so much about." She turned back to Jo. "Jo, my husband, Lord Oakland."

"How nice to meet you, Lord Oakland."

"The pleasure is mine, Lady Havenridge." The viscount had a ready smile and a warm, pleasant voice. "Caro has indeed told me much about you."

"Good things, I hope."

Lord Oakland laughed. "For the most part."

"Nick!" Caro's expression was a mix of horror and laughter.

"Oh, don't take him to task, Caro," Jo said. "I wouldn't have believed him if he'd said you'd only sung my praises."

Caro grinned, and then gestured to the duke, whom Jo had been trying very hard not to look at. "You'll never guess who this is, Jo."

The duke chuckled, an entrancing sound that curled around Jo's heart and lower organs.

She really, *really* hoped no one could see her blush.

"I believe Lady Havenridge will guess quite easily, Lady Oakland. We met earlier."

Caro's eyes widened. "You did?" She looked at Jo.

Jo frowned back at her. What did Caro think she'd done? Arranged some secret rendezvous? "I went for a walk when I arrived and encountered His Grace's son and dog. His Grace came in search of them and found me, too."

"Oh." Caro gave Jo a pointed look before turning back to the duke. "So, I assume Jo's already pleaded the Home's case, Your Grace, but let me add my voice to hers. It really is a most worthwhile endeavor. And you must know that, in addition to you, Lord Darrow supports us—" Caro laughed. "I mean *them*. Obviously, I'm no longer a part of the operation. And Oakland has agreed to contribute as well." She grinned at her husband.

He shrugged. "Not that I had a choice."

Caro's brows slammed down. "Nick, you know—"

He held up his hands to stop her. "I'm teasing." He grinned. "Mostly."

Caro gave him a warning look and then, always the saleswoman, turned back to the duke.

"I know you sent Lord Darrow to tour the Home, Your Grace, but you really should visit yourself and see what we—that is, what *Jo* is doing. Hearing of the matter secondhand, or even reading about it in Jo's letters, isn't enough to truly understand the important—the *unique*—refuge the Home offers women and children in need. *Desperate* need. Many have no other place to turn."

The duke was nodding. "I do think I should visit, Lady Oakland, though Lady Havenridge's letters have been quite persuasive and"—he hesitated for a moment—"passionate on the subject. Practical, too. I have been very impressed with her good sense." He smiled at Jo directly. "At *your* good sense, madam."

A bubble of what might be happiness and pride and something else, something odd and fluttery, formed in Jo's chest. One of her butterflies, perhaps. She felt herself start to grin—

Remember Caro's sharp eyes.

She wasn't ready to tip her hand—not that she knew herself what cards she held or wanted to play.

She swallowed the fluttery feeling and said, in a calm, even tone, "Thank you, Your Grace."

Caro put her hand on Jo's arm, reclaiming her attention.

"How *are* things at the Home, Jo? Has Polly managed to learn her way around the brewhouse? Is she getting on with Bathsheba and Esther and Albert? Are you able to keep production up to meet demand?"

Lord Oakland laughed. "Give Lady Havenridge the chance to answer one question before you ask another, Caro."

Instead of snapping at the man, which Jo expected Caro to do, Caro smiled at him.

She must *really* be in love.

"Sorry. Just tell me, Jo." Caro frowned. "It's dangerous times for the hops, though. Has Fanny kept a sharp eye on them?"

Lord Oakland cleared his throat—and Caro laughed.

"And, yes," she said, "I do realize that's another question."

At least it was a question Jo could answer without hedging.

"So far Fanny does seem to be doing a good job of keeping the bines healthy and pest-free." She smiled. "And I might be almost as obsessive as you were in checking on them, Caro. I was told Fanny would be very happy if I attended this party and stopped hovering over her."

Caro smiled back, but her eyes held the same worry they always did at this time of year. She knew how quickly the crop could be lost.

"And the brewing? Is that going well?"

Ah. Here was the time to hedge.

No. Best to be frank. Half-truths and evasions were too difficult to keep track of. You thought one would do, and then another was needed and then you couldn't remember what you'd said and what you hadn't. In no time at all, you had a tangled mess.

"We are managing," Jo said carefully, "but we've had to cut back on production."

Caro's brows slanted down.

It *was* too bad, but Caro needed to understand. "We're all having to learn new duties, myself included, Caro. It's a time of adjustment. We'll find our feet."

I hope.

"But you're here. If things weren't in good order, you'd have stayed in Little Puddledon." Caro's tone was a mix of criticism and hope.

"Er . . ."

Remember, be honest.

"I *had* sent my regrets. You're right—I'd decided I couldn't afford to be away so long—but . . ." Jo shrugged and smiled a bit sheepishly. "I suppose I *may* have been driving everyone just a trifle mad. Livy waylaid my note and penned an acceptance instead. And then she just about tied me up and threw me into Lord Darrow's carriage when it arrived."

The duke had been listening politely, but started when she'd mentioned Livy.

Oh, hell.

"Livy?" he asked cautiously, his expression guarded.

"Yes." Of course, he must know Livy well—and in the most biblical sense. He *was* a noble now—at the top of the nobility—just the sort of man whose acquaintance Livy would relish.

Well, she would pretend that she couldn't add two and two and come to the obvious sum.

"Olivia Williams. Recently of London. She came to the Home with Fanny and Polly, two of her—" Jo's nerve failed her. "Two of her *associates* when they decided to change, er, careers."

Lord Oakland laughed. "I'd had the daft idea to host a Christmas orgy at my country estate, Grainger." He grinned at Caro. "A daft idea that turned out to be brilliant. I suspect Livy got up to a bit of matchmaking."

Which must be exactly what Livy is getting up to here.

Jo finally saw the woman's plot clearly: Livy hoped Jo—or, rather, the dresses Livy had altered—would seduce the duke into offering marriage. She assumed Jo would be so overcome and starry-eyed that she'd agree—well, most women *would* jump at the chance to be a duchess—and Livy would be left holding the prize: control of the Home.

Well, day-to-day control. If I married the duke, I'd have the last word on—

Her thoughts screeched to a halt. Marriage was *not* on the agenda. She did not want to leave the charity she'd built and worked so hard to make successful, and she most certainly did not want to dive back into the *ton*'s shark-infested waters ever again.

Nor would the duke want to marry her. She was not a young, fertile female.

But that did not mean they couldn't be friends. Good friends.

Very good friends.

The image of that shocking dress of red satin and lace danced boldly into her thoughts.

This time her blush must have lit the room.

Edward had been the first to arrive in the drawing room.

He'd got Thomas settled, had met the governess—Miss Woodrow, who seemed a sensible sort and who, fortunately, was not put off by large dogs—and then had gone to his bedchamber to twiddle his thumbs and watch the clock.

Oh, and study the maze that he could see from his window. He thought Thomas would enjoy exploring it.

And Lady Havenridge?

Well, everyone liked a good maze, didn't they?

When he'd deemed it close enough to the appointed hour, he'd come downstairs—and, to his disappointment, had been shown into an empty room.

Fortunately, he hadn't been there very long before Lord and Lady Oakland appeared. He had a nodding acquaintance with Oakland—the viscount had also come to his title through a bit of an indirect and not totally welcome route—and knew of his wife. She'd been the Home's brewer—Darrow had included a note about her in his report on the charity.

And then he'd watched the door as surreptitiously as he could, hoping to see Lady Havenridge. He'd begun to worry that something had gone amiss—or that she'd decided she'd rather take a tray in her room. She hadn't seemed tired in the woods earlier—after the gingerbread had saved them from a further discussion of reproductive matters, they'd spent the rest of the afternoon exploring.

He'd almost given up—and then the door opened and there she was, dressed in a blue gown with an elegant skirt and . . .

Well, he couldn't see the bodice. She was clutching a white lace shawl around her shoulders.

To be honest, the thing looked more like a tablecloth than a shawl.

It didn't matter. His heart—and a baser organ—thrilled to see her. He tried to hide his enthusiasm, but fortunately, this wasn't a London ballroom. He didn't need to worry. No one was watching him.

He *did* hope Oakland didn't notice how often his eyes slid over to look at Lady Havenridge as she talked with Lady Oakland, but then, Oakland's gaze went to his wife equally as often.

But when Lady Havenridge had mentioned Livy? A blind man could have seen his reaction.

Livy? Matchmaking?

Lady Havenridge wasn't thinking the same thing he was, was she?

Perhaps she was. Her cheeks were suddenly quite flushed.

The high color was rather attractive.

And then her eyes met his and, to his amazement, she turned even redder.

Interesting.

He'd lay odds Livy had known he'd be here. She was very good at ferreting out information—perhaps as good as Darrow, who'd once done a bit of spying for the Crown. And according to Lady Havenridge's account, Livy had gone to some lengths to get her here. The question was—why?

Livy always had a plan—and she never thought small. He wouldn't be at all surprised if she were angling to push Lady Havenridge out and run the Home herself.

And the best way to get rid of Lady Havenridge was to marry her off.

Livy seems to have done well by Oakland and his lady . . .

True. And it was also true that Livy knew him well. He hadn't seen her since he'd succeeded to the title, but he'd always considered her a good friend as much as a lover.

At heart, her business was a matchmaking service, if of a rather base sort. Good matchmakers knew what each of their . . . customers liked. Or needed. Sometimes a matchmaker might know that better than the people she was matching.

Hmm. This might be a *very* interesting fortnight.

"Ah. And here is the guest of honor at last," Oakland said then, gesturing toward the door.

Edward looked over to see Darrow and his wife. Lady Darrow had a small bundle in the crook of her arm that must be Philip Arthur Edward Graham, Viscount Hurley.

What a large name for such a small person.

It was hard to remember—hard to imagine—that Thomas had once been that small.

The countess caught sight of their group and broke into a wide smile.

"Jo!" she said, coming over and hugging Lady Havenridge with her free arm. "It is *so* good to see you again."

And then a small frown appeared between her brows as

she looked at Lady Havenridge's shawl. Apparently, she did not find it particularly elegant, either.

"As it is to see you," Lady Havenridge said warmly—and tugged her shawl closer about her. "You look very well." She peered down at the bundle. "Oh! Lord Hurley is very handsome."

That might be a bit of a stretch. The viscount still had the disorganized, unfocused look of a newborn.

"People say he takes after me," Darrow said, coming up behind his wife with a bit of a swagger.

Edward felt a brief, unexpected stab of envy. He'd not got to have a family—mother, father, infant—with Thomas.

This afternoon with Lady Havenridge had felt like a family.

Yes, it had. His eyes slid over to look at her again.

She was looking at the baby.

Lord Hurley gave a little squeak, and Lady Darrow jiggled her arm to soothe him.

"I was afraid you might not come, Jo," she said. "That you'd think you couldn't get away." Her eyes searched Lady Havenridge's. "*Are* things going well at the Home?"

Lady Oakland snorted, which made Lady Darrow raise her brows in surprise—and Lady Havenridge shoot Lady Oakland an annoyed look.

"Things are going as well as can be expected," Lady Havenridge said. "It's not the same with you both gone. You know how I relied on you." She made a small sound, a cross between a laugh and a sigh. "Well, it wasn't until you left, too, Caro, that I realized how very *much* I'd relied on you. But the women Caro sent are settling into their positions. It might take us a while to sort everything out, but I think the Home will be fine."

Lord Hurley squeaked again, and Lady Darrow put him to her shoulder, rubbing and patting his back, swaying from side to side.

Edward remembered that motion very well, even though he'd not been around babies since Thomas was one. People did not bring their infants to see their solicitor or attend the opera.

Fortunately. Babies did not have the best manners.

And then the women started in on the hop crop. It was, to be honest, not the most interesting of topics.

Darrow was talking to Oakland, jovially warning him how his life would change once the baby arrived.

"I was on the Continent when Harriet was born," he said. "I didn't even know I had a daughter until she was about your son's age, Grainger. So I missed this helpless phase." He shook his head. "It's wonderful and terrifying at the same time."

Yes, that's true.

Oakland nodded. "Right. Caro is anxious for the baby to be born—she's getting quite uncomfortable—but I'll admit I'm more than a little nervous. Though we'll have a nursery maid, of course." He smiled. "Caro was a nursery maid years ago and was very particular about who she wanted taking care of her baby."

Grainger had hired help, too. And the women had been good, though he'd had to let the first nursery maid go. She'd acted as if, being male, he must be incapable of doing anything right around his own son.

"I find fatherhood quite agrees with me," Darrow was

saying, "though I will confess I happily hand Pip over to his nurse when he needs changing."

As if on cue, Lord Hurley's nether regions emitted an ominous sound.

"Oh, Pip!" Lady Darrow said in dismay. "You didn't!"

He had. And then, for good measure, he spit up as well.

Chapter Seven

Since it was, in large part, a family gathering, no one stood on ceremony at dinner, which meant everyone sat wherever they wished.

Or, in Jo's case, didn't wish.

Not that she'd had an opinion when she'd first found herself between Letitia and Lady Muddlegate, but she'd quickly formed a strong one.

The conversation had begun in a harmless enough manner with Lady Muddlegate smiling at her. "It is good to see you again, Lady Havenridge."

"As it is to see you, Lady Muddlegate." Jo had met Darrow's mother briefly the summer before when the woman had appeared unannounced on the Home's doorstep, having just discovered she had a granddaughter in residence. She'd still been the dowager Lady Darrow then. "And my sincere, if belated, best wishes on your marriage."

Lady Muddlegate grinned in a way that made her look thirty years younger. "Thank you. Last fall was quite the season for weddings in our family. Muddlegate and I,

Letitia and Mr. Marsh"—she nodded at the earl and Pen, sitting at either end of the table—"Darrow and Pen."

Jo smiled back. "Yes, indeed."

And *that* was where the conversation took a sharp turn for the worse. Jo sensed doom approaching when Lady Muddlegate leaned closer.

"I quite recommend remarriage, Lady Havenridge. Muddlegate is a vast improvement over my first husband, if I may be frank."

"Ah." Jo very much wanted to suggest she *not* be frank, but couldn't think of a polite way to do that.

"I heartily agree." Letitia joined the conversation from Jo's other side. "Second husbands are *much* superior. My first was also quite"—Letitia pulled a face—"unpleasant."

Jo hoped her expression didn't reveal her shock. Had Letitia been imbibing too freely? Her first husband had been Lady Muddlegate's eldest son.

She reached for her own wineglass and took a sustaining sip, bracing for the war that was about to break out around her.

To her surprise, Lady Muddlegate just sighed heavily and nodded. "It *was* too bad Walter took after his father in that."

In what?

Don't ask!

She didn't have to. Letitia told her.

"My husband had so many bastards scattered over the countryside, Lady Havenridge, that the wags came up with a name for them—Walter's whelps."

"Ah." That was bad.

Lady Muddlegate snorted. "Long before that, the

wags' parents had dubbed his father's by-blows Myles's menagerie."

"Oh." That was worse.

Jo tried not to glance longingly at Letitia's other side, where Caro was having what seemed to be a perfectly normal conversation with Pen.

Well, perhaps not. Listening more closely, she discerned they were discussing the bowel habits of newborns.

"Darrow—my deceased husband," Lady Muddlegate said, "warned Walter off several village women because they might be his half-sisters." She shrugged. "They'd dyed their hair to hide the Graham streak."

Jo's full attention snapped back to Lady Muddlegate. Ugh! That was so far beyond bad as to be completely, revoltingly horrible.

She took another sip of wine to calm her roiling stomach. At this rate, she was going to be foxed before the first course arrived.

Along with Lady Muddlegate and Letitia, it appeared. They were not neglecting their own wineglasses. Given the direction of the conversation, Jo suspected they'd indulged in a glass or two before dinner as well.

"At least *you* didn't have to worry about such things, did you?" Letitia said.

The wine threatened to go down the wrong way. *Such things?* What could the woman mean?

Something in Letitia's expression sent unease prickling up Jo's spine. She glanced at Lady Muddlegate—and saw the same look in *her* eyes.

Just smile and nod.

No. Better to know precisely what the women were getting at. After all, they were going to be spending a fortnight together. There would be no way to avoid this topic, whatever it was, if Lady Muddlegate and Letitia insisted on pursuing it.

Though Jo *would* make a point of choosing different dining companions at the next meal.

"Er, such things?"

"Yes." Letitia snorted. "Bastards. *You* didn't risk tripping over your husband's bastards at every turn, did you?"

"Ah." Well, yes, she supposed there *was* that, though it was rather rude of Letitia to mention it. "Lord Havenridge didn't care for the country, so we lived almost exclusively in Town."

Where, she assumed, the lightskirts Freddie had frolicked with either knew how to prevent conception or deposited the unfortunate results of their couplings at the Foundling Hospital.

But now women in that position can come with their children to the Benevolent Home—

Her feelings of pride and accomplishment faltered. That wasn't quite true, was it? Women with *daughters* could come. Women with sons . . .

Those women had very few options.

I really need to do something about that.

She'd look into the matter when she got back to Little Puddledon. Perhaps—

Why is Letitia staring at me as if I'm a half-wit?

"It had nothing to do with where the man resided, Lady Havenridge," Lady Muddlegate said, her tone suggesting she also thought Jo more than a bit daft. "Town or country, everyone knew Havenridge couldn't father a child."

Jo blinked.

Well, she more likely goggled. She did hope her mouth wasn't hanging open.

Everyone knew? No, not everyone. *She* hadn't known.

She took another sip of wine to give her lips something to do whilst she tried to absorb Lady Muddlegate's shocking statement. *Could* it be true? Because if it was . . .

If Freddie couldn't father a child with anyone, then perhaps his lack of an heir was his . . . well, fault *and not mine. Perhaps I* can—

Balderdash! Of course, the story wasn't true. No matter what everyone *thought* they knew, she had *intimate* knowledge of the matter. Freddie had been quite capable of copulation, but she was not about to say *that* at the dinner table.

Well, she was not going to say it anywhere.

She opened her mouth to politely but firmly change the subject—

Too late.

"You know," Letitia said, shooting a pointed glance at the Duke of Grainger on the other side of the table, a glance which, to Jo's horror, he obviously noted, "His Grace is looking for a wife."

Jo nailed her eyes to her wineglass. She was *not* going to look at the duke, even though some invisible force was urging her to do so. The poor man had just come from being hunted in London. He would not wish to feel his liberty at risk here as well.

Though he should know he was in no danger from her.

Is that true?

Of *course*, it was true! She wasn't a scheming—

Scheming . . .

Good God! Is Letitia *in league with Livy?*

"Yes," Lady Muddlegate said on her other side. "And you and he are the only two unattached adults present."

Letitia and *Lady Muddlegate?*

No, the notion was ridiculous. While Livy might have

corresponded with Caro, she would not have been so bold as to write to Darrow's mother and sister-in-law. How preposterous! No, this must be just the matchmaking urge at work, a malady that infected many otherwise sensible females.

"No one will be paying any attention to what you do," Letitia whispered. "You'll have plenty of time—"

She paused significantly. Jo was afraid to let her eyes leave her wineglass to confirm the matter, but she had a strong feeling that Letitia was waggling her brows in a telling fashion.

Please, God, let the duke be absorbed in conversation.

Or struck blind—but just until these two women moved on to more sensible topics.

"—to get to know him better." Letitia giggled. "In the *biblical* sense."

Lud!

"And then next year," Lady Muddlegate added, "Darrow can be godfather and Pen godmother to *your* child."

An odd yearning bloomed in her chest. That would be—

Impossible.

She'd had three years of marriage to prove precisely how impossible it would be.

Well, all right. Less than one year. Freddie had stopped *wasting his time*—his words—with her once it became clear she couldn't have children.

In any event, even if she *could* have children, she had no time for a husband, especially not a husband who would take her away from the Home.

Enough. It was time to take charge of this conversation. While she was not a mother herself, she'd lived with many, many mothers over the years. She knew exactly how best to redirect Letitia's and Lady Muddlegate's thoughts.

"Tell me about the girls," she said brightly, but with an underpinning of steely determination. "I've not yet seen Harriet. How is she going on, Lady Muddlegate? And your daughters, Mrs. Marsh? I'm looking forward to meeting them."

Jo took one last bite of her blackberry pie and spread the rest around so it looked as if she'd eaten more than she had.

The pie was excellent. The entire meal had been very good. She'd just had very little appetite.

At least she'd managed to keep Letitia and Lady Muddlegate from pursuing the fantasy of her marriage to the duke any further. It had not been difficult. Lady Muddlegate, having missed the first years of Harriet's life, was hungry for stories of Harriet's time at the Home, and Jo was happy to supply them. No remembered crumb was too small.

And once she'd got Letitia talking about *her* daughters, Jo only needed to offer a well-placed question here and there to keep the conversation—or, rather, monologue—flowing. Lady Muddlegate had helped with that. While she'd accepted Harriet with open arms, she'd known—and loved—Letitia's daughters from birth.

"I will tell you that Mr. Marsh has been very good with the girls," Letitia said, putting down her fork after capturing the last flake of piecrust on her plate. "I have been very lucky."

"You have made your own luck," Jo said. It was true. Letitia was due much credit here. "You've been open-minded and openhearted. It cannot have been easy for any of the girls this last year. They've undergone so many changes."

It was true. This time last year, no one in the family had

known Darrow had a daughter, and Harriet had thought her father long dead. And now . . .

Now Harriet had moved into the house where Letitia's girls had grown up and, in a very real way, taken over their place. Now *she* was the earl's daughter—but the earl's *illegitimate* daughter. Yes, her parents were married now, but that could never cure Harriet's birth. Many in the *ton* would—well, not give her the cut direct, perhaps. Few would wish to incur Darrow's wrath by doing that. But many would snicker and whisper behind her back. And they certainly would not have faulted Letitia if she'd shunned Harriet.

But Letitia hadn't.

"I'll confess when Pen told me she was going to marry the earl," Jo said, "I had serious misgivings."

As she'd told the duke earlier, she'd firsthand knowledge of the *ton*'s cruelty, and *she'd* been from the gentry. Pen was a farmer's daughter—farmers' daughters did *not* marry into the peerage. Jo had thought no one—not Darrow's tenants, not his servants, and especially not his family—would accept her.

"I'm happy you proved me wrong."

Letitia sighed. "Well, *I'll* confess it wasn't easy at first. Darrow asked me to welcome Pen and Harriet into the family when he told me he was going to propose. I said I would try, but I didn't really expect to succeed." She looked at Lady Muddlegate.

"But then we saw how happy Pen made Darrow," Lady Muddlegate said.

Letitia nodded. "And Harriet *is* a lovely girl."

Jo smiled. She couldn't help feeling a bit of pride. Harriet might not be her daughter, but she'd watched her grow and liked to think she'd contributed to her development, just as a doting aunt might.

Letitia grinned. "And it helped that I've been so happy with my new husband."

Oh, lud, are we back to that?

Apparently, they were. Letitia looked at the duke and then at Jo, waggled her brows *again*, leaned close, and—

And Jo was saved by Pen standing and saying, "Shall we leave the men to their port, ladies?"

Jo tried not to leap out of her chair, but she also wasted no time getting up and putting some space between herself and her previous dinner companions.

"If you'll excuse me," she said brightly into the air between Letitia and Lady Muddlegate as she stepped back and grabbed Caro's arm before Caro could get past her. "I've just remembered something I've been meaning to ask Lady Oakland. About an, er, problem with the brewhouse back at the charity I run. She used to be our brewster, you see."

Caro's eyes widened briefly at Jo's sudden eagerness to have a word with her, but she was nothing if not quick-witted. "Ah. I do hope it's nothing serious?"

"Oh, I don't think it is, but you'll know for certain." Jo smiled and tugged on Caro's arm, urging her to move quickly before Letitia or Lady Muddlegate discovered an interest in brewing. "But let's not bore everyone else with the details." She started to walk away.

Caro, being a good sport, played along—until they were out of earshot.

"Had a little too much matchmaking talk, did you?"

Jo kept her smile glued to her face in case anyone happened to observe them and said, through gritted teeth,

"Yes. Good God, Caro. If things go on this way, this will be the longest fortnight of my life."

"Well, maybe you *should* marry the duke."

Jo's smile slipped as she glared at Caro and contemplated strangulation.

"We'd better go to my room," Pen said, coming up to them then. "You look as if you are about to explode, Jo."

Jo thought she might well be. "Can you leave your guests?"

Pen shrugged. "Everyone's family. I overheard what you said to Harry's mother and Letitia, so I told them I needed to come with you and Caro to find out what the problem was at the Home." She frowned at Jo's shoulders. "More to the point, isn't that a tablecloth from your room?"

"Yes. I need to talk to you about that, too."

"I would think so."

It dawned on Jo that now would be the perfect time to reveal Livy's perfidy, and the only way to do that properly, to make certain Pen and Caro were fully aware of the extent of the problem, was to produce the evidence. "Let's go to my room instead. I have something I need to show you."

She led the way up the stairs and down the corridor. Once the door to her room was closed securely behind them, she whisked off the tablecloth and spread her arms wide. "See?"

Pen and Caro stared at her. Blankly.

"See what?" Caro asked.

Jo's chin almost hit the floor. "What do you mean, *what*?"

Pen and Caro exchanged a puzzled look.

"Could you give us a hint?" Pen asked.

"The bodice! There's no bodice on this dress!"

"Yes, there is," Caro said. "I can see it. It's blue. The same color as the skirt."

Jo clenched her hands. That was better than tearing her hair out.

"The dress is a bit more, er, *au courant* than you usually wear," Pen said. "It looks very nice."

Nice? Pen thought this dress looked *nice*? "It's indecent!" Jo gestured toward the wardrobe where she'd put the others. "They're *all* indecent!"

"I think perhaps you've been in the country too long." Caro laughed. "Not that you can tell what's fashionable from looking at me. And if I tried to wear your dress, it *would* be indecent. I'd be spilling out of it. Pregnancy doesn't make just your belly big, you know."

Jo didn't know from personal experience, of course, but she had heard many women say that.

"And *my* dress is designed so I can feed Pip easily." Pen smiled, shrugged. "If all the important bits are covered— and stay covered when you move—then you have nothing to worry about."

How could they not understand? "But I feel . . . *naked*!"

Caro snorted and lowered herself into a chair. "Well, you aren't naked." She pulled off her shoes and wiggled her toes. "Ahh. That feels better. Pregnancy makes your feet swell, too."

Jo was not particularly interested in Caro's feet. "I *know* I'm not *actually* naked, but I might as well be."

Pen snorted as well—and also sat down. Apparently these two were settling in for a long chat.

Which Jo would welcome if she weren't in such a pother about her clothing.

Was the dress really not that shocking?

She went over to the mirror, turned this way and that . . .

Yes, all the necessary bits were covered, but that still left a shocking expanse of flesh exposed—

Which didn't seem *quite* so shocking now. She must be getting used to it.

"You did tend to wear dresses at the Home that were a little . . ." Pen paused, clearly searching for a diplomatic way to word her comment.

Caro didn't waste time with diplomacy—she'd always been forthright, but pregnancy must have loosened her tongue as much as it had tightened her shoes. "Drab. Pedestrian. Plain."

"Caro!" Pen scowled at her.

Caro shrugged. "It's not an insult—it's just a statement of fact. We were all working women, so we wore clothes we could work in. I'd have looked ridiculous wearing a fashionable dress in the brewhouse." She laughed.

"Can you imagine Albert's or Bathsheba's expression if I'd shown up in a dress like yours, Jo? They would have thought I'd lost my mind—which I would have. Such a dress would have been ruined in minutes what with the malt and wort, water and ale. And with all the bending and lifting I did, I might, even in my less expansive pre-pregnancy state, have fallen out of that bodice."

Caro had a point. Jo looked at her reflection again. The dress was . . . pretty once one got over the shock.

"We didn't bother with parties at the Home," Caro said. "The closest we ever got to dressing up was for Sunday church. But you're at a party now, Jo. You don't have to work while you're here. You should relax and enjoy it."

"Yes, indeed," Pen said. "You've more than earned a holiday. Have some fun, Jo."

Jo stared at them. Did she know how to do that? "I . . . I like working."

She felt more than a little adrift with no accounts to go over or her to-do list in hand.

"Come sit down," Pen said. "Tell us how things go on at the Home. I believe Pip rather rudely—and messily—interrupted us earlier."

Ah. Here was something she could discuss with confidence. It was the main reason she'd come to the party.

Well, no, the main reason was Livy had virtually thrown her into Darrow's carriage.

Which reminds me . . .

She sat down and frowned at Caro. "Have you been corresponding with Livy?"

Caro didn't even try to deny it. On the contrary, she acted as if there was nothing the least bit questionable about the matter.

"Yes."

Jo felt betrayed. "How *could* you?"

"Easily. She wrote to me. I reply to correspondence"—Caro gave Jo a rather pointed look—"unlike *some* people. I wrote you, too, if you'll remember."

Guilt made Jo's shoulders hunch, but she willed them back down, away from her ears. "Well, er, yes. I've been, ah, busy."

Caro sniffed, giving the distinct impression that she saw right through Jo's evasion. Then she leaned forward—or as forward as her pregnant belly would let her. "I know it's been hard for you since I left, Jo." Now her voice was gentle. Warm.

Lud! Jo felt something inside her soften and start to give way. To have Caro understand—

No! Don't let down your guard.

"Is that what Livy told you?"

Caro snorted. "Yes. Not that she had to. I'd already assumed as much, so she was just confirming my suspicions. *You* clearly weren't going to tell me."

"Ah. Er. Well . . ."

Caro's voice was warm again. "Remember, I was there when Pen left. I *know* how you feel, Jo. I felt the same way."

Oh. All resistance hissed out of Jo, leaving her feeling as limp as an empty balloon.

Pen shifted in her chair. "I *am* sorry, but I had to think of Harriet."

"And yourself and the earl," Caro said. "It's no secret you were madly in love, Pen."

Pen shifted again. "Well . . . yes."

Caro smiled. "I don't blame you. I didn't really blame you at the time." She looked at Jo. "Neither of us did."

Jo nodded. "We were happy for you, Pen. We knew you'd made the right decision. But we still felt . . ."

"Abandoned," Caro said. "And worried about how we would manage." Caro focused on Jo again. "And so, I *knew* you'd feel that way again, Jo—abandoned and worried— when I left you just months later. I would never have done it, if I hadn't fallen so completely in love with Nick." She grinned and patted her belly. "And I would have married him just as quickly, I'm afraid, even if we hadn't antici-pated our vows with the obvious result."

Jo felt an odd twinge of . . . envy perhaps. For one mad instant, she wished she could have what Caro and Pen had. Not a husband so much as a partner, someone who shared her goals, whom she could count on to be there month after month, year after year—like Pen and Caro had been for her before their husbands had entered the scene.

She knew all too well that marriage was no guarantee

of that. She and Freddie had eventually managed to coexist, but their union had never been a partnership. The one goal they'd both had—to have a son, Freddie's heir—they'd failed to achieve. And Freddie had, in the end, abandoned her in the most final way possible.

Jo sighed. "I guess I must feel a little threatened by Livy. Perhaps I shouldn't, but I do."

Caro nodded. "That's what Livy said."

Jo scowled, annoyed that Caro had discussed her with Livy. She opened her mouth to protest—and stopped.

Why do *I feel threatened by Livy?*

She'd formed a partnership with Pen and Caro years ago. Why couldn't she form a new one with Livy? She hadn't really tried, had she?

Maybe I do *need this time away from the Home to get some perspective. Clearly, I've lost my way a bit.*

Caro was smiling at her. "I truly don't think you have to worry about Livy, Jo. Nick says she has a good heart, and Nick is an excellent judge of character."

Jo managed not to roll her eyes at that, but something in her expression must have given her away, because Caro laughed.

"And yes, I *am* madly in love and *do* think my husband is wonderful, but I'm also not a complete sawney. I've spent some time with Livy, too—just not as much as Nick has."

Right.

This time Jo looked down at her hands to mask her thoughts. One shouldn't remind a pregnant, newly married friend what her husband had likely been doing with a notorious lightskirt.

Caro snorted, but moved on. "Nick thinks Livy had

been looking for another line of work for a while—as had Polly and Fanny. The Home fits Livy's skills perfectly."

Pen said what Jo was thinking. "Caro, the Home is not a brothel!"

"I know that. But most of the women there were once in that trade. Livy understands them on a level we never could." Caro shrugged. "She was one of them."

True.

"I see your point." Pen smiled and turned to Jo. "Perhaps it's time for *you* to get into another line of work, Jo."

"What?!" Jo hadn't expected an attack from her flank—though she supposed Pen wasn't attacking precisely.

Or . . . Good God! Do I smell more *scheming?*

She looked from Pen to Caro and her eyes narrowed. They'd planned this, hadn't they? Talked it over before she'd arrived.

Yes! Pen was blushing and looking rather sheepish. She'd always been less successful than Caro at hiding a guilty conscience.

Oh, lud. And *now* Pen was examining an invisible spot on her gown. What was coming next?

"The Duke of Grainger *is* looking for a wife, you know."

"Argh." Jo couldn't manage more than that strangled sound—and then dropped her head into her hands.

"You'd be a good match for him, Jo," Pen said. "Harry thinks so, too."

And now the Earl of Darrow is getting into the match-making business?

"Please don't tell me *your* husband has an opinion on the matter as well, Caro."

Caro snorted. "Of course, he doesn't. He doesn't know you or the duke well enough."

Well, thank God for small favo—

"But *I* have an opinion."

Of course, Caro did. Was there any hope she'd keep it to herself?

No. Caro had never been one to hold back when she had some advice to share.

"You should seriously consider marrying the duke, Jo," Caro said. "You'd be perfect for him."

But Caro's advice was usually more sensible than this.

"I would not." Best put an end to this bit of insanity at once. "He'll want to marry a young woman who can give him more children."

"If he'd wanted a young woman, he'd be married already," Pen said. "He's had his pick of the eligible girls ever since he put foot on the Marriage Mart."

Caro nodded. "And he already has his heir. He doesn't need to think only of getting a breeder."

Ugh. That's what Freddie had wanted—a breeder. "I'm sure he'll want a spare."

"Well, you aren't ancient, Jo," Caro said. "I would think you could give him that and then some."

Jo wished she had a nice cup of tea in her hand so she could pour it over Caro's head.

"You wouldn't think that if you considered my history. I was married for three years, Caro. I did not have any children."

Caro shrugged. "Lady Muddlegate and Letitia seem certain that problem should be laid at your husband's door."

"They are mistaken." Caro and Pen were her friends, but she still wasn't going to discuss what had happened in her marriage bed. She shouldn't have to. *They* were married. They knew exactly what went on between husband and wife. "And, in any event, I have the Home to run, remember?"

"But Livy could do that."

Didn't Caro understand? "I don't *want* Livy to do it. The Home is *my* charity. I founded it. I—"

I'm shouting.

She took a deep breath—and then another, searching for control.

Pen laid a comforting hand on her arm. "It's all right, Jo. No one is going to push you to do anything. Just relax and enjoy your stay here."

But Caro still had the bit between her teeth. "If you married the duke, Jo, you'd still be in charge. You'd hold the purse strings and could tell Livy—"

"Caro!" Pen scowled at her. "Let it go."

Caro stopped, mouth open—and then nodded. "Right. Sorry. I didn't mean to push, Jo. I just think . . ."

"*Caro*," Pen said again.

"No, Pen, I have to say this." Caro leaned forward, holding Jo's gaze so Jo couldn't look away.

The raw sincerity in Caro's voice held her, too.

"I wasn't looking for love when I ended up on Nick's doorstep, Jo. I don't think I really believed in it. But I found it—or, perhaps it found me." Caro shook her head with what looked like bemusement and then caught Jo's gaze again. "All I'm saying is, don't bar the door. If love knocks, let it in. Love is what's important, Jo. Everything else will work out if you have that."

Caro had never before been this fanciful or, well,

maudlin. It must be the pregnancy talking—many women got a bit mawkish when they were increasing.

Jo didn't have the heart to tell Caro that love was an illusion, or, at best, fleeting. It would evaporate like the dew in the morning sun.

"Very well. I promise not to bar any doors."

Chapter Eight

Edward stood at the entrance to the maze. The sun rose early in the summer—too early.

Everyone else must still be asleep, even Thomas, but *he* was awake. Unfortunately. He'd tried to go back to sleep, but after tossing and turning for what had seemed like forever, he'd given up. He had too much on his mind.

Too much of *someone* on his mind.

Perhaps the maze would distract him. It was certainly true that it would be easier to find the center without the "help" of a young boy—or, worse, a young boy and a large dog. And then later he could guide Thomas, letting him discover as much of the solution on his own as he could.

He stepped onto the dirt path between the high hornbeam hedges.

Ahh. This was *exactly* what he needed. It was even more calming than the woods yesterday. Yesterday there had been squirrels and birds—and Bear and Thomas.

And Lady Havenridge.

Now the world narrowed—literally—to just the path

before him. The house, the other guests, all his worries were walled off by the towering hedges. He was alone—

"Damnation."

The word—more of a hiss, really—an oddly muffled hiss—came from somewhere deeper in the maze.

Damnation, indeed. Another early riser had had the same thought as he—and was likely also in search of solitude. He should go—

"Argh! You bloody bush."

He choked back a laugh. Apparently, he should go to the rescue. It sounded as if his fellow explorer was in some difficulty.

"Halloo! Grainger here. Can I be of help?"

Silence. Was the person going to pretend she—and he was quite certain the exclamations had come from feminine lips—wasn't there? That would be a harebrained thing to do, especially if she did, indeed, need some sort of assistance.

She must have reached the same conclusion.

"It's Lady Havenridge. I'm stuck."

Of *course*, it was Lady Havenridge, the woman who had haunted his dreams, disturbing his sleep. He was equal parts resigned and energized.

Fate had joined the other houseguests in conspiring against him.

Or perhaps that was *for* him. In any event, he clearly had no choice in the matter. He wasn't going to leave the woman in whatever predicament she'd got herself into.

"Where are you?"

"In the *maze*!"

She didn't add "you idiot," but she might as well have.

"Yes, but *where* in the maze?" He started walking.

"In the beginning, the middle? Have you made it to the center?"

"The middle, I suppose. I've turned down a dead end."

"Can you come toward my voice?" Though that might mean they would both wander—

"No! I *told* you. I'm *stuck*!"

How in the world could she be—

Oh.

He rounded a corner and saw her. Her bonnet was on the ground, her hindquarters were facing him, and her head . . .

Was it *in* the hedge?

She must have heard him come up behind her, because she started to turn—

"Ouch!"

Her face wasn't in the vegetation—thankfully—but it appeared that her hair was tangled in the hornbeam branches.

Do not laugh!

He was afraid he wasn't entirely successful at keeping all amusement out of his voice. "How did you manage to do that?"

She made a growling sort of noise and glared up at him, but a look, no matter how ferocious, didn't pack much of a punch when delivered from someone trapped in the shrubbery.

"I heard something in the hedge and went to have a look—and then a bird flew out right by my nose. I jumped and lost my balance." She tried to pull away from the hedge again—

"Ack!"

She was *quite* securely tethered to the greenery.

"I tried to free myself, but I think I just made matters worse."

"Hmm. Let me see how bad it is. And I beg your pardon in advance—I'm going to have to get rather close. There's very little room to maneuver."

There was *no* room to maneuver. The hedges were planted so people had to walk single file, but here in this blind alley, they were hemmed in on three sides. If he was going to reach the problem area, they would have to get *very* close indeed.

She sighed. "Do what you must."

"Very well." He stepped up against her and leaned over to survey the situation. "You've really got yourself snarled there, but I think I can free you without resorting to scissors."

She huffed, but he didn't take it personally. She was frustrated. Anyone would be.

"I'd have you shave my head if you had to."

"Blasphemy! I'd clip the hedge before I did that. Now hold still."

He reached for the first dark blonde tress. Mmm. It was so smooth. So silky. He'd like to thread his fingers through—

Focus!

He drew in a deep breath, and with it, her scent.

That did *not* help him focus.

"*Will* you get on with it?" She wiggled with impatience—which made her lovely rump dance over his poor cock with predictable results.

No, not so predictable these days.

Did I hear her breath catch?

Wishful thinking.

"If you make me hurry, my fingers will all turn to thumbs and I won't be able to untangle anything."

She snorted, but held her tongue—until he accidentally pulled her hair. "Ouch!"

"Sorry. I've almost got the first bit free."

"*First?!* How much more is there?"

"Not sure. You did an excellent job of becoming one with the greenery."

She growled. "It will not happen again."

"Well, I assume you didn't plan for it to happen *this* time. I suggest you take a companion with you when next you decide to venture into nature." He grinned down at her. "I volunteer for that duty."

"Don't be ridiculous."

He chuckled and turned back to his task. "Almost done." Unfortunately. He quite liked having her so close, his fingers in her hair.

He loosened the vegetation's last grasp on her and allowed himself one stroke to smooth the errant strands before he stepped back.

"There you go. You're a free woman, Lady Havenridge. And only a few leaves had to be sacrificed to the cause." He grinned at her as she straightened. "That didn't take long, did it?"

She gave him a pointed look. "You weren't the one bound to the hedge."

Then she emitted a long, heartfelt sigh of pleasure— that went straight to the most inappropriate part of his anatomy—and tilted her head to the right and then to the left as if to see if her neck still worked. "I do thank you from the bottom of my heart. I was beginning to worry I'd be trapped here all morning."

He frowned. That was not a pleasant thought. "I am

very happy I happened by. I wasn't entirely joking about being out by yourself, you know."

She frowned back at him. "Well, you *should* be joking. This isn't London. I go about by myself all the time."

Right. Of course, she did. She was a fiercely independent woman who liked—perhaps *needed*—to be in control of herself and her world.

The thought was rather . . . stimulating.

"The same thing could happen to you," she said—and stopped. "Well, not *precisely* the same thing. But you could be out alone and run into difficulties—twist your ankle or some such thing."

He grinned. "I quite agree. I would be very happy to have you along to supervise me and see to it that I don't run into such problems."

She snorted at him—and then her hands went to her hair.

"Oh, blast. I've lost all my hairpins." She knelt down and started searching about in the dirt.

He squatted next to her. "I suspect at least some of them have been swallowed up by the hedge." He raised his brows. "I stand ready to free you from the shrubbery again if you wish to dive in to look. The rescue might go faster, now that I've had practice."

"Don't be ridiculous." She kept her eyes on the ground. "Oh, there's one."

She was wearing a moss green dress this morning and had, fortunately, dispensed with the odd shawl. She should banish it from her wardrobe entirely. It was a crime to hide her lovely neck and shoulders and . . . His eyes skimmed the edge of her bodice, partially hidden by her hair, tumbling over—

"There's another one!" She darted forward to snag it, and then frowned at him. "If you're going to be down here in the dirt, you might as well help me look."

He grinned. He'd grinned more this morning than he had in months—perhaps years. "Oh, I'm definitely looking."

Her forehead creased—and then she blushed as she got his meaning. "Pins. You're supposed to be looking for *pins*."

"Yes, my lady." He made a show of studying the dirt.

"You are absurd." She laughed and sat back on her heels. "And how rude of me. I shouldn't take up any more of your time, Your Grace. Please—go on with your"—she waved her free hand around—"explorations."

She wasn't going to get rid of him *that* easily. She'd tortured him all night—not that she knew that, of course. And it wasn't as if he could keep his distance. It was clear to him, as it must be to her, that they were going to be thrown together constantly by this collection of amateur matchmakers. Might as well discuss the issue now, when they'd been given this perfect opportunity.

"I am at your complete disposal, my lady. How many more pins do you need to find?"

She gave him a guarded look and then counted the pins in her hand. "There should be three more, but you are probably right that some of them ended in the hedge." She smiled. "And, no, I am not going to get close to that hedge again."

She stood, so he stood, too.

"Oh, look," he said. "There was one under my boot." He bent down, picked it up, and presented it to her with a flourish.

"Thank you, Your Grace." She laughed as she took the

pin, but . . . was she going to flee back to the house? Her tone definitely sounded like a prelude to a farewell.

He would not give her the opportunity. "Were you on your way into or out of the maze?"

She hadn't expected that question. "On my way in, but—"

"Splendid! So was I. Let's explore it together, shall we?"

"Erm, well . . ."

Surely, she saw the benefit of putting their heads together—only their heads and only in the most figurative sense—and coming up with a mutual plan? If she didn't, he would point it out to her.

"I heard what Lady Muddlegate and Mrs. Marsh said at dinner last night."

She flushed. "Ohh."

Was that a moan?

"And Lord Muddlegate and Mr. Marsh had clearly been instructed to press the matter with me, because the moment you ladies left us to our port, they both pointed out your lack of a husband and my desire for a wife."

"Ohh."

That was definitely a moan.

But she recovered quickly. "You can be sure I am not going to throw myself at you, Your Grace. Have no worries on that score!"

He grinned. "Maybe I'd like you to throw yourself at me."

"W-what?!"

"I *am* looking for a wife, after all."

Her mouth hung open. He could tell she wasn't certain how to take him.

Well, he wasn't certain, either.

"Don't worry. I'm not going to throw myself at you,

either. However, I am quite, quite certain that some of the guests here *will* try to throw us at each other."

She sighed and nodded.

"So, I suggest we take this opportunity, that our early rising has given us, to discuss how we wish to handle the matter. If we can come up with a plan together, I feel confident we'll both have a much more enjoyable stay."

She looked at him. He could see she was weighing the pros and cons of his proposal.

Not that there was much weighing to be done. Any person with even a modicum of sense would see that leaving matters to chance—or, rather, to interfering, if well-meaning friends and acquaintances—was a very bad idea.

Lady Havenridge was a very intelligent woman. She reached that conclusion with alacrity and nodded.

"Very well."

Jo followed the duke down the maze's narrow passageway, an odd, fluttery feeling in her chest. He was so tall, his shoulders so broad. His hands . . .

Oh, dear, God. His hands. His fingers in her hair. His scent. His body pressed against her back, the hard, long ridge of his—

What is the matter with you? Get ahold of yourself.

Her body wouldn't listen. The fluttery feeling moved lower.

Apparently, her animal instincts had awoken after years of slumber.

Well, they'd certainly disturbed her slumber last night. She'd tossed and turned, hot and . . . unsettled. And then early this morning, when she'd been deep in a dream, an intense cascade of sensation had radiated from her feminine bits, waking her just as the pleasure was waning. Oh!

She'd wanted it back. She'd closed her eyes, trying to reenter the dream, but it was too late. It was gone.

That was when she'd decided to get up and explore the maze.

She looked at the duke's broad, strong back. *This* was the man who had caused the sensation. In her dream, he'd been kissing her, touching her, stroking her, and then, most shocking of all, he'd slid deep, deep inside her, in and out and in until . . .

She pressed her lips together tightly, swallowing her moan. She was very, *very* glad the duke was in front of her, facing away, so he couldn't see her flush.

The last time she'd felt any sort of interest in the male of the species had been when she was seventeen. Her mother had sent her into the village on an errand to Mr. Waddlesworth's apothecary. She'd stepped inside the shop—and seen Freddie for the first time. He'd looked so out of place among the dusty bottles and jars and barrels, like a Greek god who'd taken a wrong turn.

She'd felt a jolt then, but that sensation had been purer than what she'd felt last night—and now. More poetic. All hearts and flowers and knights in shining armor.

She'd still been a virgin then.

She was not a virgin now, though it had been so long since she'd engaged in sexual congress, she might as well be.

You didn't like the business much when you did *engage in it.*

True, but there had been fleeting hints of pleasure. And

listening to the women at the Home over the years, she'd concluded that not all men were created equal when it came to bedroom activities. Yes, they all had the same basic equipment, but some men were more skilled than others at using it.

Freddie had not been one for finesse in *any* matter. The duke, however . . .

Her nether regions shivered, clearly of the opinion that he would be very skilled indeed.

She ignored them—or tried to.

It was not so easy to ignore her heart and mind.

She had admired Freddie's . . . surfaces. His good looks, his manly figure, his London manners, his rank—the heir to a barony was quite the glittering personage in her little village.

Her admiration for the duke was entirely different. His rank, while far more exalted than Freddie's, was actually a strike against him—as she'd told him, she had no desire to enter a London ballroom ever again. And while he was certainly handsome, it was his intelligence, his understanding, his obvious love for his son that drew her, not his broad shoulders and long legs.

Well, yes. Those attributes certainly don't hurt.

They came to a junction, and the duke turned right.

Jo stopped. "I thought we were going to the center of the maze."

"We are."

"Then shouldn't you turn left? You're headed back to the beginning."

The man grinned. "Oh, ye of little faith." He nodded to his hand where it rested on the hedge, its long, clever fingers pale against the green leaves.

Just how clever are they?

Stop!

The duke might be looking for a wife, but she was *not* looking for a husband. She had the Home to run.

Caro's words about not barring doors slithered into her thoughts, but she chased them right back out. Caro was in love—and very pregnant. Her reasoning was clouded.

But Pen told me to have some fun . . .

She'd wager she could have a *lot* of fun with this man.

"If this maze is laid out like many are," the duke was saying, "we should be able to reach the center by following the hedges on our right. The turns that seem to head back are there to fool you so you won't take them." He laughed. "Of course, if it was designed on a different plan, then, yes, we *are* going the wrong way. We'll see, shall we?"

When was the last time I ventured off anywhere without a plan—besides this trip, that is? I—

Stop! It's only a maze. Don't make such a to-do about it.

She shouldn't make a to-do about any of it. She'd go on this small adventure with him, and then maybe tonight they could go another, more . . . intense adventure in her bedroom—and not just in her dreams. It wasn't as if she had to worry about conceiving. They could have some . . . fun without taking any vows.

A shocking thought. She didn't do things like that.

Why not?

Perhaps Livy had indeed done her a favor when she'd pushed her into Lord Darrow's traveling coach. A fortnight of being a little reckless might be a good thing, a needed holiday before she settled back into her real life.

No need to decide now. She would see where this maze took her.

She grinned back at him. "Lead on, then, Your Grace. I

will follow—but I reserve the right to tell you 'I told you so' when we end up where we began."

Did his smile get a little . . . wolfish?

"Well, where *we* began, if you'll remember," he said, "was with you caught in the bushes."

She laughed. "How unkind of you to remind me of my mishap, sir!"

No one had ever teased her this way. Or looked at her quite this intensely. It was very . . . stimulating.

"I was delighted to be able to assist you." His voice was low and rather stimulating, too.

She'd jammed her bonnet back on her head when she'd got free of the hedge, but she'd not had the patience to do more than shove her pins into her pocket, leaving her hair tumbled over her shoulders. The duke reached out now to trace one tendril from her cheek down her neck and over her breast.

Even more stimulating.

I should slap his hand away—

Too late. It's already gone.

Unfortunately.

The touch had been tantalizingly light and far too brief.

And now his smile was pure sin. "Come on. We've a lot to discuss"—his smile widened to a grin—"I hope."

Right. The plan. They *should* join forces. They really had no choice. Clearly, the other guests and, from what Pen had said last night, even their host and hostess were not going to leave them alone on the matter. If they presented a united front, they would spike the matchmakers' matrimonial guns.

Jo followed the duke down one passageway after another, turning and twisting and doubling back. She would have been quite lost if she'd been on her own.

Well, there was a time or two when she thought the duke *was* lost. She'd been about to say exactly that when they made one last turn and stepped into the maze's center.

"Oh!" It wasn't a large space, but after being hemmed in by the tall green hedges, it felt expansive.

And then she saw the statue.

"Oh!"

A naked male figure with outspread wings was bent over an equally naked female figure. They had just kissed—or were just about to do so.

"Oh, indeed." The duke sounded as surprised as she was. "It looks like a copy of Canova's *Psyche Revived by Cupid's Kiss*."

It was certainly reviving something in her. She averted her gaze, spotted a bench, and sat down, careful to keep her eyes off the passionate pair.

Which meant she had nowhere to look but the duke's face as he sat down next to her.

It was a small bench, perhaps designed with a lovers' tryst in mind.

Lovers . . .

Stop!

She pulled her knees close together so as to take up as little of the seat as possible.

The duke put one arm along the back of the bench, his hand resting right behind her shoulders. He wasn't touching her. He might not even be aware of how close he was to her—but she was aware of it. Very, *very* aware.

"Now, as to how to handle the matchmakers," he said. "I suppose we could announce, in no uncertain terms, that we are *not* interested in marrying each other, but what fun would that be?"

When was *the last time I had fun?*

Fun was for children. She was too old, with too many responsibilities, too many worries, to engage in anything so unproductive. So frivolous.

Pen told me to have fun.

Yesterday afternoon had been fun. Sharing a picnic. Looking for newts, splashing in the stream with this man and his son and their dog.

Her eyes started to stray toward the very naked couple on the verge of another fun activity.

No. Don't look.

She pulled her focus back to the duke.

"And, to be honest," he was saying, "I doubt it would work. Lady Muddlegate and Mrs. Marsh are both recently remarried and have a missionary's zeal on the subject, don't you think?"

"Yes, indeed! You heard them at dinner. I hope never to be stuck between those two at another meal."

"See? If we act as if we are indeed considering at least the possibility of marriage, you won't have to be. They will stumble over themselves to see that we sit together."

"True." That *would* be a plus.

"And if we go off by ourselves—to get away from them—they will likely waggle their brows and exchange significant looks, but they won't try to stop us." He grinned. "On the contrary, they will congratulate each other on their matchmaking success."

She nodded. She thought he was quite right. "So, we'll pretend to an interest."

"Not exactly." He grinned. "I want to be completely honest with you, Jo. May I call you Jo?"

Hearing him say her name rather than her title—well, Freddie's title or, rather, Freddie's cousin Oswald's title now—sent warmth curling through her. She nodded, not trusting her voice.

"And you must call me Edward."

"Oh! That is far too bold." Calling the duke by his Christian name would raise eyebrows indeed. But, well, she could see that if she continued to "Your Grace" him, no one would believe their tale of a romantic relationship.

"I suppose I could call you Grainger."

He pulled a face. "No. That's the duke—not *me*. Call me Edward. I *much* prefer it." He gave her a beseeching look that reminded her forcefully of his son. "Please, Jo?"

She hesitated.

"Come on. You can do it."

"Well . . ." It shouldn't be so difficult, but it was.

Why? Does it feel like I'm . . . committing to something?

"Well, it *is* two syllables as opposed to your one." He raised his brows. "Would it help if I called you Josephine?"

That made her laugh. "Oh, please don't."

"Please don't . . . who?" He raised his brows higher and gestured, palms up, fingers moving toward him as if pulling the word from her lips.

Mmm. Fingers. Lips.

"Edward," she said, partly to dispel those thoughts. "Josephine is what my mother called me when she was angry at me."

He nodded. "Jo it is then. So, Jo, I will confess that there is no *pretending* to a romantic interest on my part. I *am* interested. You know I'm in need of a wife. And Thomas is in need of a mother."

Oh, hell. Reality had finally shown up to this party.

"And *there* is the main problem with your plan. Well,

one of two, really." She held up a finger. "First, I *can't* marry you—I've got the Home to run."

His Grace—Edward—grinned at her. "Livy can run it, and you can supervise Livy."

Good God! Her eyes narrowed. "Are *you* in league with Livy, too?"

She'd already concluded that this was the man Livy had had in mind when she'd loaded that trunkful of scandalous dresses onto Darrow's carriage—and then pushed Jo inside.

Edward looked genuinely surprised. "No. Of course not."

"But you do know her."

"I *knew* her. I haven't spoken to her in over a year." He smiled. "But I do consider her a friend. And I trust her. If she wants the job, then I think you can trust her, too, Jo. She'll work hard and do what's best for the Home." His smile broadened. "And, as I say, you can supervise her, just from a distance."

She gave him a hard look, but decided not to fight that battle now, especially as her treacherous female bits seemed to want to take the duke's side.

"Well, perhaps you will find my second point more persuasive, then. We can't mislead Thomas. Did you know he's already asked me to be his mother?"

Edward's brows shot up, but instead of looking horrified, she thought he looked . . . pleased.

Oh, hell.

"He did?"

A breathless feeling—panic?—clutched at her throat. She spoke quickly, her words tumbling over each other.

"Yes, he did, but it was very shortly after he first met me, before you came looking for him. He couldn't have meant anything by it. He doesn't know me. But he *does* know you are looking for a wife. I'm sure he—"

Edward put his hands on hers, likely to stop her mad rush of words.

The move was very effective. The words did stop, because her tongue stopped working—as did her lungs and heart. Her body could only do one thing—feel. Feel the weight and warmth of his hands, the touch of each separate finger—

His palm and fingers would feel wonderful cupping my breast the way Cupid's—

Don't think about that sculpture! We are talking about Thomas.

"Thomas is an excellent judge of character," he said.

She was going to scoff at him, thinking he was teasing her, but she stopped when she saw he was serious.

She might not know him well, but she knew one thing beyond a doubt—he was a good father. He loved his son.

And so she needed to point out what was obvious to her but might not be as obvious to him.

"He does seem to be a very sensitive child." She leaned toward him a little, held his gaze.

He'll not like me putting my nose in his business, but so be it.

Jo had long practice with sticking her nose into other people's business when a child was involved. Children often didn't have the words to speak up for themselves, especially to a parent whose love they didn't want to risk losing.

"I think your search for a wife is wearing on him."

The duke didn't snap her intruding nose off. Instead, he nodded.

"I quite agree. It *has* been hard on him. I've spent far too much time away from him at boring Society events—balls and soirees and what have you." He grinned at her. "I'd be delighted to put the hunt for a wife behind me."

Something fluttered in her chest again.

She squelched it. She must not lose sight of the fact that to him, she was a convenient means to his end. Oh, not in a cruel way—she was certain he meant her no harm. It was just that his focus was on his needs and those of his son—as they should be.

And it was also true that women had been trying to get him to propose ever since he'd acquired the title. He'd likely lost perspective.

He's not cocky or overbearing, though.

"Thomas is worried that any woman I marry will supplant him in my affections," he said, "and govern me the way the wicked stepmother in Cinderella governed her namby-pamby husband." He scowled. "I don't understand how any man could allow his child to be mistreated that way."

"Er, yes. Quite right." Jo had never looked at that fairy tale from a father's perspective before. When she'd thought of it at all, she'd focused on the women, the evil stepmother and stepsisters. But now that Edward pointed it out—yes, the father of that story was very much a villain, especially as, at least in the real world, men held all the power.

The fellow had likely let his animal urges blind him when he'd married the evil harpy, but that didn't excuse his continued blindness to his daughter's plight. Infuriating!

"A father must look out for the needs of his children,"

she said. "And any woman marrying a man with children must be willing to be a mother as well as a wife."

Oh, Lord. She'd said precisely the right—and the wrong—thing. Edward's smile was blinding. She couldn't keep from smiling back, but . . .

He might see her as the answer to his prayers, but she wasn't. She couldn't marry him. Her life was in Little Puddledon at the Benevolent Home.

Isn't it?

Of course, it is.

But, for the first time, she felt a thread of doubt.

Chapter Nine

Blast. He'd been too enthusiastic and had alarmed Jo. He could feel her withdraw, could see it in her eyes, in the way they widened and then shuttered and slid away, hiding her thoughts from him.

One would think he would know how to court a woman.

One would be wrong.

He'd met Helen when he'd been young, studying law with her widowed father. They had spent hours and hours together, working—Helen had helped with duties usually assigned to a male secretary—and at the home she and her father shared and where Edward had taken his meals. They had fallen in love easily, naturally, gradually, helped along, he suspected, by Mr. Moore. The wily old man had been too dependent on his daughter to want her to marry some fellow who would then take her away from him.

And now that he was the duke, he spent his time fending women off rather than trying to attract them.

Until now.

Jo is right to be hesitant. It is far too soon to think about marriage. We've only just met.

In person, he reminded himself yet again. *We've corresponded for almost a year.*

It felt as if he'd known her forever.

But there was no rush. He'd begin now and see where things went.

"Yes," he said cautiously. "I mean to keep Thomas very much in mind and offer only for a woman who is willing— no, *happy*—to be a mother to him."

She nodded, an abrupt motion that gave him the distinct impression she'd decided she would not be that woman and was now going to push him away.

"Keep this in mind, as well, Edward."

Zeus, a bolt of pure pleasure shot through him at the sound of his name on her lips.

"Thomas sees matters with a child's eyes. He doesn't— he can't—comprehend adult concerns."

"Er, adult concerns?" He knew she didn't mean lust and desire. So, what could she—

Oh.

"Yes." She looked away—and then back quickly when her eyes encountered Cupid and Psyche. "Thomas doesn't understand that some women can't have children. You want a wife who is young and fertile, who can give you more sons, give you daughters, give Thomas brothers and sisters." Her voice turned hard and tight. "That eliminates me."

Alarm bells went off in his head, and he sensed a yawning pit open before his feet. A false step now could be fatal.

She'd been married three years and had not had a child. Did she think she couldn't have children?

At dinner last night, he'd heard Lady Muddlegate and Mrs. Marsh talk about Freddie's lack of by-blows. They'd been right—Freddie had no bastards. It was common knowledge, at least in London.

When Darrow had told him about the Home and Lady

Havenridge last year, he'd done some asking around himself to see what he could discover about the deceased baron. One of the people he'd asked was Livy. She made it a point to know all the gossip—her business depended on titled gentlemen, after all. She wanted to be certain she knew every detail about them—their preferences and their vices. He hadn't thought to inquire about illegitimate children, but Havenridge's lack of them was one of the first things Livy had mentioned.

Of course, it *was* possible Jo couldn't conceive. It was merely that the truth of that matter hadn't been conclusively established.

It was far too early to bring up that topic directly. But indirectly . . .

Even if they never got to the point of a proposal, his experience might help her in some way.

"I would, of course, welcome more children," he said, carefully. "But I know all too well that no marriage is guaranteed offspring. My wife and I were married for five years before we had Thomas." He hesitated, and then pushed ahead. "And it wasn't for lack of trying."

"Oh."

She clearly didn't know what to make of that.

He would move on to the other part of her statement.

"And I've spent hours and hours with young women since I stepped onto the Marriage Mart." He grimaced. "Let's just say I may be too old to fully appreciate them. They seem so . . ." How to put it? "*Young*. Not as young as Thomas, of course, but still, more like a daughter than a wife."

She nodded slowly. "I've often wondered why older men marry girls just out of the schoolroom." She flushed and shot a glance at their passionate marble companions.

"Well, I suppose I know why. It's just . . ." She wrinkled her nose in distaste. "I have to tell you—"

"Woof!"

He was not destined to hear what she had to tell him, because Bear, followed closely by Thomas, bounded into the clearing right then.

"Papa! Miss Jo! We found you!"

"That you did," Edward said as Bear tried to wash Jo's face for her while she laughed and dodged. "Bear! Some manners, if you please. Sit!"

Bear sat, but gazed adoringly at Lady Havenridge.

Or perhaps *he* was the one staring—not quite adoringly, he hoped. That would be a bit too revoltingly poetic.

"Bear likes you, Miss Jo," Thomas said.

Is Thomas gazing adoringly as well?

He did not want his son hurt—but there was nothing he could do to ensure that he wouldn't be.

Zeus, this business of finding a wife while a father was a complicated one.

"You were very clever, Thomas," Jo was saying. "How did you find us? I couldn't make it through the maze on my own. Your father had to show me the trick of it."

"I was looking for Papa." Thomas grinned. "I didn't know I'd find you, too, Miss Jo."

Oh, Lord. Thomas was far too happy he'd discovered them together. He did hope the boy wouldn't be too disappointed if nothing came of this . . . friendship with Lady Havenridge.

I'll be disappointed enough for both of us.

He felt a faint—a very faint—twinge of alarm at that thought. He was getting in too deep here, too fast.

And I don't care.

Oh, hell.

He *should* rein himself in.

"Bear needed a walk," Thomas said. "So, I decided to take him out. I asked Douglas—he's one of the footmen—where you were, Papa, and he told me he thought you might be in the maze. So, I went there. When we got to the entrance, Bear used his nose, didn't you, Bear?"

Blast! Bear was using his nose for something else now, sniffing around the base of the statue—which drew Thomas's attention to the artwork.

"Papa, that man has wings! What is he doing with the lady? Are they wrestling? They don't have any clothes on."

And now Bear was watering Psyche's toes.

Edward glanced at Jo. Her lips were pressed tightly together. She gave him a wide-eyed look of . . . amusement? Embarrassment?

In any event, it was clear she was not going to help him out here.

"It's a statue of, er, a pair of ancient lovers, Thomas. The winged fellow has just kissed the lady."

"Lovers? Kiss? Ick!" Thomas's face twisted in suitable young-boy disgust. "I hope you and Miss Jo aren't going to kiss and wrestle like that when you are lovers, Papa."

Jo now made a strangled sound, a mix of a gasp, part . . .

Had that been a giggle?

A nervous one.

"Thomas!" Edward tried to keep the shock out of his voice, but it wasn't easy. "Where in the world did you get the idea that Miss Jo and I were going to be . . ."

His courage failed him, and he frowned instead of saying the word.

It was one thing for the boy to hope Edward would marry Jo so Jo would be his mother. It was quite another to talk about *lovers*.

"Lady Adrianna said it last night, Papa. And then Woody—that's what the girls call Miss Woodrow—shushed her. But Lady Bianca said it was true, that her mama and grandmama *both* said you'd be lovers by the time the party was over because you're the only two unmarried grown-ups here. And *then* Lady Cassandra said you needed a wife—which you do!—and Miss Jo needed a husband and you were a powerful duke, so it was almost like a fairy tale."

Thomas glanced at the statue and wrinkled his nose again. "Though not *that* sort of fairy tale." He looked at Edward. "Right, Papa?"

"Er." He really did *not* want to get into the subject of lovers, but he also hoped Mrs. Marsh's daughters were correct, and he and Jo did find their way to, at a minimum, do some kissing. "Right. We will not be engaging in any fairy tales."

Though he *did* hope for a happy ending.

"Do I look like I have wings? And I can't imagine Miss Jo would go about without a proper dress on, can you?"

Well, he *could* imagine it—had been imagining it all night in fitful dreams and twisted sheets.

"But, more to the point, Miss Woodrow was right. The girls shouldn't say such things. And neither should you, Thomas. Look—you've put Miss Jo to the blush."

She *was* a very interesting shade of red, but it was probably unfair of him to blame Thomas for it. Dare he hope she was also thinking, in delicious detail, of what lovers did? What *they* could do? She wasn't a virgin, after all.

"I'm sorry, Miss Jo. I didn't mean to embarrass you."

"And you didn't, Thomas. Your father is just joking."

She gave Edward a look he couldn't quite decipher.

He shouldn't get his hopes up, but something else was already rising inappropriately.

He shifted position on the hard bench.

"Even Harriet said it would be a good thing if you married Papa, Miss Jo. She likes having a father and said I would like having a mother." Thomas grinned. "But I already knew that."

Zeus, how I love this boy.

Could Jo come to love Thomas, too? She was listening to him intently, as if what he said was important. Most adults, in his experience, never gave children their full attention.

Well, most adults never gave *anyone* their full attention. They were too busy thinking about what *they* were going to say, and so they heard only what they expected to hear. Such focused, intent listening was a rare and beautiful skill.

"Even if Papa didn't have to marry someone, Miss Jo, I'd want him to marry you."

And sometimes, even if you were listening with only half an ear, you heard something that opened your eyes.

"I don't *have* to marry anyone, Thomas."

He'd been found on a remote branch of the family tree, hadn't he? Should some disaster befall him and Thomas, the official squirrels could just scamper back amongst the family foliage to find another poor sap to wear the ducal coronet.

"You don't, Papa?"

Thomas must be wondering why he'd spent so many nights away from him, searching Society's ballrooms for a wife. He was now wondering the same thing.

"I don't." He looked at Jo. "But I might like to."

Jo turned red again.

"Woof!"

Edward looked over at Bear—

Oh, blast.

"Bear," Thomas said, "you weren't supposed to do *that* here!"

Edward and Thomas went off with an only slightly re-pentant Bear to find a gardener and a shovel to clean up the evidence of Bear's visit. Jo, having wrestled her hair back into some order, went off to find Pen to clean up a different mess.

Pen was married to the earl. She could ask her husband to ask—no, *tell*—his mother and sister-in-law to stop spec-ulating about Jo's business, at least in front of Letitia's daughters. The proverb was very true—little pitchers *did* have big ears. Letitia's girls were just the age to be avidly interested in anything that hinted at romance.

And there had been far more than *hints* here. Lovers! Lud! She'd thought she was going to expire on the spot when Thomas had repeated what the girls said.

It wasn't only mortification you felt.

She paused, her foot on the first step up to the terrace, and took a deep breath.

No, it hadn't been only mortification. It had been . . . *wanting*, too. Desire. Something she hadn't felt in years.

Even before Freddie had stopped visiting her bed, she'd stopped enjoying what they did there. Not that she'd ever *really* enjoyed the business, but after the first few months when she hadn't conceived, there'd been too much stress, too much pressure to hope for pleasure. Soon every time she'd felt the weight of Freddie's body on hers, she'd also felt a crushing sense of failure. She'd tensed. When he'd come inside her, it had hurt.

I bet it wouldn't hurt if Edward—

Lud! Her face—her entire body—felt as if it had burst into flames.

There *had* been those dreams last night. That odd sensation in her nether regions . . .

Which were now making themselves known here in the morning light.

Edward is looking for a wife. You are not looking for a husband.

Right. But . . . there *was* this odd pull she felt toward the man.

There's nothing odd about it. It's called desire. It's natural.

She frowned. Of course, that was all it was. She must not let herself get swept away as she had with Freddie.

She started up the stairs.

You aren't going to get swept away. You aren't seventeen any longer. And you don't have to marry the duke to go to bed with him.

She stumbled and grabbed the railing to catch herself. Was that really true?

Yes. Such behavior was quite common in the *ton*. As long as they were discreet, as long as they were careful not to raise Thomas's hopes—and as long as Edward understood that she wasn't making any promises—they could have some . . . fun.

Like Cupid and Psyche.

She pictured in far too much detail the sensuous lines of that sculpture, and her nipples hardened. She'd like to feel Edward's fingers, so careful, so deft when they'd freed her hair from the shrubbery, touch her there.

And touch another hard nub lower down on her anatomy.

Maybe I could find out what that odd tingling cascade this morning was.

If anyone could re-create that sensation, it would be Edward. It *should* be Edward. After all, it was his fault she felt so unsettled.

Well, yes, he'd had no control over his appearance in her dream. That was true. Still, this was her best chance to see what all the fuss was about, why so many women at the Home enjoyed sexual congress.

She started climbing the stairs again. She had a fortnight—minus a day. She would see what happened.

She frowned. No, she would *not* wait and see—she'd take control of the situation. She was not going to be the shy, passive girl she'd been when she'd married Freddie. That girl was long gone.

For once it was a good thing she couldn't conceive. It made everything so much less complicated. She and Edward could . . . cavort without any worry that there would be permanent consequences.

A permanent consequence in nine months' time.

This could be just for fun. An experiment to see if she liked it.

To see if it makes me feel less lonely.

Her foot paused above the next step. Am *I* lonely?

She *had* been talking to her dog rather a lot. Livy might have been right about that.

Well, she would find out. Tonight, after dinner, when Thomas was already in the schoolroom, she would talk to Edward and see if he was interested in exploring the matter.

But first she had to find Pen and tell her to muzzle her relatives.

She continued up the stairs, across the terrace, and into the house.

And stopped. Where should she look for Pen? At the Home, she would just stop by Pen's bedroom, but if she did that here, she might encounter Darrow as well.

She felt herself flush. Surely, they wouldn't be up to any . . . fun in the middle of the day?

She didn't want to risk finding out.

"May I help you, madam?" One of the footmen had noticed her doing an impression of a statue.

"Yes. Thank you. Can you tell me where I might find Lady Darrow?"

"I believe she is—"

"Here, I am," Pen said, coming down the corridor. "Thank you, Charles."

"Very good, my lady." The man bowed and took himself off.

"Is it hard to get used to having servants?" Jo asked, watching the man depart.

"It was at first." Pen studied Jo's face for a moment and then smiled. "I was on my way to walk around the lake. Would you like to join me? I've just fed Pip, so I should have some time before he summons me again."

"That sounds perfect." There was less chance of being overheard outside.

They went back out the door, across the terrace, down the steps, and off on the path that would take them to the lake.

"Didn't you have servants when Havenridge was alive?" Pen asked.

"Barely." Jo had never discussed her life before the Home in any detail. It wasn't a time she liked to remember. "Money flowed through Freddie's fingers like water. He was always dodging the duns. We made do with a skeleton staff—it was all we could afford, and even then, too often we came up short."

She did not want to put herself in that position ever again. Money was tight at the Home, yes, but *she* was in control of their expenditures—or as in control as one could ever be in this world. It was one reason she kept such careful accounts.

"I have to say, Pen—and I probably said as much when you told me you were marrying Darrow—I was truly worried that you'd have a hard time of it. That Letitia and even the servants and the people on the estate wouldn't accept you. I'm delighted to have been proven wrong."

Pen smiled. "To be honest, I was worried, too. Everyone here remembers me, of course. People don't leave the estate except through the graveyard. And you know my father wasn't precisely an asset to the community."

Pen's mother had died when Pen was very young and her father had drowned his sorrows in ale. Pen had been the one to see that the family's land got farmed—which had made her so good at tending the hops at the Home.

"Oh, there *have* been a few awkward moments," Pen said, "but most people are happy with me because I make Harry so happy." She grinned, her cheeks a bit flushed. "And just about everyone is happy that Harry now has the title. For one thing, they don't have to worry about their daughters—as you heard at dinner last night, Harry's father and brother couldn't be trusted to keep their breeches buttoned. But they also see how hard Harry works. They appreciate that he's trying to improve and modernize operations." She shrugged. "Well, *most* of them appreciate his efforts. There are always a few people that don't like change, of course."

"Of course." Jo heard the respect and pride in Pen's voice. How wonderful it would be to be married to a man one could be proud of instead of constantly embarrassed by.

Well, if one wanted to be married, that was.

"And they are happy that I've started a charity school for the children."

Jo stopped, grabbing Pen's arm in her excitement. "You have?! Oh, excellent! I've been meaning to ask you about that."

Pen laughed. "I *thought* you might be happy. It's not a Benevolent Home—I leave that to you. But a school . . ." She sighed. "I would have loved it if there had been just such a school when I was a girl."

Jo nodded, and they started walking again.

"You—and Caro—have done very well for yourselves, Pen. Who would have thought all those years ago when we were starting the Home that one day you would be a countess and Caro a viscountess?"

"And you could be a duchess!"

"I . . . That wasn't my point. What I meant was that, yes, you have risen in station, but more, you are intelligent, accomplished, skilled women—facts that an earl and a viscount were smart enough to recognize." Jo smiled, shrugging slightly. "And to fall in love with, of course."

It was true. Ten years ago, they'd all been so young and

naïve. It had been very much a case of the blind leading the blind. But they had not ended in a ditch. They'd succeeded beyond their wildest dreams.

Pen and Caro had moved on with their lives, which was good.

Do I feel left behind?

No, of course not. Someone had to run the Home.

Does it have *to be you?*

"I didn't mean you would or should want to improve *your* station, Jo," Pen said. "I meant that the duke—like Harry and Oakland—should recognize *your* worth and love you and offer for you because of who you are."

Well, at least they'd got round to the love part, which was the point of this discussion. "Er, about that."

Pen just about leapt into the air. "Yes? Are you really thinking about marrying the duke, Jo?"

"Dear Lord, Pen. I just met the man yesterday."

"But you've been writing him for close to a year, haven't you?"

"Yes, but that's not the same thing."

"No, but it's something. Maybe it's almost better because you've shared your thoughts before you've seen each other and been overwhelmed by physical urges."

Did Pen really believe that romantic twaddle?

Though the physical urges bit is *more than twaddle.*

Still, Jo gave her a look.

Pen smiled blandly back.

"You should stroll about the lake with him or, even better, take him to the temple." Pen pointed to a stone building visible on a hill. "The path up branches off just a little farther ahead." She grinned. "It has a lovely view and is *very* private."

And then the woman had the gall to waggle her brows.

Well, that was the perfect opening to raise the issue that had sent her looking for Pen in the first place.

"I might do that, but I need your help, Pen."

Pen grinned. "Oh, I hardly think you need *my* help! I'm sure the duke can, ahem"—more brow waggling—"*handle* any *needs* you have."

Jo would *not* roll her eyes. "I think you are not getting my meaning. You heard Letitia and Lady Muddlegate last night."

Pen nodded. She'd already admitted as much.

"Well, earlier this morning, when I was in the maze with Ed—with the duke—"

Blast it if Pen didn't give a little skip—but at least she managed to keep her tongue between her teeth this time.

Just barely, from the look of it.

"—Thomas found us. He told us Letitia's girls had told him that the duke and I were going to be *lovers*." Saying it aloud made Jo angrier.

She was happy to see Pen's brows angle into a frown. "Oh, dear. That's not good."

Thank God Pen saw the problem immediately. "It's not good at all. I don't know what will transpire between me and the duke. I confess that I'm thinking of exploring the possibility of some type of closer relationship with him."

That wasn't convoluted enough to dampen Pen's obvious enthusiasm, but she did manage to restrain herself. Her eyes gleamed, but she kept her features schooled to interested concern.

"But I don't want to get Thomas's hopes up." Jo flushed. "Even if, er, *some* things happen, that doesn't mean I'm marrying his father."

Pen nodded, but did she truly understand?

She must—*she* was a mother. Still, best not to leave any doubt about the matter.

"I don't want Thomas to get hurt, Pen. He's only a young boy. Of *course*, he wants a mother. It would be beyond cruel to make him think I'm going to fill that role if I'm not."

Pen nodded again, but with a look about her that said *Oh, I hope, I hope you* will *be his mother*.

Jo scowled. "Promise me you or Darrow will rein in Lady Muddlegate and Letitia before they do any more damage." She cleared her throat of a lump that felt like desperation. "Please?"

That might have sounded like begging, but Pen nodded. "Don't worry, Jo. We'll have a word with them."

Jo snorted, but she'd delivered her message and felt confident Pen would act on it. Time for a change of subject.

"How is Harriet getting on with the baby? Does she like being a big sister?"

Pen's eyes lit up. "Oh, yes. Harriet has been wonderful. Harry says . . ."

Jo listened—she *was* sincerely interested—and nodded, interjecting a judicious *oh!* or *really?* when appropriate for the rest of the walk.

Chapter Ten

Jo stood in the Long Gallery and looked up at a full-length portrait of one of the earl's Elizabethan-era ancestors. The poor fellow was togged out in a garish yellow doublet and hose with a big white ruff around his neck and a large yellow plume on his hat. He looked like an enormous bumblebee.

She was attired in the shocking red dress of satin and lace.

Far too little satin and lace.

The last bit of fortitude with which she'd donned the gown in her room earlier deserted her. She looked with more than a little envy at the man's ruff.

She'd timed her arrival in the drawing room for just before the butler announced dinner. She'd wanted to limit, as much as possible, her exposure to Letitia and Lady Muddlegate. At least it appeared that Pen had indeed had a word with them. Oh, they'd clearly been watching for her—they'd given her a smile the moment she'd stepped through the door . . .

Well, it had been rather more than that. Yes, they'd

smiled, but then their eyes had dropped to her bodice and their smiles had got wider and more . . . knowing.

Dear God, it was a wonder she hadn't blushed to match her dress!

All right, she probably had.

She'd made it through dinner—this time at Pen's right with Edward next to her and Caro directly across the table—without spilling her wine or dumping any food in her lap. And she'd managed—discreetly—to suggest Edward meet her here as soon as he could get free. And then, when the ladies had left the men to their port, she'd excused herself. The very last thing she wanted to do was sit and drink tea with Letitia and Lady Muddlegate. That would be straining their control—and hers—past the breaking point.

So now she was hiding in the Long Gallery, admiring— or at least inspecting—Darrow's ancestors. She—

"I'm very glad men's fashions have changed."

She shrieked, slapped her hands over her mouth to muffle the sound—too late, of course—and spun around to find Edward standing there.

"Oh, I'm sorry. Did I startle you?"

She dropped her hands and scowled at him. "No. I always scream and jump when someone speaks to me."

Did she sound as breathless as she felt?

Calm down. You're a mature widow now, not a young virgin.

She felt a bit like a nervous virgin.

Perhaps he was nervous, too, because she thought his laugh sounded a little breathless as well.

"Pardon me. Next time I'll engage a footman to go before me, announcing my approach." He grinned. "Though that would defeat your effort to make this meeting less . . .

public." He gave her a pointed look. "We really don't have to sneak about, you know."

"We are not sneaking about." Though now that he mentioned it, the sooner they left the house the better. It would not do for a servant to find them together like this. Word would go through the house—the estate—like wildfire. "We are just being discreet."

"I'm not certain I comprehend the difference, but we don't need to be discreet, either. We are unattached adults."

He *must* see the problem.

"Yes. And you are a father. The father of a son who would like a mother—and, it seems, would like *me* for a mother. I don't wish to get Thomas's hopes up."

He shrugged. "I believe Thomas's hopes are already up."

"Yes, but we don't need to raise them any higher." One would think the man would be less a dunce about this. "Oh, do let us go outside."

He grinned. "That sounds like an excellent idea. I'm not fond of family portrait galleries to be honest."

"No?" If she walked toward the door, perhaps he would come along. "Why not?"

It worked! He was finally moving in the right direction.

"Well, perhaps I would have a different opinion if I'd been born to the title. But not having grown up at Grainger nor having had any contact with the ducal line . . ." He shrugged. "I always feel as if these stuffy, imperious strangers are staring down at me, judging me—and they are not happy with what they see." He pulled a face. "I half expect to see their painted noses wrinkle, as if they can smell the stink of the shop as well as the current *ton* can."

Jo snorted. "A good lot of the *ton* are silly fribbles. I think you were fortunate not to grow up as the heir. Too often noble young men fritter their lives away, gambling and drinking and—" She flushed. "Doing other things, waiting for their father to die."

She looked straight ahead. She could feel his eyes on her profile, but she was not ready to talk about Freddie. They would have to at some point. She knew that.

This was not that point.

She went to open the door to the terrace, but Edward got there first.

"Allow me," he said, bowing.

She snorted again. "I can open the door myself, you know."

"Indeed, I do know it, but even though I worked for my bread, I did manage to learn some manners." He swept his arm toward the terrace. "After you, my lady."

"Oh, very well." She stepped outside. "Sometimes I think the Americans have the right of it. We should get rid of the peerage entirely. People aren't dogs or horses. It's not their pedigree that gives them value. *All* men and women have value—equal value regardless of who their fathers and grandfathers were."

He closed the door behind them. "Zeus! Am I in the presence of a radical? Next you'll be reciting from Thomas Paine's *Rights of Man*."

She laughed and started across the terrace to the stairs. "Rights of *Wo*man! That's another problem with the current system. Why shouldn't title and property pass through the female line? Clearly women are capable of managing things. Look at Queen Anne. Queen Elizabeth."

She'd missed this sort of conversation. Not that she and Pen and Caro had discussed politics often. Any free time they'd had they'd spent coming up with plans to keep the Home afloat financially. But given that they served women and children, groups most of society discounted or ignored entirely, it was impossible to avoid the topic completely.

Livy might have some interesting thoughts on the matter.

Jo stumbled and had to grab for the balustrade.

Why have I never asked her?

"Careful." Edward caught up to her and offered her his arm.

She looked at it.

"It's not a snake, you know."

"I can manage by myself, thank you." *And if you're going to insist on being so prickly, he is never going to touch you, is he?*

Good point.

"Oh, very well." She put her hand on his arm.

It was rather . . . pleasant to feel its broad, solid strength and be forced close to Edward's side. She took a quick breath—and inhaled his scent, a mix of port and linen and, well, *him*.

Edward gave her a cautious look—he must think her demented—but just nodded and returned to their conversation as they made their way down the steps.

"If my title had passed through the female line, I'd still be working as a solicitor."

She glanced up at him. "Would you be happier?"

He looked away into the distance as if considering the question, and then shrugged.

"I don't know. I'd have said yes, at least in the beginning. I'd built a comfortable life for myself and Thomas. I felt in control—or as in control as anyone can feel with a young son. And I *liked* my work, my clients."

He looked back down at her. "And then everything changed. Thomas and I went from a small house with a maid-of-all-work to a sprawling pile—*several* sprawling piles—and a host of servants and other dependents. It was very disorienting. Having a background in the law helped, of course, but I still had to learn a lot quickly." He shook his head.

"I swear the servants—especially the butlers—still know more about being a duke than I do. But I *did* learn, and now I care about the estates and, more importantly, the people who live and work on them."

Edward's words gave her a warm feeling of . . . pride? No. Their connection was far too tenuous to claim pride. Admiration, perhaps.

"Your dependents are fortunate. Many peers look upon their estates simply as sources of wealth to be used to fund their lives of dissipation."

That had certainly been how Freddie had viewed his properties.

Edward gave her a searching look. He must have heard the bitterness in her voice. Was he going to mention Freddie?

Not yet. Not yet.

Fortunately, if that had been his initial intention, he thought better of it.

"Oh, yes, I know that all too well. I had many such fellows as clients over the years and so had a front row seat on all the problems such behavior causes. You can be certain I was not going to be *that* sort of landowner."

She nodded and looked away, out over the lake—and remembered how full of pride and respect Pen's voice had been when she'd talked about her husband.

Jo's throat clogged with something that felt suspiciously like longing. *If I married Edward—*

Don't think about marriage.

Her grip on his arm must have tightened, because he looked down at her. "Everything all right?"

"Oh yes. Everything is fine."

I just have to decide how I'm going to ask you to engage in sexual congress.

Lud! She looked straight ahead, hoping he'd not ask her why she was behaving so oddly, and wrestled with the question of seduction as they walked, her steps easily matching his, her hand still on his arm.

"Now that I feel I've got the estate issues sorted out," Edward was saying, "I find I'm turning my attention more to the House of Lords and my duties there. While I don't plan to take on primogeniture—I do know a hopeless cause when I see one—there *are* several issues I'm interested in pursuing."

He grinned at her. "Such as the plight of women and children. I imagine you could give me some advice on those matters."

She perked up. Here was something she *could* address easily. She opened her mouth—

No. If she started in on that, several hours would go by and she'd be no closer to her goal than she was now. She had not donned this shocking red dress to discuss parliamentary priorities.

They had reached a crossroads—literally. The path split. She could either keep to the lake—or, well, change course.

It was time to take action if she was ever going to.

"Shall we go up to the temple?" She pointed up to the circular building. "Pen says it has a nice view."

She wouldn't tell him what else Pen had said.

Well, no. She *would* mention part of their conversation. "I should tell you that I took the opportunity this morning to ask Pen to have a word with Lady Muddlegate and Mrs. Marsh, to tell them to mind what they say around Letitia's daughters. Pen agreed they shouldn't have been talking about us being lovers in front of the girls."

She glanced up at him as she said that last bit.

Mistake.

"Ah," he said, his voice low and full of . . . *sin*. "But *are* we going to be lovers?"

Well, at least the topic was now open for discussion.

Edward wasn't entirely certain what was going on.

Hell, he hadn't the faintest *clue* what was going on. Thomas had interrupted his conversation with Jo in the maze this morning before he'd been certain they'd had a meeting of the minds. And then he'd spent the rest of the day out riding with the men—and thinking about Jo. Remembering her scent, the feel of her hair sliding through his fingers, the press of her body against his. Light, tantalizing details that had whetted his appetite for more. For a deeper, longer encounter.

And *then*, before dinner, he'd watched the door to the drawing room, waiting for her. He'd tried to be discreet about it while carrying on a conversation with Oakland and Lady Oakland, but he'd been getting more and more concerned as the minutes ticked by and Jo hadn't appeared. Had something happened to her? But then surely Lady Oakland would have said something.

He'd started to ask—and then, *finally*, Jo had stepped into the room.

Causing him to completely lose his train of thought.

"It *is* a very nice dress, isn't it, Your Grace?" Lady Oakland had said—or perhaps giggled would be a more apt description.

He'd looked at the woman, and she'd waggled her brows at him, causing her husband to choke on his wine.

"Give a man some warning before you do that," Oakland had told his wife as he'd used his handkerchief to mop up the spirits that had detoured through his nose.

Edward had heard this with only half an ear because Jo had been walking toward him.

It was indeed a very nice dress—red and lacy with a low-cut bodice—but his eyes and all his attention had been focused on the woman *in* the dress. She'd looked equal parts defiant and nervous, brave and vulnerable.

He'd wanted to take her in his arms in the middle of the Earl of Darrow's drawing room in front of all his highly interested guests and hold her. Kiss her.

Instead, he'd just smiled. Widely. Like a love-struck fool.

Was this love? It was certainly strong, focused, and more than a little desperate.

And getting more so.

When the butler called them into dinner, Edward had played his assigned role, protecting Jo from Lady Muddlegate and Mrs. Marsh, escorting her down the table to sit next to Lady Darrow. And then, as he'd bent to pull out her chair for her, she'd whispered her message in his ear—meet her in the Long Gallery as soon as he could after dinner.

He'd all but collapsed into his chair next to her.

He was certain the meal had been delicious, but he couldn't recall anything that he'd eaten. And the other men had been highly amused—and not fooled at all—

when he'd downed his port in record time and had excused himself.

He hadn't gone so far as to say he was retiring early. He'd not wanted to hear all *those* jokes.

And then he'd found Jo jumpy and nervous and wanting to argue political theory with him. Yet when he'd broached her favorite topic—women and children and their needs— she'd not taken the bait.

Now perhaps they were getting somewhere. She'd flushed quite violently when he'd asked if they were indeed going to be lovers, but she hadn't looked away. More to the point, she hadn't hauled off and slapped him. She—

"I don't know," she said.

Well, that was better than a *no*. And she *did* still have her hand on his arm.

Well, she'd *had* it on his arm. She'd just removed it and had stepped away. Hell. Was she going back to the house now?

No, apparently not.

"We need to talk," she said. She looked up at the temple again. "But let's wait until we get up there."

"Very well."

So, there was still hope. And she was right. They *did* need to talk. Thomas and Bear had interrupted their earlier discussion.

They weren't free to frolic for a few days and then move on. They were connected through her charity, partners of a sort who would need to work together for years.

And, of course, there was Thomas's welfare to consider.

And *then* there was the host of bystanders, all *far* too interested in what should be an extremely private matter.

They walked in silence, no longer touching, up the path through the woods. The only sounds were those of nature—a hawk's cry, a rustling of dead leaves, a squirrel chattering—and the thud of their heels on the ground, the swish of Jo's skirt.

"Oh! Look!" Jo stopped when they emerged from the woods and stared, not at the temple, but out over the lake. "Pen was right. The view's quite beautiful, isn't it?"

"Indeed, it is." He was looking at her, but then turned his attention to the view *she* meant.

He hadn't thought they'd gained much altitude—the hill they'd climbed hadn't been particularly long or steep—but from this vantage point, they could see the entire lake.

And several other stone structures. "Some previous earls must have been very fond of follies."

Jo nodded. "Puddledon Manor has a folly, too, but only one—a Gothic cottage."

And then, for some mysterious reason, she flushed.

Hmm. I wonder if the cottage has a bed?

He'd admit that when Darrow had told him he was going to be a father again, he'd done the calculations. Perhaps everyone did that when a child arrived so close to a wedding day. And he'd concluded that young Pip might well have got his start in Little Puddledon, though he'd wondered at it. He couldn't imagine Darrow braving a houseful of women to engage in such behavior, nor could he see Lady Darrow consenting to consort at the village inn where everyone must know her. And while frolicking out-of-doors was always a possibility in the summer, it seemed unlikely.

If *he* felt observed here, think how many more eyes had been avidly watching the earl and his not-yet countess.

Jo had now turned to examine the temple, so he turned to look at it, too. It clearly had classical aspirations with its dome, Corinthian columns, circular portico, and regularly spaced niches graced with statues.

Jo walked over to have a closer look, so he followed her. She climbed the steps—

"Oh!" She stopped so abruptly, he almost ran into her.

"Oh, what?" He looked—and saw a naked woman unsuccessfully—or half-heartedly?—trying to cover her private parts.

Oh, indeed.

"That looks like Aphrodite," he said.

Jo emitted an annoyed-sounding huff. "I don't know why Darrow's ancestors chose to litter the landscape with naked people."

He tried to swallow his laugh, but he wasn't entirely successful. It emerged as a gulp and a snort. "It *is* rather a classical tradition."

"I *know* that. It's just . . ."

It's just time to get to the point.

He didn't want to hurry her, but he also didn't want to launch into another academic discussion. They did not have all night.

Or, well, he hoped they were going to do something else all night—something besides talking. Something that, yes, involved naked people—them. In bed. Together.

And if they weren't going in that direction, he'd like to know it now so he could stop hoping for something that wasn't going to happen.

"Jo, you didn't bring me here to critique the statuary."

She let out a long breath. "No. I didn't."

He waited. She frowned at Aphrodite. Then she frowned at him. Then she frowned back at Aphrodite.

"It's not an easy subject to broach," she told the statue.

He could just say it himself, but he was finding this

oddly entertaining. And it was true she was an extremely independent woman. She might not appreciate him taking the, well, words out of her mouth.

"I promise to try not to have a fit of the vapors." He bit the side of his cheek to keep from laughing. "Just say it, Jo, without any more roundaboutation."

"Yes. Right." She took a deep breath and told Aphrodite, "I'd like to, er, discuss the, ah, possibility of becoming lovers."

She was now redder than her dress.

Chapter Eleven

Jo glanced over her shoulder. "Assuming you're interested, of course."

How awkward—and annoying. The man was just staring at her. "If you're *not* interested—"

He held up a hand to stop her. "Oh, I'm interested. *Very* interested." His voice was low, his eyes intent. His lips curved into . . .

Was that a *predatory* smile? Well, she was not some helpless little mouse to be snatched up by a hungry hawk.

"I said *discuss* the *possibility*. We may decide—*I* may decide—that the notion lacks merit."

She thought he was biting his tongue, but whether it was to keep from speaking or from laughing, she couldn't say.

"At this point I am suggesting only"—she closed her eyes briefly as she said the words, because some things, while sensible, were still mortifying—"*sexual congress*. As a first step. A trial, if you will. If I don't like it"—she looked at him, well, *glared* would probably be a more accurate description—"and I would have to *really* like it if I'm going to consider changing the course of my life, a life I've worked very, very hard to build and which I find extremely satisfying." She stopped and took a deep breath. She might have been letting her emotions get out of control.

Wasn't this going to be just for fun? You weren't going to consider marriage seriously, were you?

She hadn't intended to, but she discovered she couldn't completely separate the notion of marital relations from marriage in her mind.

"If I don't like it, then that is where the matter must end," she said rather forcefully, perhaps trying to firm her own resolve.

Edward looked calmly back at her and nodded.

She'd expected some argument.

Perhaps that would come later.

"I know you are looking for a wife—and a mother for Thomas. However, I am not at all certain I wish—" No, that was the wrong way to couch the matter. She needed to be sure he understood.

"I am almost certain I do *not* wish to marry again."

He nodded, and that hot, sinful smile flickered over his lips. "Then I shall have to try my best to persuade you."

Oh, lud, his voice when he said *best*. It made her shiver.

It made a very specific part of her shiver—and brought a storm of nervous butterflies back to her stomach.

She tried to give him a stern look, but she suspected she wasn't very successful.

"I warn you, you will have a very difficult time of it. My first marriage was not especially pleasant, and now I have my charity to run. I cannot see how I can marry you and still manage it. How can I live at the Home in Little Puddledon and be your wife and Thomas's mother? You certainly aren't going to move to the village."

Why are you throwing up all these objections? Didn't

you decide you wanted *to explore bedroom matters with the man? You will lose this opportunity. Edward is going to wash his hands of you.*

He didn't. Instead, he nodded and said, quite calmly, "I see. Let's discuss the matter, shall we?"

"Er . . ." This was not how she'd imagined her seduction would go.

Well, she'd not really been able to imagine a seduction at all, much as she had hoped *something* would happen when she put on this scandalous red dress. Had she thought Edward would overpower her, sweeping away all her doubts, reservations, and inhibitions?

I probably would have fought him tooth and nail.

The slightest hint that someone wanted to pressure her to do anything that wasn't her own idea always put her back up.

"There's a bench over there with a view of the lake," he said. "We can sit and be comfortable."

"Very well." She strode over and sat at one end. This bench was larger than the one in the maze. There was room enough for her and Edward and for fat old Prinny to plop himself down between them.

Unfortunately.

No, not unfort—

It is *unfortunate if you're still hoping for some sort of seduction.*

Perhaps Edward would sit—

No. He settled at the far end and turned toward her.

She turned to face the lake—and nerves launched her tongue into motion again.

It was finally time to talk about Freddie.

"When I said earlier that young men waiting to inherit often fritter away their lives, I was speaking from personal experience, as you likely surmised. Freddie gambled and drank and—"

And she couldn't say it this time, either.

"Well, it's a wonder I wasn't tripping over his bastards, even in Town."

Edward gave her a searching look, opened his mouth—

Is he *going to tell me Freddie couldn't father children? Lud! He must think me as much of a ninny as Lady Muddlegate and Letitia do.*

"I know what you are going to say, but you're wrong. I assure you, Freddie was capable. I am *not* a virgin."

"Yes, I understand, but I'm not certain you do."

Her back stiffened. And now he was going to insult her intelligence? If so—

He laid his hand on hers, his touch warm. Comforting. Calming.

"Remember what I told you in the maze, Jo? I was married to Helen for five years before we got Thomas." His fingers tightened on hers—and then he reclaimed his hand and sat back.

"You may be right that you can't have children. But you may be wrong. Helen was certain she was barren, until she found she was carrying Thomas."

Sorrow shadowed his face then, and he looked away, out over the lake.

Oh. Her heart ached for him. He must have—*they* must have been so happy to discover they were going to have a child, and then nine months later . . .

It was so wrong when birth brought death. Overwhelming joy and pain at the same time in the same heart.

She wanted to reach out to him as he had done to her, to offer comfort, but she was too late. He'd shaken off his melancholy and managed to smile.

"And Lady Muddlegate and Mrs. Marsh are correct about Havenridge, you know. I asked around once I discovered I was supporting your charity to find out what I could about you and your departed husband. Havenridge had a reputation with the Fashionable Impure—a girl never had to worry after he left her bed that she'd have a squalling reminder of his visit nine months later. I take it they thought it was his best quality."

"Oh." She frowned. *Could* it be true that Freddie—

No. Surely he would have known it if it were, and he had been quite clear on the matter—there was nothing wrong with him. The fault lay with her. He had told her so repeatedly.

"But what I had been going to say before we got off on, er, reproductive matters was, from what I could tell, Havenridge didn't change his behavior when he succeeded to the title."

She snorted. "Very true. I suppose habits learned early are hard to break."

No, that wasn't entirely fair, was it? She really had tried, over the years, to see the matter through Freddie's eyes. "I do sometimes wonder if he *would* have changed if he'd been able to have a son."

This time it was Edward who snorted.

Her surprise—and skepticism—must have shown on her face, because he gave her a very direct look.

"As I said earlier, I spent years working with the nobility when I was a solicitor. There are many who take their responsibilities seriously, but there are just as many who don't. Like your departed husband, they drink and gamble and"—he paused—"*carouse*. Their parental status has nothing to say to the matter."

Well, yes, she did know that. Many of the women at the Home were there as the result of some irresponsible lordling's carousing.

He frowned. "It is, frankly, one of the things that worries me about Thomas's position. He is now the heir to the dukedom. He will, eventually, go to school with other sons of the nobility. They will become his friends, and, someday, will join him in the House of Lords, governing the country. I hope . . . I will try . . ."

He shook his head. "I *am* trying to see to it that Thomas does not become another silly noble fribble. That he grows up to be a responsible, thoughtful man." His gaze held hers. "But I know I can use the help of a sensible, clear-eyed woman to achieve that end."

She felt both flattered and flustered. She wanted to help—

No. Well, yes. She did want to, but she couldn't. She had the Home. She had women and children—girls—depending on her.

Fortunately, Edward didn't press her. He smiled and moved on.

"What *does* surprise me, however," he said, "is how *you* came to marry a man such as Havenridge. By all accounts, he'd always been a self-centered, harum-scarum ne'er-do-well. You are . . ." He shook his head bemusedly. "None of those things. Really, you and he are as different as chalk and cheese."

She sighed. She'd asked herself that exact question over the years.

"I'm not the same person I was then. Just as your years as a solicitor have formed you, my years running the Home have changed me. For one, I'm not so easily dazzled now."

She would have said she was completely immune to dazzlement, but she was feeling more than a little bedazzled by her current companion.

"And Freddie *was* dazzling. He was handsome. Charming. Everything a young girl dreams of."

Edward looked more than a little skeptical. "You must have been very young."

She smiled. "Yes, I was. And foolish. But then young girls are brought up on fairy tales, aren't they? Encouraged to dream of a handsome prince, who will ride in on his white horse, sweep them off their feet, and carry them away to live happily ever after."

Edward snorted. "Or of a titled lord with several thousand pounds per annum."

Yes, Jo could see his point. He *had* just come from the Marriage Mart.

"It would be much better if girls were raised to rely on themselves," she said. No, it was more than that. "It would be much better if girls—women—*could* rely on themselves. If they had more of a say in their own lives. More freedom, more power, to choose their own paths, independent of any man."

Edward nodded. "Yes, indeed. That is one reason why your charity is so important."

He said it matter-of-factly as if it was something he believed, not something he was saying to flatter her into doing what he wanted.

A rare mixture of happiness and pride bubbled up inside her.

"But how did you even meet Havenridge?" he asked. "Did you have a Season?"

Now *that* was funny. "Oh, no. I'm the middle of seven

girls, remember. Papa was a village vicar. There was no money for a Season."

A puzzled frown furrowed his brow. "But you must have gone up to Town?"

Why would he think that? "No. The first time I set foot in London was the day I married Freddie. We left Upper Swallowden right after Papa pronounced us man and wife." She'd been so excited . . .

So stupid.

"But didn't you tell Lady Muddlegate and Mrs. Marsh that Havenridge hated the country?"

Oh, right. "Yes. Freddie *did* hate the country, but he liked the wild parties Lord Arnold, the Marquess of Drumm's youngest son, used to throw at Hades."

Edward's eyes widened. "Hades?"

Jo laughed. "That was the name of Lord Arnold's estate. Papa warned me to stay well away from the place when Lord Arnold and the rest of the Hell-born babes, as Papa called them, were in residence. I half expected to see the Devil dancing on the lawn up there." She shook her head. "But Papa didn't tell me to stay away from the village. Mama happened to send me on an errand to the apothecary when Freddie was there buying comfits."

Lud, how she'd stared—gawked, really—at Freddie. At his gleaming Hessians, well-fitted breeches, meticulously tailored coat, and snowy white cravat. At his artfully styled blond hair, his strong chin, blue eyes—

And then he'd smiled at her and any remaining shred of good sense had gone flying out the window.

She sighed. "It is likely impossible for you to comprehend the, well, *impact* that the sight of a London gentleman has on a young girl, especially one who's never been out of her village."

She could see from the skeptical look on Edward's face that it was indeed impossible, but that he was too polite to say so.

Well, looking back, she found it impossible to believe, too. How could she have let a man's appearance, no matter how pleasing, blind her to his character?

To be fair, Freddie had been charming, too. That had likely been what had seduced her more than his handsome face. Even after they were married and she'd discovered how terribly uncharming he was at heart, there were still moments when he'd smile and she'd fall under his spell again.

"I thought I was in love. I *was* only seventeen." She sighed. "Yet that's old enough to make a bad decision with lasting consequences. You know what they say: 'Marry in haste; repent at leisure.'"

She was *not* going to make the same mistake again.

"How hasty *was* your courtship?" Edward was having a difficult time imagining this serious, intelligent, *cautious* woman doing anything in haste, even when she was seventeen.

Hell, weren't they sitting here debating—at rather some length—the wisdom of a bit of carnal play? Not that he had any personal experience with such assignations, but from all he'd heard they were usually conducted in a far more spontaneous and, well, *passionate* way—especially at a house party where each person had a private room with a sturdy door and a comfortable bed near at hand. He'd thought it was just a matter of a few heated looks, a glancing touch, a furtive kiss, and—voilà!—it was off for a night of passion.

Or, as Jo had said with amusing—to him—embarrassment, a night of sexual congress.

Of course, in this instance, he was hoping for more than a night. He was hoping for a lifetime.

Well, at this *particular* moment, he was hoping they would leave this blasted temple with its exceedingly hard stone bench. Soon.

He shifted his weight as unobtrusively as he could.

"From the time I first saw Freddie until Papa pronounced us man and wife—two weeks."

He blinked. "Pardon me?" He could not have heard her correctly. "Did you say . . . two *weeks*?"

She scowled at him. "Yes. Two weeks. A fortnight. Fourteen days." Her brows rose. "The length of this house party."

"Ah." He blinked again. "That, er, *is* rather quick."

He was too smart to ask the obvious question.

He didn't need to ask. She was too smart not to know what he was—what anyone would be—thinking.

Her brows snapped down again. "And no, we did *not* anticipate our vows. Not that there would have been a permanent consequence if we had—well, besides my losing my virginity, and the women at the Home say there are ways to fake that, *if* that little bit of skin is of great importance to some man."

Her look dared him to say that it was—and promised to eviscerate him if he did.

He was not about to go off on *that* academic tangent either. The bench was only getting harder. He wished to reach their goal—sexual congress in a nice *soft* bed—tonight.

Or, at least he hoped it was their shared goal.

"So, what *was* the rush?"

She frowned at him and then frowned at the lake. "Freddie's father had threatened to cut off his allowance if he didn't marry a respectable woman within six months. Unfortunately for Freddie, all the London women and their families knew him too well. None wanted anything to do with him. So, two weeks and one day before his father was to make good on his threat, Freddie came to Hades to drown his sorrows."

Her lips twisted. "And found me, the answer to his prayers." She looked back at Edward. "Not that Freddie prayed."

Somehow it did not surprise him that Lord Havenridge had not been particularly pious.

She sighed and looked back over the water. "And, to be brutally honest, I think my pride was much to blame. My older sisters had all married village vicars like Papa. I thought myself superior to them." Her tone was bitter with perhaps a note of self-loathing. "I thought that I was destined for greater things than being *just* a vicar's wife. So instead of being properly skeptical that a London gentleman would fall madly head-over-heels in love so quickly with me, I thought I was finally being recognized for who I was, for my"—her lips twisted in clear self-disgust—"*specialness*."

He put his hand on hers. "You *are* special, Jo. Perhaps not in the way you thought then, but look at yourself now. It took intelligence and strength of will to found the Benevolent Home and keep it running all these years. You

are doing important work, giving women and children—
or at least girls—a safe place to live."

She smiled at him, her face, well, *glowing*, and turned
her palm up to grasp his hand.

He thought he might be glowing himself, happy that
he'd apparently said precisely the right thing.

And had meant it, of course. It was true.

She was looking down at their joined hands now.
"The irony of it is, if Freddie had only waited, he would
have saved himself—and me—so much pain." She looked
up, her eyes meeting his. "The week after our wedding,
Freddie's father went out riding, missed a fence, and broke
his neck—and Freddie became Baron Havenridge, with
access to all the estate's funds."

"Ah." That did seem an unnecessarily cruel twist of fate.
His mind circled back to her wedding. "I can understand a young girl thinking she was in love and wanting to
marry after such a short acquaintance, Jo, but your mother
and father weren't seventeen. Didn't they try to stop you?"

"No." She shrugged. "Freddie really *was* quite charming.
I imagine he hoodwinked both of them as well."

"Not bloody likely."

Her eyes widened. "I beg your pardon?"

"Think of it, Jo. If all of Town knew Havenridge was
a very dirty dish, it's hard to imagine your parents didn't
know it, too. Surely the London papers reached your
village."

He snorted. "I'm all too familiar with the way the
gossip columns avidly cover the *ton*. They *must* have been
slavering over such a delectable tidbit as the heir to a
barony desperately searching for a wife to placate his
father and keep his funds flowing."

And that wasn't the worst of it. "But even if your

parents hadn't read the London tittle-tattle, they had their own eyes to inform them. Didn't you say your father called Freddie and his friends Hell-born babes and warned you off going near them?"

She blinked at him. Bit her lip. "Oh. Yes. I always thought . . . I guess I blamed myself . . ."

"Don't. Your parents should never have let you marry the man."

She smiled, shook her head. "Oh, but I wanted to, desperately. Seventeen-year-old girls can be very strong-willed."

His reaction was swift and intense. There were few things he believed with such absolute certainty as this. "And that is where a parent needs to be equally strong-willed."

Her brows shot up.

He took a breath, trying to modulate his voice which was, admittedly, bordering on the strident.

"Not that I've had to deal with a seventeen-year-old daughter, of course. And Thomas has not seriously butted heads with me yet. But I know that when he does, it will be my job to protect him—and I *will* protect him to the best of my abilities."

He searched her eyes, willing her to understand. To believe him. "I imagine Thomas and I will not always agree on such matters. I hope I will be able to keep an open mind, to be persuadable by a well-argued case. But in regard to someone who presents such a clear danger as a man of Havenridge's stamp?" He scowled. "No. Pigs would fly before I'd let a fellow like that anywhere near Thomas, or anyone else I loved. For your father to allow you to *marry* Havenridge, to put yourself so completely in the cur's power—"

Jo was staring at him as if he was demented—and he did feel a bit mad with the anger coursing through him.

Why do I care so much? It's long in the past.

But it was *wrong*. That offended his sense of justice. And Jo had suffered. Was still suffering, if this conversation was any indication. Her father—and her mother—had failed her.

He took her hands in his. It wasn't his place, but he couldn't keep from saying this.

"I suspect the answer lies with your younger sisters, Jo. That your parents saw your marriage to Havenridge not only as an improvement in *your* station, but also as an improvement in *theirs*—as a way to open Society's doors to the younger girls. Perhaps your *parents* wanted more than just another vicar for you and your sisters."

Jo stared at him—and then laughed rather grimly. "Well, if that *was* their plan, Freddie's suicide drove a stake through it."

He tried not to flinch at her wording, but she was right. If Havenridge had been deemed sane at the time he'd pulled the trigger, he'd have been considered *felo-de-se*— a felon. All his property would have been forfeited to the Crown, a *literal* stake driven through his dead chest, and his body dropped at midnight into a pit at a public cross-roads. Since his heir *had* succeeded him, he must have been declared *non compos mentis*.

Not that insanity was a flourish anyone wanted on their family crest.

"It doesn't matter now," Jo said. "It was a long time ago."

Something in her expression—in the brave front that didn't quite hide the sadness in her eyes, in her determined but fragile cheerfulness—called to something deep in him. He wanted to hold her, keep her from feeling any more pain.

Not smother her, never that. Or control her. But to stand *with* her.

If she would let him.

He couldn't put that all into words—nor, he felt certain, would she want to hear it now.

So, he wouldn't use words.

He leaned forward and kissed her.

Chapter Twelve

Jo had seen Edward's face still, seen his gaze sharpen, focus on her with such intensity her breath caught, but she'd not known what to make of it.

And then he'd touched his lips to hers.

Oh! It was hardly more than a brush, soft, light, over almost as soon as it began, but it sent *such* a jolt through her. It galvanized and reanimated parts of her she'd thought quite, quite dead.

Parts she'd not known even existed.

Or . . . or perhaps it was more like rain, falling on drought-parched ground. Seeds, long dormant, awakened to push up out of the dirt and bloom.

Something was unfurling deep inside her.

Edward had pulled back and was watching her now, waiting for her reaction.

She hesitated. Up to this point, her talk of becoming lovers had been just that—talk. She could still change her mind. She could smile, stand up, say it was time to go back to the house. She felt certain Edward wouldn't press her or even make her feel guilty for having lured him out here under false pretenses.

They *hadn't* been false pretenses. She hadn't promised anything—she'd just suggested they discuss the possibility of an affair.

An affair she thought she wanted.

But can I trust myself? I was so wrong about Freddie.

Yes, but she'd been seventeen then. She was not seventeen now, and Edward was nothing like Freddie.

And this isn't a marriage. I'm not vowing to obey or serve Edward for as long as we both live. This is only for a fortnight, if that. For . . . fun.

This was her time to take a holiday from her duties. From being responsible. To hie off across that figurative field, chasing pleasure. Everyone here expected her— wanted her—to do just that.

She *did* like to make people happy—even herself.

She kissed Edward back.

Or tried to. Her nose bumped into his; her mouth got only a corner of his mouth.

He laughed, and then his arms swept round her, bringing her up against his chest. His mouth came down on hers—

There was nothing soft or light about *this* touch. It was insistent. Hungry.

Suddenly, she was hungry, too. All her arguments, all her weighing of pros and cons, all *thought* spun away.

Edward's tongue traced the seam of her lips. What did he want?

Her body knew. Her lips parted, and he slid in, deep, filling her.

Oh, dear God.

She was *drowning*. Heat swirled through her. Her breasts felt full, her womb heavy. The opening between her legs throbbed. She wanted him there, too, just like in her dream, gliding in, deep, deeper, stroking . . .

And then his hand touched her breast, his fingers *so* close to the top of her scandalous bodice. She needed him to stroke her there, too. Needed him—*desperately*—to push the cloth aside and—

He lifted his head, taking away his lovely mouth and tongue and all the hot, wet sensations they'd created.

She wanted to cry.

"Edward! Don't stop!" She reached for him to pull him back, but he dodged, laughing.

Though the laugh did sound a little shaky, so she forgave him.

Almost.

"Consider this a pause only, Jo. I suggest we move inside. I, for one, would like a soft bed—this bench is quite hard." He grinned. "And if we keep on in the direction we are headed, we risk scandalizing the wildlife."

Now *that* sounded promising!

Jo was setting a brisk pace back to the house.

Edward followed along behind. He was having a little difficulty walking. Their interlude in the temple had been very . . . stimulating, and his most stimulated organ had yet to resume its normal, polite proportions.

It was likely rather shocked at having been so suddenly resurrected.

Well, lagging behind *did* have its benefits—he could admire the view. Mmm. Jo had a lovely stride. Which must mean she had lovely, strong legs under those skirts. He was very much looking forward to seeing them, feeling them wrapped tightly around him.

He had to slow his steps even more.

Jo stopped and looked back at him. "*Will* you hurry along?"

He grinned. "*Will* you take my arm? I'm delighted you're so eager to get busy, but if we're observed, I'd rather not have it look as if I'm chasing you. Someone might feel compelled to come to your rescue—and you don't want to be rescued, do you?"

It appeared as if she couldn't decide if she was amused or annoyed, but she did wait for him to catch up.

"And it's sometimes true that delay makes the consummation all the sweeter. It's the anticipation, don't you know? Do take my arm." He offered it with a flourish. "And I shall try to tease you with suggestive talk so you are ready to leap into bed the moment the door shuts behind us."

She gave him a doubtful look, but did put her hand on his sleeve. "I can't believe—"

Woof!!

Edward's head snapped up, his eyes leaving Jo's to see—

Bear bounding across the lawn toward them.

Oh, blast. There went any hope of an immediate trip to the bedroom.

And the fact that *that* was his first thought and not to wonder why his dog was out running loose spoke volumes.

He had to get his animal urges under control.

Well, first he'd get *this* animal under control.

"Sit!" he commanded as Bear reached them.

Bear sat. He didn't look the least bit repentant of whatever sin he must have committed.

"There's Thomas," Jo said. "And the girls."

"And the governess, Miss Woodrow." Edward's heart—

and cock—sank. Hell, there might be no bedroom activity at all at this rate.

The children, all in their nightclothes, ran up, the governess, huffing and puffing, still quite a distance behind.

"Papa! Bear was only hungry!"

"Miss Jo, the dog stole Lady Cassie's dinner!"

"Your Grace, that dog took my sister's food."

Jo laughed and held up her hands, calming the hubbub. "Children, please! Perhaps we can begin with introductions. I believe you've all met the duke?"

The girls nodded and curtseyed.

"I am Lady Havenridge, though I hope you will call me Miss Jo. I know Thomas and Harriet, but I haven't yet had the pleasure of making *your* acquaintances." She smiled at Mrs. Marsh's daughters. "Though of course I know you are Harriet's cousins."

Lady Adrianna, the oldest, took charge. "Yes, Lady Havenridge. We are."

"Please—Miss Jo."

The girl nodded. "Yes, Miss Jo. I am Lady Adrianna." She gestured to her sisters. "And this is Lady Bianca and Lady Cassandra."

"How lovely to meet you," Jo said, sounding quite sincere. "Now, what seems to be amiss? *Did* Bear eat your dinner, Lady Cassandra?"

The children all started talking at once again.

"You know," Jo said after a moment, in a quiet but firm tone, "I really *can* listen to only one person at a time, and I believe I was talking to Lady Cassandra." She smiled at the girl who, if Edward remembered correctly, was two years older than Thomas. "I'm sure you're quite capable of explaining the matter to me all by yourself, aren't you, Lady Cassandra?"

Jo really was splendid at this. Her calm good nature was very soothing, even to him. She would make an excellent mother.

And wife.

And, yes, she also did an excellent job of running her charity, but surely Livy or someone else could do that? It wasn't as if Jo would be washing her hands of the place. She'd still have a say—a *large* say—in the Home's operations, just at a distance.

Sometimes a bit of distance was actually a good thing. It allowed one to see all the facets of an organization . . .

You're rationalizing.

True. And no matter how persuasive he found his arguments, this wasn't his decision to make.

Still, if Livy is truly interested . . .

Livy was very good with people.

Well, very good with *men.*

Yes, but she looked out for the girls who worked for her, too. She was kind. Perceptive. Intelligent.

Of course, none of that mattered if Jo decided she didn't want the position he might wish to offer her.

Lady Cassandra nodded—and gave her sisters A Look before beginning her story. "I wasn't hungry at dinner so I wrapped my meat pasty up in my napkin and tucked it under my bed to have later." She turned accusatory eyes on Bear. "But then *he* crept into my room and ate it while we were playing spillikins."

It must have been a *very* spirited game of spillikins. Edward could not imagine Bear creeping anywhere.

At least the dog had finally found the grace to hang his head—or perhaps he was just making himself comfortable. His body followed his head down, and he stretched out on the grass.

By this time Miss Woodrow had caught up to the group.

"Your. Grace," she panted. She was clearly not used to running any distance. She looked at Jo. "Lady. Haven"— pant—"ridge?"

Jo nodded, smiled, and said calmly, "Take a moment to catch your breath, Miss Woodrow, and then perhaps you can help us understand matters. Lady Cassandra was just telling us that Bear ate her dinner."

Miss Woodrow nodded. "I'm afraid he did." She looked somewhat sternly at Lady Cassandra. "But Lady Cassandra should *not* have been hiding food in her room."

Lady Cassandra stuck out her lower lip in a bit of a pout. "I *was* going to eat it," she said, sullenly. "Just later."

"You didn't have to scream at Bear," Thomas said a bit roughly. "You hurt his feelings."

They all looked at Bear. He didn't appear the least bit, er, hangdog.

"I'm sorry Bear took your food, Lady Cassandra," Edward said, "but—"

Jo put a discreet hand on his arm, stopping him—and causing him to notice Lady Cassandra had gone a bit pale.

Blast. He hadn't thought he'd spoken sternly, but, then again, he was large and male and a stranger to the girls. He should tread carefully.

And from what Lady Muddlegate and Mrs. Marsh had said, it sounded as if the previous Earl of Darrow had not been a model father.

"But"—Jo picked up where he'd left off—"dogs *do* have a very acute sense of smell and will eat almost anything they find. Do you have a dog, Lady Cassandra?"

The girl shook her head. "Papa didn't like dogs."

"He liked dogs, Cassie," Lady Adrianna said. "He just

didn't like them in the house." She looked at Edward and Jo. "They stayed in the kennel. They were hunting dogs."

Edward found himself irrationally irked by Lady Adrianna. She was rather overbearing. Perhaps it came from being the oldest daughter.

Or perhaps she reminded him a bit too much of her meddling mother.

"Miss Jo has a dog," Harriet said. "His name is Freddie. Why didn't you bring Freddie with you, Miss Jo? I'd hoped to see him again."

Jo laughed. "You know why, Harriet!" Then she smiled at Harriet's cousins. "Bear is very well-behaved compared to Freddie. Freddie growls."

"Though only at men," Harriet said.

"And maybe boys. Miss Jo said she didn't know about boys," Thomas added.

"True. And, to be honest"—Jo looked back at the most injured party—"I suspect Freddie would have stolen your meat pasty, too, Lady Cassandra. He wouldn't have been able to help himself."

Lady Cassandra looked as if she accepted that and might finally be willing to let her feelings of ill-usage go.

"Perhaps it is time to shake hands—or paws—and make up," Edward said, smiling and making an effort to soften his voice.

Miss Woodrow's eyes widened. "Shake *paws*?"

Apparently, Thomas had yet to show off Bear's tricks. The boy corrected that oversight now.

"Yes, Miss Woodrow." Thomas turned to his dog and pointed to Lady Cassandra. "Bear, shake Lady Cassie's hand."

Bear heaved himself up and walked toward the girl—who darted behind Miss Woodrow.

"You don't have to be afraid," Thomas said, perhaps a little smugly. "Bear won't hurt you."

Bear planted his rump on the ground and extended a paw.

Lady Cassandra peered around the governess. She hesitated, but then stepped forward, gingerly reached out . . .

"Oh! Look!" she said, a mix of wonder and glee in her voice. "I *am* shaking Bear's paw!"

Then her sisters and Harriet—and even Miss Woodrow—each had to take a turn.

Miss Woodrow straightened after hers. She was smiling, but there was also a small line between her brows.

"Thomas,"—her gaze moved to Edward—"Your Grace, Bear is a delightful dog, but I think tonight, because of all the, er, confusion and because I'm not entirely certain we found all the bits of pasty in the schoolroom, it might be best if he slept somewhere else."

Edward nodded. Likely a wise decision. "He can stay with me, of course." He turned to his son. "As can you, Thomas, if you want."

And there goes any hope of furthering my amorous ambitions.

Perhaps it was just as well. No need to give Lady Marsh's daughters any more encouragement to contemplate his and Jo's romantic connection.

"Oh, I'm sure Thomas will be fine in the schoolroom, won't you, Thomas?" Miss Woodrow said.

Damnation! There was no need for Thomas to be brave. He wasn't used to being around other children—and these were all girls and older than he.

He felt Jo's hand on his arm once more and looked down to see her understanding smile. She was right. He should encourage Thomas's independence—or at least not *dis*courage it.

"Yes, Miss Woodrow, I will," Thomas said and then smiled at him. "Don't worry, Papa."

Good God, now the boy was looking after him!

"Could Bear come back upstairs tomorrow, Miss Woodrow," Jo asked. "Once things are put to rights, that is?"

Miss Woodrow nodded. "Indeed, he can, Lady Havenridge. We've just got to clean Lady Cassandra's room and give it a good airing to get rid of the scent."

Then Miss Woodrow put a hand on Thomas's shoulder and smiled. "Let's go back now, shall we? We need to finish our game of spillikins before bed." She looked at Edward. "I will tell you, Your Grace, that Thomas was beating us all to flinders."

"Thomas is very good at spillikins," Harriet said.

Thomas grinned. "I *am* good, aren't I?"

Edward's heart twisted. He didn't think he'd seen that look of pride and confidence on Thomas's face before.

He needs to be around other children, learn how to deal with them. It's part of growing up.

"Yes," Lady Adrianna said, not unkindly, "especially for a boy."

Thomas scowled at that, opened his mouth, and—

"Well," Jo said, heading off what might have become a new argument. "It's getting dark. His Grace and I were finishing our stroll. Shall we all walk back together?"

Chapter Thirteen

Edward and Bear led the way down the narrow, winding stairs from the schoolroom, Jo following carefully behind, one hand on the rail and the other lifting her skirt so she wouldn't trip.

When they'd got back to the house, it had been clear Thomas had wanted them to come up to the schoolroom with him, so up they had gone and had stayed to watch Miss Woodrow and Thomas finish their game—and Thomas win.

And then Edward had offered to play.

It had been the right thing to do. Thomas had been thrilled—well, so had Miss Woodrow and the girls.

Jo had been . . . somewhat less than thrilled. She'd been happy to help sort the bobbery on the lawn, but then she'd hoped to go directly to her room and to bed.

With Edward.

But he was a father. She understood that his son's needs must come first, so she'd sat in one of the chairs, putting a hand on Bear to keep him from getting into any more mischief, and had watched Edward get down on the floor with the children.

And had fallen a little more in love with him.

She almost missed a step, but grabbed the rail in time.

Edward must have heard her small gasp, because he stopped and looked back. "Are you all right?"

"I'm fine." *Except I might be losing my heart to you.*

He gave her a concerned look. "Only a few more steps. We're almost there." He grinned. "And if you feel yourself going, call out so I can brace myself."

She laughed. "Don't worry."

No, this isn't love. It can't be. I just admire the man, that's all.

The girls and Miss Woodrow certainly admired him. The adulation had been a bit thick in the air, though to give Edward credit, he'd seemed oblivious to it. Sprawled on the floor, playing with the children, laughing, teasing, challenging them, he'd looked to be having pure, uncomplicated fun.

He was so good with them. He should have more children of his own.

Which was one more reason this affair they seemed about to embark on could be only for now and not forever.

And it *was* going to be for now. It had taken some courage to get this far—she wasn't going to turn back, even if that might be the more sensible thing to do.

And furthermore, if everyone was going to link her name with Edward's anyway—she'd seen the looks Letitia's girls and Miss Woodrow had been throwing her—she might as well make it true and get some enjoyment from the situation.

"Thomas and I used to play spillikins all the time before the blasted Season took over my life," Edward said now. "I'm relieved to see I haven't completely lost my touch."

Mmm. Touch.

Her breasts ached with the memory of his almost-touch at Aphrodite's temple.

She'd watched his hands as he'd played with the children. His fingers were so much broader than theirs, he should have been at a decided disadvantage. Yet he was so dexterous, his touch so precise, he could pluck the most precariously placed stick free without disturbing the rest of the pile—when he wanted to.

But having fun—letting the *children* have fun—had obviously been his goal. Not winning. She'd noticed that he'd often go after the sticks that had no hope of being safely freed, but which, when moved, fell in such a way as to open more chances for Thomas and the girls.

"You could have won. I saw what you were doing."

Edward had reached the bottom of the stairs. He grinned up at her and her foolish heart turned over.

Don't! Don't start writing a romantic fairy tale.

"Ah, I've been caught out, have I?" He laughed. "Thomas is on to many of my tricks, so I have to try harder to lose convincingly."

She took the last few steps and stood beside him.

It's too late. The story's beginning is already written.

Yes. And the middle was about to be. But the end would not be a happily-ever-after. It couldn't be, not and let her stay at the Home.

It will be a happily-for-a-fortnight.

That would be—*had* to be—enough.

"You should have played, too," he said as they started down the corridor.

"*I* am not particularly skilled at spillikins. And Bear needed supervision." She rubbed the dog's ears. "Who knows what else Lady Cassandra might have hidden away in her room?"

He laughed—and glanced around. There was no one else in view, so he leaned closer, waggling his brows in a mock lascivious way. "Shall we see what you've got hidden in *your* room?"

That made her giggle. She'd never giggled with Freddie.

I am just going to have fun and not worry about the past or the future.

"No food. I'm afraid Bear will be sadly disappointed."

He stopped at the first door they came to. "Bear is not invited to the party. I'll get him settled and then come along."

Her heart—and her female organs—shivered with anticipation.

He smiled in a rather knowing way as if he could sense her . . . excitement. "Which door is yours?"

Well, this was convenient—and more evidence of collusion. Clearly, Pen had had matchmaking in mind when she'd assigned bedchambers. "The next one down."

His eyes widened—and then he grinned. "Is it? It's a wonder I didn't notice earlier. I even think there's a door in my room that must open onto yours. If I can, I'll come to you that way. Less risk of advertising our"—his grin widened—"intentions."

That ship had sailed for good up in the schoolroom, but she just nodded. She didn't trust her voice.

She watched Edward disappear into his room. Then she walked quickly to her door, opened it, closed it—

And collapsed against it, her knees suddenly turning to jelly.

Idiot! What is the matter with you? This is no time to turn lily-livered. You want this.

Yes, but . . .

No buts. She'd made her decision. She was going through

with it. It wasn't as if she had to worry about conceiving. Or about spreading gossip—gossip had already spread. She would just be making it true.

She could have . . . fun without qualm or scruple.

If this was going to be fun. That remained to be seen. Though all indications were hopeful.

I should get into my nightgown—

Lud! Embarrassment—and perhaps some other form of heat—flooded her. She'd worn that scrap of cloth last night. She might as well have been naked.

Still, it was all she—

She heard a light knock, a creak of hinges, and a door opened on the far side of the room.

"Here I—oh!" Edward stopped when he saw her still plastered against the door to the corridor. He'd shed his coat and waistcoat . . .

She stared at his chest. There was only a thin layer of linen between her and his naked skin.

How will it feel?

"Er, would you like a glass of brandy? There's a decanter in my room."

She nodded. A little liquid courage sounded good. After a glass—or two—her stomach might not feel quite so tight and jumpy.

"I'll be right back."

She watched him disappear, heard a deep woof from the other room and a low murmuring that must be Edward talking to Bear, a clinking, and then he reappeared, a decanter in one hand and a glass in the other. He didn't say anything, just poured the brandy and approached her cautiously.

"I don't know why I'm being so silly." But she didn't

leave the door's support. She looked at the single glass. "Aren't you having any?"

"I thought we'd share, if you don't object." He handed her the brandy. "You first."

She took a sip. The fiery liquid burned down her throat and warmed her stomach, steadying her. She handed the glass back.

Edward smiled. His eyes searched hers.

She resisted the urge to look away.

"We don't have to do this, Jo. We can just talk if you'd like." He spoke quietly, calmly. Then he shrugged, still smiling. "Or I can go back to my room—and Bear—now."

"No. I want to do this."

His right brow winged up. "You don't sound—or look— very enthusiastic." His voice grew softer, gentler. "You're not afraid of me, are you, Jo?"

"No!"

She might have said that a little too forcefully.

"You don't need to be. I am not going to force you. I swear I will stop at once if you tell me to."

"I am not afraid. I'm just nervous. I don't do this often." *Oh, God, did I really say that?*

"I know." He took a swallow of brandy and handed her the glass. "I don't do this often, either. In fact, the last time was over a year ago."

She'd just taken a sip—the spirits tried to shoot out her nose.

"Really?" That was hard to believe.

"Really." His brow winged up again as he took the glass back. "Does that disqualify me?"

"No, of course not. I just thought . . . I mean, I assumed . . . You must know that Freddie . . ."

He put his finger gently on her lips, stopping her. "I am

not Freddie, Jo. Oh, I'm no saint, but I've also never been one to, er, copulate indiscriminately." He traced his finger slowly along her bottom lip. "I'm very much a monogamous sort. Always have been. Always will be."

His finger—and his words—were doing very odd things to her. Her lips—*both* sets—began to . . . throb. Her heart started to pound . . .

But she still heard the hope—the *dangerous* hope—in his voice and knew she had to fight the drugging sensations and respond.

"This doesn't mean I'll marry you, Edward."

She thought she saw a shadow briefly darken his eyes before he nodded.

"I know." He took one more swallow of brandy and put the glass down. "But I can't promise not to hope for it." He smiled. "And I warn you I'm going to try my best to persuade you to change your mind."

"You won't succeed."

She likely said that as much to bolster her flagging will as to warn him.

His gaze sharpened; his smile grew . . . hotter. "Is that a challenge?"

She opened her mouth to retort, but then discovered she didn't know what she wanted to say. *Was* it a challenge? Did she *want* to be persuaded to give in, give up her life's work for . . . what?

Happiness? Love?

Nonsense. I am *happy. And I don't believe in love. I—*

He kissed her.

Oh! All her reservations—all *thought*—dissolved at the feel of his mouth on hers. Her body took over. Her lips parted.

His tongue, tasting of brandy, slid in warm and deep.

Need roared back. She wound her arms around his neck, pressed her body against his. Close. Closer. She wanted to be part of him.

He raised his head, taking his lips away—and she . . .

Well, she might have growled.

He laughed. "I quite agree, Jo, but I believe your lovely dress is in the way. May I remove it?"

That sounded like an excellent idea. Frankly, if he didn't do so soon, the cloth might spontaneously combust.

"Yes. Please."

"My pleasure." His lips curved up slowly, knowingly. "And yours. I promise."

Then his mouth brushed her temple. His fingers—those oh-so-clever fingers that she'd watched play spillikins— untied her skimpy bodice and slipped it down slowly, tracing a burning path over her skin.

She moaned. The butterflies were back in force. She put her hands on his shoulders, braced herself—

She might have growled again. His shoulders were still covered in linen. She wanted to feel his *skin*. *She* was going to be naked. Her dress was sliding to the floor now, and Edward was loosening her stays. It was only fair that he—

Ah. Her stays were gone, her shift following quickly after. And now Edward's hands were cupping her breasts, a touch she'd been craving since seeing Cupid with Psyche.

She forgot the point she'd wanted to argue.

His thumbs stroked her nipples, causing them to harden. She moaned again. She was melting with need. The opening between her legs was damp, swollen and eager . . .

This is just like my dream, the part I couldn't remember.

But it *wasn't* a dream. This time she was very much awake.

"Shall we get into bed now, Jo?" Edward whispered by

her ear, the words tickling over her skin, sending more heat rushing through her.

"Y-yes." She frowned and plucked at his shirt. "But you're still dressed."

He grinned. "Only for a little while longer. I promise I'll be naked soon. Now, come. Let me get your stockings off."

She should assert herself. She wasn't a child, after all. "I can do that."

"I know you can, but what fun would that be?"

She blinked at him. Fun?

There's that word again. I—

Oh!

Edward grasped her waist, lifting her up as if she weighed nothing to sit on the edge of the mattress. Then he knelt on the floor, his face level with—

How embarrassing! She pulled on his shoulders. "Oh, *do* get up!"

He didn't. Instead, he grinned at her and then eased her legs apart to press a kiss on her inner thigh, close, *so* close, to her core.

All thought of modesty, any remaining shred of embarrassment, vanished. She spread her legs wider, tilted her hips to encourage . . .

No, he was moving in the other direction, down her leg, sliding her stocking slowly, slowly lower, kissing the inside of her knee, her calf, her ankle.

Ohh. That was lovely.

He pulled the stocking and slipper off and then repeated the sensuous torture down her other leg.

She was panting now, her nipples hard, the opening between her legs even wetter, if that were possible. She *wanted* him. Desperately. Urgently. Her life might depend upon having him inside her.

She'd *never* felt this way before.

Then he stood. His hands grasped the hem of his shirt, and she watched, sprawled wantonly on the bed, drugged into a stupor by desire, as he pulled it over his head, revealing his flat belly, broad chest, and muscled arms.

Mmm.

He dropped the shirt on the floor, and his clever fingers moved to his fall, freeing his long, thick cock.

Mmm.

Her core clenched in anticipation.

She was beginning to understand the attraction of sexual congress.

Then he climbed into bed. She opened her arms, and he came to her, pulling her close, wrapping her in his warmth and strength.

"I don't want to hurry, Jo." The words sent more shivers through her. "But I don't think I can go slowly."

She grinned at him. "Then go quickly."

He did. His weight carried her back onto the mattress as he kissed her mouth, her jaw, her throat.

"Edward." She moaned. "Edward."

His clever hands and lips moved to her breast. Each rasp of his tongue, each stroke of his fingers made the opening between her legs ache more, made her more . . . desperate.

"*Edward.*" She tugged on his shoulders. "I need you *now.*"

"Now, Jo? Are you certain?" His voice was strained and breathless, too. Good.

"Yes." She tugged on his shoulders again. "Now!"

"Then you shall have me."

He rose up over her. She felt his tip touch her entrance and she braced herself—

Ahh. There was no pain, no discomfort. No feeling of being invaded. Just pleasure, a cascade of pleasure as Edward slid deeper and deeper, all the way to her womb, filling her. His body—hot and hard—pressed her into the bed, but she didn't feel trapped or dominated or used.

She was surrounded by him, inside and out, and it was glorious. She felt . . . at home. At peace—

No. Not at peace.

"Edward!" She tightened her hold on his shoulders—and tightened inner muscles she'd not known she had. She was *so* close to . . . to the pleasure she'd felt in her dream.

But this was not a dream. This was real. Edward was real. He was here. He was *in* her. "Move!"

She tilted her hips to underline her message and encourage him to act.

"Move?" he whispered by her ear. "Like this?" He rocked his hips. His cock slipped back and then in. Deep.

Ohh. That was wonderful. But not as wonderful as she felt certain it was going to be.

"Yes! Again. Faster."

"*So* demanding." There was laughter in his voice, but also a note of strain. He must feel the same passion that was consuming her. Good.

He began stroking in earnest then, long, slow, deep strokes.

Too slow. She dug her fingers into his back. "Edward!"

He took her meaning.

Oh! This was far better than her dream. It was like nothing she'd ever felt before. Hot. Wet. Intensely carnal. All thoughts of polite behavior, of restraint, of decorum fell away, and her body took over.

No, not just her body. Her heart, too. She delighted in what Edward was doing to her, but she never lost sight of the fact that it was *Edward* doing it. Not some man— *this* man.

Whom she loved.

Her mind froze. *Oh, God, I do love him, don't I?*

And then her womb and channel clenched, and her body tumbled over the edge Edward had pushed it to. Wave after wave of exquisite pleasure washed through her. And, as her pleasure ebbed, she felt Edward stiffen and his warm seed pulse into her.

If only it could *take root.*

No. It was better that it couldn't. Her stay here was a holiday, a magical time out of time. A time to have fun, to enjoy and create memories that she could savor later, when she was back at the Home and her *real* life. She wasn't building a future.

Edward collapsed onto her, his weight pressing her down into the mattress. He was hot and sweaty and heavy—and she didn't mind. Mind? She *liked* being so close to him. She wanted this moment never to end.

She tried to memorize every detail. She slid her hands down his back to his muscled arse, pressing him even closer. She wanted him to stay—

She felt his cock relaxing, withdrawing, slipping away. All too soon he would leave her.

And all too soon—in less than a fortnight—I will leave him and go back to the Home, back to my real life.

Edward turned his head, kissed her cheek. "Mmm."

Do I have *to leave him?*

She lay next to Edward's warm, sleeping body, turning that question over and over.

* * *

Edward woke gradually. He was warm, contented, deeply relaxed in a way he hadn't been in years.

I feel married again.

His eyes flew open. *Good God! Is that true?*

He stared up at the bed canopy. It was too soon to feel this way. Yes, he wanted to marry Jo, but that wasn't the same as *feeling* married.

It's only because we had sexual congress.

No. Well, yes, they *had* done precisely that—twice. The first time and then again in the middle of the night. But this feeling ran deeper than simple physical satisfaction.

He looked over at Jo lying next to him, snoring slightly, her hair spread over her pillow.

She was not at all like the young London girls. She had a depth that came with living, from suffering hardships, making mistakes, and yet finding a way through. Flourishing in spite of difficult times.

Or maybe *because* of them. He'd certainly been changed by Helen's death and having to raise Thomas on his own. Jo wouldn't be the same woman if she'd had a happy, long-lived marriage. For one, she'd never have started the charity she was so devoted to.

She was smart. Sensible. Sensitive. Beautiful.

And *very* independent.

Thomas liked her. *He* liked her. But she had to like *them* enough to change her life.

She certainly wasn't swayed by the thought of being a duchess. If anything, it was a tick in the debit column.

And she was not about to rush into anything.

Well, they were only here for a fortnight—less than that now. He would not think about the past or the future. He would just enjoy the days—and nights—with her, exactly as she seemed determined to do with him. And then, when it was time to leave, they would discuss the matter.

He looked over at her again. The bedclothes had slipped down to her waist now, exposing her beautiful, naked breasts. Should he . . . ?

No. He looked back up at the canopy. He'd already woken her once. That was enough.

Well, it didn't *feel* like enough, but he should try to restrain himself. She'd not had conjugal relations for over ten years. To engage in such activities three times in less than ten hours was likely too much. He didn't want to risk making her sore. There was always tonight.

But, Zeus, that middle-of-the-night coupling had been glorious. He'd woken hard and then got harder as he'd inhaled Jo's scent, heard her soft breathing, felt the mattress shift as she moved.

He'd *tried* to go back to sleep, but it had not been possible. So, he'd run a fingertip lightly over her breast to see if she might wish to play and had felt her nipple tighten. He'd stroked the curve of her arse and had heard what he'd have sworn was a purr. And then he'd touched her entrance and found she was already wet.

And then she'd opened her eyes and smiled at him, and he'd been lost.

He'd tried not to rush, but, once again, he'd not been able to go slowly.

It hadn't mattered. She'd been ready. *Very* ready. He'd felt her come apart on his first stroke, and it had taken him only one thrust more to find his own release.

God, he wanted to do it again and again.

You should go back to your room. Leave Jo in peace. Thomas might come looking for you—

"Good morning."

Ah, Jo was awake. He looked over at her. She'd rolled onto her side to face him—and was grinning.

What was so amus—oh.

He followed her gaze down to the rather pronounced tent in the bedclothes just below his waist.

"I bet I know what *you're* thinking." She giggled.

He grinned back at her. It was too early for Thomas to be out of the schoolroom. He had time. *They* had time.

Especially as, so far, they'd been so very quick about the matter.

"I guess I'm not very good at hiding my thoughts, am I?"

"No, but that's all right. As it turns out, I'm thinking the very same thing."

"You *are*?" The bedclothes twitched, but he tried to ignore that eager organ. "Are you certain? You aren't too sore for another visit? It can't have been that many hours ago that I paid my last call."

"I'm not sore." She laughed a bit breathlessly. "I'm making up for lost time."

Ah, time. Did she pause, too, thinking of the precious minutes passing?

He was not going to waste another second.

Nor was she, apparently. She leaned over and kissed him, running her hand down over his stomach to his cock.

"Ahh." Her touch was tentative, light, her fingers dancing up and down his length, driving him mad with desire.

"Do you like that?"

"Y-yes." *Try for some self-control. Go slowly this time.*

"What about this?" She wrapped her hand around him and—

Maybe next time.

He rolled, taking her onto her back, and lifted himself over her.

She was ready. She took him in her hands, guided him to her opening—and then sighed in what sounded like deep contentment as he slid inside.

Or perhaps that was him sighing.

He paused to savor the moment. He felt so welcome, so warm, so . . . at home.

And then need urged him into motion—his need and Jo's. She arched into him, her muscles tightening, her small pants and moans exhorting him to greater effort as he stroked in and out and in.

She caught her breath, stiffened—and made a small sound of pleasure as she came.

He came an instant later, pouring into her his love, his hope, his life.

And then he collapsed onto her body, completely, thoroughly sated and more than a little dazed. He felt her hands skim over his back, cup his arse.

He never wanted to move again.

But he had to. He was heavy. It must be hard for her to breathe.

He lifted himself and stretched out on the bed next to her. "That was . . ." He searched for the proper word. His thoughts were still a bit addled.

She put her head on his shoulder, cuddled next to him, and smiled. "Wonderful."

"Yes. It was. Wonderful." He kissed her slowly, thoroughly. "Though some day we must see if we can manage to make it not quite so quick."

She smiled. "Mmm. I thought you said you were going off to your own bed after we did this last time." She petted his poor cock. Flaccid and exhausted as it was, it still managed to twitch and warm with pleasure at her touch.

"I was going to. I kept telling myself to get up, but I couldn't tear myself away from your lovely, seductive, *bewitching* presence."

She laughed and pressed a kiss to his chest. "Are you calling me a witch?"

He grinned. "Aren't you one? You have certainly cast a spell on me. You—"

"Eeeekkkk!"

He bolted upright. That had come from the room next door—the one he was supposed to be in.

"Woof! Woof!"

"Zeus! That's Bear." He vaulted out of bed.

"And likely the maid seeing to the fire," Jo said as he dashed toward the connecting door. "Edward!"

He paused. "What is it?!" He spoke rather sharply, but there was no time to waste. The maid was still screaming and Bear was still barking.

"You're naked."

"Oh. Right." He looked around.

"Take the coverlet," Jo said. "You don't have time for shirt and breeches."

Another piercing scream underlined the need for haste.

"She must not like dogs." Jo's voice held a note of criticism. "Bear's not going to eat her."

Edward just nodded. He grabbed the coverlet, wrapped it around himself like a toga, and opened the door, sparing a brief prayer of thanks that his cock was no longer preceding him like a lance into battle.

Chapter Fourteen

Jo picked up her teacup. She was seated in a wing chair in Pen's sitting room, Pen and Caro arrayed on either side of her, blocking all escape routes.

"Thank you, Mary," Pen told the maid who'd brought in the tea tray. "That will be all."

The girl curtseyed, threw Jo a wide-eyed look, and fled.

Jo took a sip of tea and tried to look nonchalant.

She should not jump to conclusions. It *could* be that Pen and Caro merely wished to discuss the Home's operations in more detail. They'd got distracted the other day with all that silly talk of love and marriage.

Now perhaps they could be serious. She'd like to get Pen's advice about how best to support Fanny's efforts with the hops. And Caro would surely have some thoughts on their ale production. Caro was the saleswoman after all, the one who'd taken charge of persuading tavern keepers to offer Widow's Brew. She—

Oh, don't be ridiculous. The reason that footman had been lurking in the corridor outside her room, pouncing the moment she'd stepped out of, er, hiding, had *not* been that Pen and Caro had a burning desire to discuss the Home's operations.

"That was quite some excitement earlier," Pen said.

Jo bit her tongue. *Don't say anything.*

It was always a mistake to rush into speech. Much better to let your opponents talk and get an idea of what precisely they were thinking. Of where the traps were so you could take care not to stumble into one and spring it.

Not that Caro and Pen were her *opponents*, precisely.

And it *had* been quite the farce that had played out in Edward's room: maid screeching, dog barking, duke trying to hold the dog, calm the maid, and not let the coverlet slide off his body and thereby display every naked noble inch to the crowd that had gathered in the corridor.

A crowd that had included footmen armed with fire pokers.

She bit back a nervous giggle.

At least she'd had the sense to stay out of sight. Mostly. She *had* taken a peek around the doorjamb.

No one had *to see you. They all must know the room Edward came from is yours.*

But the maid—and the onlookers in the corridor— couldn't know what Edward and she had been doing in her room.

Please! What else could *you have been doing? Of* course, *everyone knows. Which is why you are here now, drinking tea with Pen and Caro.*

Oh, if only the maid had come just a little later. Edward had been on the verge of returning to his room. Five more minutes—well, ten—or perhaps fifteen—and they would have kept their . . . arrangement secret.

For today. What were the odds it would stay secret

with a houseful of interested eyes on them? A houseful of interested, *matchmaking* eyes.

Zero.

Apparently, Pen and Caro had learned the silence trick, too. They sat mumchance, staring at her.

She stared at them—

Oh, bollocks. This is ridiculous.

She cleared her throat. "Er, yes. It was. Quite."

Caro grinned and waggled her brows. "What was the duke doing in your bedroom?"

Quick, think of something!

"I heard a noise." That was true. The maid's scream had been *quite* a noise. "He rushed in to see what it was."

"He rushed into *his* room," Pen said, immediately seeing through Jo's weak attempt at subterfuge, "*from* yours."

Caro's brows were waggling so much they might as well be dancing. "*And* he was naked."

"He was wrapped in a coverlet." Which had been true when the maid saw him.

Caro rolled her eyes. "He was naked *under* the coverlet. Ergo, he must have been naked when he was in bed."

Don't blush.

Jo held her cup closer, putting it right under her chin, hoping that if she *did* have any heightened color, Caro and Pen would blame the steaming tea.

"Perhaps he sleeps that way." *Don't blush, don't blush!* "It *is* summer."

Pen and Caro exchanged an exasperated look.

"Jo," Pen said, "there's no need to tie yourself in knots. We're *happy* for you."

"And it's not as if it's a surprise," Caro added. "It's what you said you planned to do."

"What?" Jo frowned. She put her cup down with a clink.

She'd not said she was *planning* on going to bed with Edward. And she hadn't said anything at all to Caro.

But I did say something to Pen.

She turned reproachful eyes Pen's way.

Pen's eyes widened. "Was I not supposed to tell Caro? We'd just been talking the night before about how you should marry the duke."

"I am *not* going to marry the duke."

Jo might as well have saved her breath. No one seemed to have heard her.

"It was *my* plan!" Caro said, almost crowing. "Well, I suppose it was really Livy's plan."

Livy again, the schemer!

A red haze of fury swirled before Jo's eyes, momentarily blinding her. She'd like to strangle the jade.

Livy's not here. Perhaps I can wrap my hands around Caro's *throat.*

Caro was blithely going on, clearly oblivious to Jo's rage.

"She's the one who suggested it, and I thought it was brilliant." Caro looked at Pen. "Remember how I wrote you?"

Pen nodded. "Harry and I had already hit upon asking Grainger to be Pip's godfather, and we were leaning toward asking you to be his godmother, Jo, but once Caro suggested *this* idea, everything fell into place. It was perfect—it *is* perfect!"

Caro and Pen finally looked at Jo, *really* looked at her.

"Oh," Pen said. "You aren't happy."

That was quite the understatement.

"No. I'm . . ." Jo couldn't begin to describe how she felt. Bamboozled. Betrayed. Angry.

And pressured. She *hated* feeling pressured.

"I cannot believe you two conspired against me like this."

"Oh, not against you, Jo!" Pen said. "*For* you."

"We didn't want to say anything to you about it before you came. We thought that would make you . . ." Caro paused, clearly searching for some diplomatic wording. "Uncomfortable."

"Defensive." Pen smiled. "And, well, you *can* be a bit pigheaded at times."

Pigheaded?!

Jo's eyes narrowed. She'd show them pigheaded.

"And Livy *did* say she thought you might not come if we told you," Caro added. "We didn't want to give you another reason to hide at the Home."

Hide?!

"You likely would have been self-conscious if you'd known in advance," Pen said. "That would have made you . . . awkward." She smiled. "We just thought we'd put you and Grainger together and see what happened."

"What developed naturally." Caro grinned. "And something *did* develop!"

Pen and Caro were almost bouncing on the edge of their chairs with excitement.

"Oh, good Lord." It was hard to be angry when these two were so obviously delighted with themselves. "Has it occurred to either of you that what *developed* was the decision of two unattached adults to engage in a pleasant affair?"

Pen and Caro were still too caught up in spinning their fairy tale to hear what Jo was saying.

"Harriet told me she ran into you and the duke last night on the lawn," Pen said, "which made me think you must have taken my advice and gone with him up to the Temple of Aphrodite."

"The goddess of *love*." There went Caro's eyebrows

again. Pregnancy must have seriously compromised the woman's ability for rational thought.

Jo scowled at Pen. "You didn't tell me it was a temple to Aphrodite."

"Oh?" Pen shrugged, her gaze sliding away from Jo's. "It must have slipped my mind."

Right. Pen had never been good at hiding a guilty conscience.

"It seemed appropriate, though," Pen went on. "After all, you did say you were . . . how did you put it?" Pen's grin got wider and now *her* brows waggled. "*Thinking of exploring the possibility of some type of closer relationship* with the duke." She laughed. "Not precisely poetic, but I got your drift."

"You must have done a lot of *exploring* last night." That was Caro.

Pen tapped Caro on her arm, as if admonishing her to behave.

"And *then*"—Pen went back to recounting her daughter's observations—"Harriet told me you and the duke came up to the schoolroom. And while the duke played spillikins, *you* watched him very, very intently. Harriet said all the girls—including Miss Woodrow—decided you must be over head and ears in love with him."

Jo moaned and dropped her head into her hands. How embarrassing.

No, my feelings are the least of it.

It was *Thomas's* feelings that were important. It would never do to get his hopes up.

Lud! His hopes were probably already up. Sky-high up. And it would be even worse now. The story of Edward, Bear, and the maid must have made it to the schoolroom.

She would try to limit some of the damage. "Please

don't encourage Harriet in that foolishness, Pen. Thomas wants a mother. It's not fair—it's not *kind*—to encourage him to think I'm going to marry his father."

Pen's—and Caro's—jaws dropped in unison, and they exchanged an incredulous look.

It would be funny, if Jo were in any mood to be amused.

"But, *aren't* you going to marry the duke?" Caro asked.

"Yes, Jo, aren't you?" Pen frowned at her. "Thomas may want a mother, but more to the point, the duke wants a wife. Harry says he's been haunting Society's ballrooms ever since he had the title dropped on his head."

Pen wasn't telling her anything Jo didn't already know. "And I assume he'll keep haunting them until he finds a woman he wishes to marry."

It shouldn't hurt to say that, but it did.

"I think he already has," Caro said.

Pen nodded. "Harry says—"

Jo was getting heartily sick of hearing what Harry said.

"—Grainger doesn't have a reputation as a womanizer. The last woman whose name was linked with his was Livy, and he ended that at least a year ago, when he succeeded to the title." She shrugged. "And Livy's a professional. As far as Harry knows, besides Livy, the only other woman in Grainger's life was his wife." She grinned. "And now you."

Caro nodded. "I can't imagine he'd share your bed, Jo, if he didn't want to make you his duchess. And he *especially* wouldn't consort with you in such a . . . well, *public* isn't quite the right word, I suppose. But . . ." She looked at Pen for help.

"In such an *observable* way," Pen said.

There were indeed far too many eyes trying to observe Jo's business.

However, Pen and Caro were misconstruing the situation entirely. "We *meant* to be discreet. We didn't know the maid would come in and then be afraid of Bear. It really was poor-spirited of her to scream so."

Pen and Caro exchanged looks of exasperation.

"Jo," Pen said, "if you are going to . . . form an attachment at a small house party—"

"—that's not an orgy," Caro added.

Pen and Jo both stared at her.

Caro grinned. "I just thought I should mention that, since I met Oakland at what was supposed to be an orgy."

Pen rolled her eyes and turned her attention back to Jo. "I'll grant you this is a bit of an awkward situation—you and Grainger being the only unmarried adults here."

"Though we did rather plan it that way!" Caro added, not especially helpfully.

"Yes." Pen gave Caro another quelling look and continued. "But you have chosen to make yourself a couple."

"Indeed! Very much so."

"Caro," Pen said, "*will* you stop that?"

Caro just grinned. "Why don't you just admit that you love him, Jo? And then marry him and make everyone happy."

"But I *don't* love him." Even Jo thought that sounded like a lie.

But it wasn't a lie . . . was it?

"Oh, I don't know *how* I feel." Her head was starting to pound. She *hated* being indecisive. "I like him. I admire him. Of course, I do. Anyone would. But I *can't* love him. It's too soon—I've made *that* mistake before. I won't make it again."

She saw Pen's mouth start to open—she knew just what she was going to say—and Jo was having none of it.

"And yes, I *know* I've written to him the last year about the Home, but it's not the same thing."

Jo leaned forward. She'd never talked about her marriage, so it wasn't surprising they didn't fully understand.

"I don't want to go back to London Society. I hated it—and it hated me—when I was part of it before. And as a duchess? That would be a *thousand* times worse than being just a baroness."

The thought of all those stuffy, supercilious people staring at her again was, frankly, terrifying.

"I don't want to give up my independence. I *like* being in charge of my life, setting my own goals. And I don't want to leave the Home. It's *mine*. *I* built it—with your help but it was *my* idea. I won't give it up. I can't."

All right, maybe she was losing control here. Her voice had definitely risen to a rather hysterical pitch.

She took a deep breath—more of a gulp—and then scowled at Caro. "And yes, Livy might *think* she could run the Home, but she *can't*. She's too new. She'd . . . change everything."

Jo pressed her lips together. And now there was a note of panic in her voice.

"We just want you to be happy, Jo," Pen said quietly. "I know it was hard for you when I left, but you never made me feel like I was abandoning you. You didn't try to make me stay. You let me go, because you knew my happiness lay elsewhere."

Caro nodded. "Yes, Jo. I never thought I'd be the one to say this—you know how much of myself I put into the Home's brewing business—but you have to follow your heart. Go where you will be happiest." She looked Jo in the eyes. "Ask yourself if you're still happy at the Home."

"Of *course*, I'm still happy at the Home."

Aren't I?

Lud! She wasn't entirely certain.

Edward followed Thomas and Bear down the stairs from the schoolroom, weighing how best to explain his relationship with Jo to the boy. Dealing with the hubbub in his room earlier seemed like child's play in comparison.

And it had been *quite* the hubbub. Bear was a large dog with a deep bark. Even Edward had been taken aback by how loud the sound had been, how it had filled the room, reverberating from every corner. Add to that the maid's high-pitched screeching and it was a wonder he could still hear.

Edward's arrival on the scene had only caused the girl to scream louder, as if she were afraid he was going to pounce on her, throw her to the ground, and ravish her.

And *then* he'd heard shouting and feet pounding down the corridor. The door had flung open to reveal several sturdy footmen armed with fire pokers.

Fortunately, they stopped on the threshold to evaluate the scene.

It probably helped that none of them wished to be the one to bash a duke's head in.

He saw them look at his bed—see that it was still in possession of its coverlet—and then look over his head at the open door to Jo's room.

He thought he'd heard a muffled gasp behind him.

Zeus! He did hope Jo had had the sense to put on some clothing.

By then the maid had finally stopped shrieking, only now she looked—and sounded—to be on the verge of tears.

"Oh, Your Grace, I'm so very sorry. I'm afraid of dogs, and yours is such a big one. I wasn't expecting to see him. He . . . I . . ."

He tried to put her at ease as quickly as he could. The crowd, seeing no one in danger of death or ravishment, had dispersed—which meant this delicious story would be shooting through the household and up to the schoolroom.

Time was very much of the essence.

"That's quite all right. No harm done. Very understandable. Bear *is* very large."

He'd done everything but literally push her out the door. Then he'd leapt into some clothes and run up the stairs to find Thomas.

Too late. The way the girls—even Miss Woodrow—looked at him made it all too clear that word of the morning's adventure had preceded him.

Thomas was in very high spirits, chatting about the spillikins game of the night before as they went down the stairs. It wasn't until they stepped outside that he got to the part about how happy he was that Miss Jo was going to be his mother.

Oh, hell.

Best be direct.

"Thomas, we don't know that Miss Jo *will* be your mother."

Thomas looked up at him. "But I heard Lady Adrianna say you were in Miss Jo's room this morning and—" He frowned. "She was going to say something else, but she stopped when she saw me."

Thank God for that. He was getting heartily sick of Lady Adrianna.

Bear had headed off across the lawn toward the woods, so Edward and Thomas followed.

"*Were* you in Miss Jo's room, Papa?"

"Yes." There was no point in dancing around *that* fact. Thanks to the maid, the entire household must know by now.

How much more to tell the boy was the issue.

An issue apparently decided for him by Mrs. Marsh's eldest daughter.

"But then you *have* to marry Miss Jo. Lady Adrianna said so—and Miss Woodrow agreed. If you don't, Miss Jo will be *ruined*." Thomas looked at him reproachfully. "Which sounds very nasty."

Edward chose his words carefully. "Miss Jo will not be ruined, Thomas. For one thing, she is a widow, and widows are allowed more . . . freedom in their behavior than young, unmarried girls."

Thomas thought about that—and of course didn't accept it without question. "Why?"

"Why are widows allowed more freedom?" There was an obvious answer involving virginity or lack thereof, but he was not about to discuss that with a child Thomas's age.

"I suppose because they are generally older and have run their own households." He grinned as he guessed what Jo might answer. "They are no longer under any man's supervision—husband or father—and are free to make their own decisions."

And *there* was the best way to explain the situation.

"Miss Jo likes being independent, Thomas. I'm not sure she wants to marry again."

"But what if you've given her a baby?"

Edward missed a step and stumbled. He'd thought—

hoped—that had been what Lady Adrianna had stopped short of saying.

It turned out Mrs. Marsh's eldest daughter was not the only busybody amongst her progeny.

"Lady Bianca said you were *naked* when the maid saw you coming out of Miss Jo's room, so that meant you must have given her a baby. And *then* she said that if you don't marry Miss Jo, the baby will be a bastard and being a bastard was a *very* bad thing. And then Harriet said no it wasn't and Miss Woodrow had to stop them from fighting."

Ah.

"*Did* you give Miss Jo a baby, Papa?"

I hope I did.

He couldn't say that. And he likely couldn't dodge the question entirely, not with Letitia's girls in the schoolroom.

Best to be as truthful—and vague—as possible.

"I don't know, Thomas." Ah, he saw a clear path. "Remember how I told you it took me many years to give your mama a baby—to give her you? So, I think it's unlikely I gave Miss Jo one last night—or would give her one even if she and I, er, see each other every day we're here."

Thomas nodded, seeming to accept that explanation.

They were almost at the trees now, and Edward was just about to breathe a sigh of relief. Surely the subject of Jo and babies would be forgotten in the excitement of newts and frogs.

But Thomas had one more question.

"Don't you *want* to marry Miss Jo, Papa?"

Oh, God. He wanted that more than anything.

"Of course I do, Thomas. But she has to want to marry me back."

Chapter Fifteen

Jo had never been so happy to close a door behind her as she was to close her bedroom door that night. She leaned back against it, shutting her eyes as the day's disastrous events paraded before her, beginning with the screaming maid, proceeding to the extremely uncomfortable conversation in Pen's sitting room, and carrying on through each excruciating minute till she was finally able to escape here.

If only it hadn't rained. She would have got out for a long, calming ramble and the other guests might have forgotten about the contretemps with the maid, Bear, and the *almost* naked duke.

To be honest, she wasn't sure the coverlet really counted enough to justify that qualifier.

But it *had* rained. Everyone had been stuck inside, and everyone had had an amusing observation—*several* amusing observations—to make about the morning's events.

She took a deep breath.

All right, yes. That was an exaggeration. Lady Muddlegate and Mrs. Marsh had had observations. They'd only made them once or twice.

Well, in Letitia's case, three or four times.

But it didn't matter. The others didn't need to say a word. Jo could *feel* them thinking about her. She—

She heard a knock on the door that connected her room with Edward's, and her heart jumped into her throat. She'd thought he was still downstairs playing billiards with the men.

There was another knock, and the door cracked open. She heard Edward's voice.

"May I come in?"

She nodded—and realized he couldn't see her.

"Y-yes."

And then the door opened all the way and he was standing there, grinning, decanter in one hand, brandy glasses in the other.

Relief washed through her. She'd been on edge, every muscle tight, and just seeing this man caused all that tension to drain out of her.

She wasn't alone any longer.

Well, yes, of course she wasn't *alone*. She knew that. There was another person in the room. But that wasn't the sort of aloneness she meant. For the vast majority of her marriage, she'd felt alone even when Freddie had been standing right next to her.

Even when Freddie had been in bed with her. Been *in* her.

But with Edward . . .

With Edward she felt she had a partner, someone who would take her side or at least have her best interests at heart. Someone she could trust to—

Careful! You're getting in too deep here.

"You *do* know it's acceptable to come all the way into a room after you've closed the door, don't you?" he asked.

She stayed where she was, suddenly wary, not of him but of herself. "I was thinking."

He smiled and gestured with his chin to the table and chairs near the fire.

The table covered with the cloth she'd worn as a shawl the first night.

"Come sit and think." He lifted the decanter and poured the brandy. "And drink." He held a glass out to her.

"And talk," she said, finally pushing away from the door. "We need to talk."

Perhaps talking will keep me from feeling so much.

He nodded. "Yes, we do."

Freddie had run anytime she'd tried to start a serious conversation, so she'd stopped trying. It would be so nice to—

Stop!

She heard a noise in Edward's room as she took her glass. "Is that Bear?"

"Yes. I believe Lady Cassandra's room has been aired sufficiently so that Miss Woodrow was willing to let Bear return, but Thomas thought I should keep him." He grimaced. "He thinks I need the dog more than he does."

Jo grimaced, too, as she settled into one of the wing chairs. Might as well get the subject everyone else—or at least Lady Muddlegate and Letitia—had been talking about out of the way. "That was quite, er, something this morning."

He laughed as he sat down. "It was. But don't worry. I believe the housekeeper has decided I can do without maid service for the rest of our stay. We should not have a reenactment of *that* again."

And that, of course, made Jo think in graphic, *longing* detail about what they had done before the maid's arrival.

Is it sexual congress that is making me feel this connection to Edward?

How odd that the same basic act could have such different results. With Freddie, it had made her feel more isolated. Alone and lonely. With Edward . . .

Oh, dear. Edward's brows had risen. Was he going to ask her what she was thinking?

She rushed into speech. "The housekeeper could have found a girl who liked dogs, couldn't she?"

"I suppose so." His eyes gleamed. "I suspect she was more concerned about my lack of clothes than Bear's lack of manners."

And now she was remembering every detail of Edward's body.

She reached for another topic.

"I thought you were playing billiards."

He pulled a face. "I was going to, but then Muddlegate and Marsh decided to play whist with their wives, and Lady Oakland was feeling tired so Oakland went upstairs with her. That left me alone with Darrow."

"You still could have played."

"Indeed. However, Darrow had been instructed by his wife to have a word with me concerning my intentions with regard to you."

"Ohh . . ." Jo moaned and closed her eyes. Why did Pen have to meddle in her life?

"He apologized for it—felt he was sticking his nose where it didn't belong—but, finding himself alone with me, he jumped at the opportunity to complete his assignment."

She took a sip of brandy. "I hope you told him that it was indeed none of his business."

"No. I told him I hoped to marry you."

She choked and had to take a moment to mop up her dress and sort her breathing from her swallowing before she could speak. "Edward!"

"It's the truth, Jo. I *do* hope it."

"You can't!"

"I can. In fact, as I said, I do." He grinned. "And why shouldn't I? You aren't married." He tilted his head toward the bed. "We are compatible." His grin slid into a mock leer. "*Very* compatible."

She rubbed her forehead. She felt a headache coming on. This was all happening far too quickly. "You need a young wife who will give you more children."

"I don't want a young wife." He frowned. "And while I would welcome more children—as I think I've said—the thought also makes me . . ." He shrugged, looked away. "*Anxious* I suppose is the right word."

"Anxious? Why—oh." She remembered his history.

"Indeed. Children are wonderful. Childbirth is not. It is painful and frightening. Women die. *Helen* died."

She nodded and took another sip of brandy. She wanted to tell him that things were not that bleak, to argue that his wife's death had been . . . bad luck. That while many women died, most lived.

But he knew that already. She wouldn't—*couldn't*—insult him by appearing to belittle his experience.

So, she would move on to another topic.

"Pen had a footman waylay me this morning the moment I left my room." Thinking about that conversation in the sitting room made her angry all over again. "It seems she and Caro have been corresponding with Livy."

Ah! Surely, he would dislike being manipulated as much as she did.

She sent him a pointed look. "Did you know they were

all—Pen, Caro, and Livy—scheming to get you to marry me? Livy even secretly altered my gowns, made them far more revealing, hoping that would entice you into seducing me."

He laughed. "Well, it worked, didn't it?"

Her brows slammed down. "What do you—"

He held up a hand. "No, don't take umbrage, Jo. Your gowns are very nice, but in truth it was the woman in the dress who seduced me." He chuckled. "Literally. I believe you are the one who first proposed an affair."

Well, yes. He did have a point there.

"Which I was eager to agree to. But I'm certain I would have fallen under your spell even if you'd been dressed in sackcloth." His brows rose. "Which, if you'll forgive me for saying so, you basically were when we first met out on the lawn."

He might be right about that as well.

"I'm a working woman. I need to dress sensibly. I'm not"—she gave him a speaking look—"nor do I *wish* to be, a *lady* who dresses to be gawked at, who does nothing more than promenade and gossip. I know that type too well. I lived among the *ton* for three years, remember."

Oh, *lud*, how she knew that type. The horror of her London years came roaring back.

"I was only a minor member of the nobility then, only a baroness, when Freddie was alive. To be a duchess . . ."

She shook her head, repressing a shudder. Surely Edward must understand that was too much. "I can't do it."

She looked over at him.

He was scowling at the fire, his jaw tight . . .

Oh. That's right. He understood too well.

"Believe me, Jo, I know how horrible Society can be.

Remember, I was a solicitor before I was the duke. A good number of the *ton* look down their long noses at me, too."

He turned to her. Smiled. "Let's face them together. Bite our thumbs at them." He leaned toward her, his eyes holding hers, his voice eager. "We can skip all the balls and soirees, Jo, and focus on more serious things when I have to be in London for Parliament. And we can stay in the country the rest of the year."

She heard the need in his voice. It pulled at her. She wanted to say yes, wanted to make him happy—

No. I don't have to make him or any man happy. I need only make myself *happy.*

But how to do that? Which path was the right one?

It would help if the entire burden didn't fall squarely on her shoulders.

But that's a woman's lot in life, isn't it?

"Edward, you are asking me to upend my life for you, while, if you'll forgive me for saying so, you are giving up exactly nothing."

He frowned, and then nodded. "Yes. I see that. But I can't put aside my title and all its duties, Jo. I feel a responsibility to everyone who depends on me." A corner of his mouth crooked up. "Including a certain charity in Little Puddledon."

That was something else they needed to discuss. "You won't withdraw your support for the Home if I don't marry you, will you?"

All the good humor vanished from his face, and when he spoke, his voice was cold. "Do you really think I would do that?" He stood. "If you *do* think it, then clearly you do not know me."

Was he going back to his room?

She jumped up, put a hand on his arm. She couldn't bear it if he left her, especially not this way.

"No, Edward, I *don't* think it. Truly, I don't. But I had to raise the issue. Don't you see? You aren't the only one who has people depending on you. I have to think about all the women and children at the Home. I can't risk their happiness. Their security. Their *lives*."

She could see he was still offended, but at least he was listening.

"Some men *would* try to use their position to force me to do their will. You must know that." She looked away, at the fire. "Freddie would have." She swallowed. "Freddie did."

"Jo—"

She shook her head and he stopped. The compassion in his voice threatened her control. She didn't want to cry. "Oh, I learned to stand up to him soon enough. It wasn't so bad. But I *won't* be pressured."

He took her hands then, and she turned to look up into his eyes. She saw warmth and understanding there. And honesty.

"I won't pressure you about anything, Jo. Of course, I will support your charity no matter what you decide. I believe in the work you are doing. And, even if you find you can't marry me, I hope we can always be friends."

Warmth spread through her, a heady mix of joy and pride, of relief and . . . comfort? Trust?

"How about this," he said. "We will both keep an open mind for the rest of the time we are here. I know it will be hard with everyone so interested in our business." He frowned. "Or do you know now that you can never come to love me enough to choose me over the day-to-day running of the Home?"

She hesitated. *Could* she honestly consider marriage? On the one hand was the life she knew—the life she'd worked so hard to create. A life of independence, of dedication to the charity she felt so passionate about. A life where she had respect and a position of some authority. The safe, comfortable choice.

On the other? Edward. And Thomas.

And love.

You thought you loved Freddie, and look how very, very wrong you were.

Edward is not Freddie, and I am not seventeen.

True. But when Edward touched her, when he took her to bed, she felt young and starry-eyed again.

On the other hand.

That's three hands.

"I don't know." She frowned at him. "I can try."

Edward smiled. "That's all I'm asking. Try to remain open to the possibility while we . . ." His smile turned rather salacious. "Explore the issue."

She glanced at the bed, thinking of all the exploration they'd done last night.

She'd very much like to do more tonight.

It would only be wise to thoroughly research the matter. That was the way to making an informed decision.

She grinned. "Very well. Let's begin at once."

Chapter Sixteen

Edward walked up the path to Aphrodite's temple, Jo striding beside him. It was early—very early—on the last day of the house party. Young Philip Arthur Edward Graham, Viscount Hurley, had been christened yesterday. Now all that was left was to say good-bye.

A panic akin to what he'd felt when Helen was dying gripped him.

No. He was overreacting. He was saying good-bye to Jo, but only for now. Not forever.

Well, of course not forever. He was the main benefactor of her charity. He'd promised her that would not change no matter what she decided about marriage.

And she would need his help. They'd discussed starting a home for mothers and sons, and Jo had suggested acquiring a tatterdemalion farm that bordered the Home's property. He planned to visit the place to look it over and help her evaluate its suitability. And then they would have to work out the legal and financial details. The project's funding would be borne by the dukedom, of course, just as the bulk of the money to run the Home came from those coffers.

But his hope that he could announce their betrothal today? *That* was dead.

It wasn't a complete surprise. He'd felt her vacillating the entire house party. Sometimes he was certain she was going to say yes, and other times he felt a deep, debilitating dread, positive she would say no.

He'd tried to woo her during the day with words and at night with his body, but he could only plead his case. He was the barrister, not the judge. Jo was the one who would decide the matter.

And then, at the christening, when they'd stood together as godparents, he'd felt the tide turn against him for good.

Was *that* the problem? He remembered all too well, when he'd thought he and Helen would never have a child, how holding—even just seeing—a baby could set off an emotional storm of longing and loss and despair.

He'd wanted to ask her, but by the time they were alone and he could have done so, the gulf between them had grown too wide.

Well, it was a difficult conversation to have at the best of times. And, to be honest, he was afraid words might betray him now. He'd foolishly allowed hope to live in his heart, the outrageous hope that Livy was right and Jo's inability to conceive during her marriage could be laid solely at her husband's door.

He'd allowed himself to hope that Jo might be increasing now.

He could *not* say that. And it was only a hope. A dream. Time would reveal the truth of the matter.

And if she is carrying your child, she'll have to marry you.

He frowned. Jo would not like being coerced.

Ha! Not like it? She would *hate* it.

He scowled down at his boots. He wanted her to marry him, but he wanted her to be able to choose freely.

Bear, the ostensible reason for this early morning jaunt, was somewhere up ahead. He could track the dog's progress by the chattering, screeching complaints of the squirrels and jays, who did not appreciate a large dog invading their territory.

Last night in bed, he'd made one last—well, *several* last attempts to persuade Jo to have him, to show her with his body what he couldn't say with words, how much he loved her.

She'd been a willing, even eager participant, but he could tell she was just collecting memories. Saying goodbye, turning a page.

Zeus, how he wished it were a fortnight ago and he was walking this path for the first time, all the days—and nights—with Jo still ahead of him.

He looked at her—well, at the back of her bonnet. She was staring down at the ground.

If this were yesterday morning, they'd be talking. Laughing. Teasing.

But this was today. The last day.

One thing hadn't changed—she still refused to take his arm. She was so bloody, *maddingly* independent.

And yet it was in large part her fierce independence that so drew him to her. That and her kindness. Her intelligence, her sense of fun, her sensitivity—especially to Thomas—

And her body.

He *was* a man after all.

He would take her friendship if she decided that was all she could offer him, but he wanted so much more. He wanted everything.

They'd reached the temple. Bear was there before them, sniffing Aphrodite's feet. He woofed a welcome, wagging the great fan of his tail, and then went back to exploring the olfactory delights that lurked in the folly's corners. The click of his nails on the marble floor sounded especially loud in the sudden quiet.

Well, Edward supposed that it was actually no quieter now than it had been the moment before. It just felt as if everything had paused, holding its breath, waiting with a sudden sense of expectation—or, to be honest, doom.

It had been evening the first time he'd been here with Jo. The shadows had been beginning to soften, lengthen. The line between what was real and what was imagined— dreamed of, hoped for—had begun to blur. Anything had seemed possible.

Now the sun was bright and sharp.

Within hours she would leave, and the magic of this fortnight would be over.

"Well—"

They both spoke at the same time. Stopped. Stared at each other.

Before this morning, they would have laughed together. Now, he bowed and said, formally, awkwardly, "Please, you first."

Jo nodded, accepting the burden—and speaking first *was* a burden, he realized. He was being a coward to put the onus on her, but he did it anyway. She might be stronger than he in this.

He hated feeling so . . . helpless. So powerless to control matters, to make what he wanted happen. But that was the way with life, wasn't it? He couldn't stop Helen from dying. He couldn't protect Thomas from hurt and disappointment. And he couldn't make Jo marry him.

Jo moistened her lips, opened her mouth—and then turned to walk toward the stone bench.

Oh, God. The bench where they'd first touched, first kissed.

Perhaps Jo felt some of the same pain he did, because she changed course, veering away to follow the curve of the portico, stopping only when she came to a spot where all they could see was trees—nice, calm, restful vegetation.

Well, not entirely restful. A squirrel objected to their presence from a nearby branch.

Bear took exception to that and came over to bark a rebuke, which sent the furry-tailed rodent scampering down the trunk and off into the underbrush.

"Edward."

Here it comes.

He gripped the balustrade, braced himself . . .

"I love you."

His heart leapt with joy. He turned to grin down at her.

She wasn't grinning back.

Hell. There's a but *coming.*

He braced himself again.

"But I can't agree to marry you. Not yet."

He must have made a small sound of distress, because Bear interrupted his rodent watch to look up at him.

Jo looked away, out into the woods. "I'm sorry. I know it's not what you wanted to hear, but—"

He interrupted her, panic suddenly loosening his tongue. He was not going to—he *couldn't*—accept that answer without trying to change her mind.

"Why can't you?"

She frowned at him. "It's obvious."

"Not to me."

She stared at him. He stared back.

She finally gave a little huff, rolled her eyes, and said, in a tone that suggested she was addressing a halfwit, "You're a duke."

"Yes. And I was once a solicitor. But when it comes down to it, I'm just a man." He tried to lighten matters by waggling his brows suggestively. "As you know very, very well."

She flushed, but he could see she wasn't going to give in.

"I have my work. The Home is in Little Puddledon. That's where I need to be—not with you at Grainger or at any of your other properties."

"But you don't *have* to choose." He took a breath, tried to modulate his voice. "Livy can manage the Home, can't she?"

Jo shook her head. "No. Especially not now, when we are setting up a second home for mothers with sons. Livy might be able to handle one of the places, but not both."

He almost suggested they rethink the new project, but he stopped himself in time. Jo would dismiss that argument out of hand, and, being the father of a son, he would have to agree with her.

He was an attorney. He would offer up another argument.

"Yes, but think, Jo. Wouldn't it be better to have Livy in charge of one place and to find someone else to fill the second position? If you had two women doing the day-to-day work, you'd be free to concentrate on planning. With two homes, there will be more planning to do."

She frowned again. Was she wavering?

"I would still need to be in Little Puddledon."

"I don't know about that. If you chose the right people,

people you can trust, you can rely on letters—just as you and I have done over the last year."

"Mmm."

"And you—*we*—could certainly visit regularly."

He would dangle some other charitable tidbits in front of her. She was an ardent reformer. He'd heard her talking to Lady Darrow about the school the countess had started for the tenant children here.

"And think of all the good you could do on my estates."

Did he see a flicker of interest in her eyes?

"Do you have schools?"

"No—or should I say, not yet?"

She gave him a pointed look that he took as a warning not to push her too much—or too obviously.

He would move on to other enticements.

"I could certainly use your advice on what policies I should support in the House of Lords to further the well-being of women and children."

Her eyes were definitely gleaming now.

But she controlled herself. "No. It's not just that you're a duke, Edward. Oh, that's part of it. But more than that, it's just too soon." She shook her head decisively. "I made *that* mistake with Freddie. I can't do that again."

But you aren't seventeen and I'm not Freddie.

He didn't say it—he kept his lips tightly sealed. He didn't want to risk putting her back up.

"Don't you see, Edward? It's too soon for *both* of us. We've been on holiday, away from our real lives, thrown together with no other responsibilities. Things will look different once we are home. Once I am back in Little Puddle-don, and you are back in London."

"No, they won't." He sounded as sulky as Thomas sometimes did when he told him to finish his beans.

Well, he *felt* sulky. He didn't want to go back to London with all its two-faced toadies. Not now that he'd found Jo.

Jo frowned at him. "Think! Isn't it true that you were worn out from the Marriage Mart when you came to Darrow? And then you met me, and I wasn't pursuing you. That must have been a relief. And *then* it turned out that Thomas liked me, even asked me to be his mother."

"Yes! See—"

She waved him to silence. "How do you know what you feel isn't largely because you see me as an answer to your problem? A tidy . . . solution that frees you from having to trawl Society's ballrooms any longer?"

His stomach twisted. "No. That's not it. I—" He shook his head. *Come to the point.* "How can you say that, Jo? I love *you*. I want to marry *you*. Not anyone else."

She frowned, put her hand on his arm. "You may think you do, Edward, but—"

He shrugged off her touch, suddenly angry. "I know how I feel, Jo. I am willing to agree to wait to see if my feelings change, but I don't think they will. I'm a grown man who has lived thirty-five years. I know my own mind."

Jo's brows snapped down. "And *I* am a widow of thirty-four years. I know *my* own mind as well." She poked him in the chest. "*You* were happily married—I was not. *You* are a man—I am not."

He was tempted to make a salacious joke about that, but fortunately his brain kept a tight rein on his tongue. He swallowed the words.

"Women give up *everything* when they marry, Edward, even our identities. I'd become your duchess. Your wife. Thomas's stepmother. No one would see *me* any longer."

She looked away from him, off into the woods. "I do

love you, but I need to be sure I love you *enough*. I need time away from you, from this"—she waved her hand, taking in the temple and, he knew, the house party in general—"unnatural environment. From Pen and Caro *scheming* to get me married to you."

She looked back at him. "You know I decided to marry Freddie too quickly. I am older and wiser, yes, but I will admit I don't *feel* older. I feel just as bowled over, as dazzled, as I did then." She flushed. "And, well, more seduced. I love what you do to me in bed, but we can't live our lives in bed."

Unfortunately.

She didn't say the word, of course, but he thought he heard a note of regret in her voice, a longing that echoed his own.

Bear had come round to fill the space between them. Edward felt the dog bump against his leg and bent down to scratch his ears, thankful for the small distraction.

"I just need time and some distance, Edward, to sort out my feelings."

That was fair. "Very well. Let's agree in . . . how much time would you say you need away from my handsome, charming self?"

Jo snorted and rolled her eyes, just as he'd hoped. "A month or two, I suppose. I know at first I'll miss you terribly."

That sounded promising.

"But I imagine that will wear off in a few weeks."

Not so promising.

"Why don't you write me in—let's say in two months' time," he said, "to let me know what you've decided."

Should I mention now that she might be carrying my child?

No. She'd snap his nose off—and perhaps remove other parts as well—if he did.

"And I should come down to Little Puddledon anyway," he said. "Well, I *should* have visited months ago. But especially now that we are talking of starting the Home for mothers and sons. You can show me the site you have in mind, and we can discuss more of the details." He swallowed, looked away briefly. "And I promise not to pressure you if you decide I am just your friend and not your lover."

Jo nodded. "Yes. That sounds reasonable." She put her hand on his arm. "It's not just having to leave Little Puddledon, Edward. I *hated* London. Or, well, I suppose it was Society I hated—all those people staring at me, whispering about me."

His hand covered hers. "I don't like Society much, either, Jo. People stare and whisper about me, too. But I think I can face them more easily if I have you at my side."

She looked up at him, her eyes softening as if she was swayed by his words.

He would not allow himself to hope . . . too much.

"And you'll be a duchess, Jo. You can look down your nose at them." He grinned. "Though I do think we should spend most of our time in the country when I don't need to be in Town for Parliament. London has its attractions, but it's very dirty and noisy."

Something else had caused her eyes to cloud. "Oh, Edward. The *ton* never forgets a scandal. The old cats are sure to remember Freddie's suicide—*and* that it was a result of losing at cards to the previous Duke of Grainger."

He shrugged. "Let them remember. We can't change the past, Jo."

She frowned, but he could tell she was worried.

"Come, Jo. You are one of the bravest women I know. You aren't going to let a few gossipy women—and men—control what you do, are you?"

"N-no." Her chin came up, her voice grew stronger. "No."

"There you go. I have complete confidence in you." And he would allow himself some hope.

"And now we should go back. Thomas will want to say good-bye to you."

Jo nodded. "Yes. And I wish to say good-bye to him. He's a wonderful boy, Edward."

He grinned. He hoped Jo's obvious love for Thomas would be one more prod moving her in his direction.

He even managed to keep her hand on his arm all the way down the temple steps before she reclaimed it.

Chapter Seventeen

The Darrow traveling coach swayed to a stop in front of the Benevolent Home for the Maintenance and Support of Spinsters, Widows, and Abandoned Women and their Unfortunate Children.

Jo stared out the window as she waited for the coachman to open the door. She'd been in a fit of the dismals ever since she'd left Darrow, but had thought her spirits would lift when she finally reached the Manor.

They hadn't.

The old brick building looked . . . different. Smaller.

No, it's the same. I'm the one who has changed. The Home doesn't feel like home any longer.

Nonsense. She was just tired from traveling. She'd bounce back and be her normal self soon enough.

"Thank you, Zachariah," she said as the coachman let down the steps.

The man smiled. "I hope ye had a good journey, milady."

"Yes, I did. You are an excellent—"

"Jo!"

Jo looked over to see Winifred hurrying toward her and brightened a bit. That's right. The Home was more than just a building. It was the people in it that made her feel like this was where she belonged.

Winifred's gaze had already swept past her.

"And Zachariah! I've been looking forward to seeing you again."

The coachman laughed. "I know ye weren't looking for *me*, Winifred. It's me horses yer wanting to see."

Winifred grinned. "Aye. Though it *is* good to see you as well."

Clearly, Jo had been forgotten.

She'd assume Zachariah would think to unload her trunk— not that she needed any of those altered dresses here—and would leave these two to wax poetic over horseflesh. There was one creature at the Home who she felt certain would be happy to see her.

"Where's Freddie, Winifred?"

Winifred couldn't manage to tear her eyes away from the lead horse, but she did answer. "With Livy in her office."

Jo stared. Livy had an office?

She had a bad feeling about this. "Where?"

That got a bit more of Winifred's attention. The woman managed to glance over, looking slightly abashed. "Oh. I mean *your* office, o' course."

Jo's stomach dropped—and then her ire rose. So, Livy had taken over her office, had she? Well, they would just see about that! Jo was not about to let the woman usurp her position without a battle royale.

She strode around the house to *her* office, knocked briskly, as a warning only—she was not about to ask permission to enter her own office—and opened the door.

She had just enough time to see Livy was indeed sitting in *her* seat at *her* desk before Freddie erupted into a paroxysm of joyous, demented barking. He leapt up from his usual place at what should have been *her* feet and bounded over to greet her.

She crouched down to hug him and have her face enthusiastically washed.

"Jo," Livy said, having the grace to vacate Jo's chair. "You're back."

Jo tried to glare at her, but it was hard to do that when she had to keep dodging Freddie's tongue.

"Yes, Freddie," Jo said, finally capturing her dog's face in her hands. "I'm happy to see you, too, but *do* try to restrain yourself a little." She managed to stand and then reclaimed her seat at the desk. Freddie rested his head in her lap, and she stroked his ears.

She immediately felt calmer, more in control.

Livy had taken one of the chairs on the other side of the desk. Now she leaned forward. "I'm *dying* to hear all about the house party, Jo. Tell me everything." Her brows tented. "But first, how are Nick and Caro doing? Caro *sounds* happy, but it is sometimes difficult to discern the truth of the matter from letters. And I don't know her well, of course."

Jo had opened her mouth to take Livy to task for her egregious meddling, but was stopped by the note of sincere concern in the woman's voice.

"They both seem very happy," she said.

Livy beamed at her. "Oh, good! I *thought* Caro would be perfect for Nick." She sighed happily. "While I've always considered myself a matchmaker, the matches I've made in the past were just for a few hours. Caro and Nick were my first try at making a match for life."

And then a distinctly mischievous gleam appeared in her eyes. "And my second try was just a fortnight ago. Tell me how I did with that, Jo." She waggled her brows. "Did Edward like your dresses?"

He had, but . . .

"Livy, I cannot believe you had the audacity to take your scissors to my wardrobe! There was hardly anything left to those bodices. And the new dresses you slipped into my trunk were just as scandalous."

Though she had got used to them after a day or two. She was wearing her old travel dress now—it felt odd to have so much fabric near her neck.

Livy was eyeing that dress with obvious distaste. "It's criminal how you hide yourself in such dowdy gowns, Jo. You have a very nice figure."

Jo flushed. Well, what else should she expect from a former madam?

"Though I grant you there aren't any gentlemen in *this* vicinity worth trying to impress," Livy said. "Edward, however . . ." She brightened. "*Did* he like your gowns?"

"Er."

"You may as well tell me. I'll find out anyway. Caro will write me."

Of course, she would. And Livy would likely report everything Jo said to Caro.

Blast it, I'm surrounded by spies.

"Yes, he liked them."

Livy gave a little bounce in her seat. "And . . . ?"

"Why do you think there's an *and*?"

Livy pinned her with her far-too-perceptive gaze. "Reading people is part of my job, Jo—or was part of my job, my old job." She grinned. "And, also, I know Edward. You're perfect for him—even more perfect than Caro is for Nick."

Jo frowned at Livy, and then looked down at Freddie.

Were his warm, brown eyes urging her to confide in the woman?

But Livy wants to take over, Freddie.

Freddie whined as if to ask why that would be so bad.

He had a point. It *would* free her to marry Edward. She already missed him with a deep, deep ache.

"*Did* he propose, Jo?" Livy bounced again. "Do tell!"

And chances were good—hell, it was inevitable, really— that Livy would weasel the truth out of her eventually.

"Yes, he did."

"Huzz—!" Livy slapped her hands over her mouth to muffle her cheer, and then said, calmly, "You should marry him."

"I can't."

Even Jo heard how weak that sounded, how little conviction there was in her voice.

"Yes, you can!" Livy said. "If it's the Home that worries you, I can run that."

Livy leaned closer, almost vibrating with intensity now, and Jo was suddenly reminded of Caro. Caro had had the same energy.

"You can trust me, Jo. I liked managing things while you were away. I know I can run this place. Let me try. Please? And then, if you don't like what I'm doing, you can fire me. You'll be married to the man who owns the estate, after all."

"But, Livy—"

Livy swept on. "I *want* to do it. Please give me a chance."

Jo saw the passion and sincerity in Livy's eyes, heard it in her voice.

"I was getting bored in London, Jo. And, well, hard and cynical, I suppose. I told myself I was doing some good by giving women in need a way to support themselves.

I tried to be careful, make it as safe for them as I could. I was very particular about the men I would take on as clients—I never wanted to send a girl out to some brute who would hurt her."

Livy stopped. Took a breath. When she spoke again, her voice still held passion, but she was clearly striving for a bit more control.

"But now that I see what you are doing here, I see this is a better way to help women—women *and* their children."

Her gaze held Jo's. "I know from firsthand experience how desperate these women are. I was one of them." She pressed her lips together as if gathering her composure before saying, "I was once a governess in a viscount's household."

Jo wasn't really surprised. Livy was far more articulate than most of the women at the Home—*and* she could read and write, add and subtract.

"But then I made the colossal mistake of fancying myself in love with the eldest son. I came from the gentry and had visions of marrying into the nobility." Livy snorted derisively. "A governess marrying the heir to a viscountcy? That sort of thing only happens in fairy tales." She half smiled and shrugged. "Or, well, here I suppose, with Caro."

She sighed. Shook her head. "I might have come to my senses eventually, but discovering I was pregnant hastened my enlightenment."

"Oh!" Jo hadn't meant to say anything, but the sound— more of a gasp, really—escaped before she could stop it.

Livy nodded, her voice grim. "I was tossed out into the street without a reference within hours of telling my lordling lover that he was going to be a father."

Jo bit her lip. She wanted to ask the obvious question,

but didn't want to poke a wound that, while years old, had clearly left a deep scar.

She didn't need to ask. Livy gave her the answer.

"I lost the baby just a few days later."

Pain flashed over Livy's face and she looked away. "If I'd held my tongue, no one would have been the wiser, and my life would have been very, very different."

It was, sadly, not a unique story, but every time Jo heard it, her heart broke a little more. "I'm so, *so* sorry."

Livy managed to regain her composure—barely. She looked back at Jo. "I'm not." And then she glanced away again and swallowed before she continued.

"Well, I *am* sorry about the baby, but I am not sorry my life changed. I've had far more independence than I would ever have had as a governess. If I'd stayed, I'd have become a mousy little creature, forced to lurk in the shadows, never seen or heard, only there for the children."

Jo could not imagine Livy as such a pale, fading female. Yet she was right. Jo had observed it herself. Oh, not so much with governesses, though it was true Miss Woodrow, while obviously well regarded by Pen and the earl, had never appeared without her charges in tow. But with servants in general and female servants in particular.

Or perhaps the mouse-like role extended to almost all women who followed the narrow path Society had laid out for them. She certainly had far more independence now than she'd ever had as her father's daughter or Freddie's wife.

Or would have as Edward's duchess.

Was that true?

No. She felt confident Edward would never try to take her independence from her. If she decided to marry him, they would have a partnership, both in their marriage and in the operation of the Homes and any other charities they took on.

And if I decide not to marry him?

She, too, liked the woman she'd become.

Something settled in her, and she felt a new sense of calm. No matter what happened, she would find a way to carry on.

"Give me a chance, Jo," Livy was saying. "I know I have a lot to learn—but I also know I *can* learn. Teach me. Please?"

Livy did seem committed to the Home's purpose, and even if Jo chose to stay in Little Puddledon, she'd need someone to run the new Home for mothers with sons.

"Very well. Let's get started."

Chapter Eighteen

Edward sat in his study going over the estate books.

Well, *trying* to go over the estate books. His concentration had been shot to hell ever since he'd left the christening party.

He checked his calendar again. Tomorrow would mark two months plus one week since he and Jo had gone their separate ways. Where was her letter? Had it gone astray? He felt certain she would have done as she'd promised and written him.

Or had she thought he'd not been serious about his need to hear from her?

No. That might have been the case if they'd been only lovers, but they were business partners as well. She needed to tell him when it would be best for him to come to Little Puddledon to explore the site for the new Home they wished to establish. She was too passionate about her charity not to follow up on that.

Passionate . . .

He heaved a deep sigh.

He'd been doing that a lot recently.

He'd *tried* to remain optimistic and cheerful, especially

for Thomas's sake, but here in his study he'd often let his spirits flag.

That's not the only thing that's flagging.

Hell.

Thomas had chattered on and on about Jo as their coach had rolled home from Darrow to Grainger. He was happy the boy liked her, but he'd found it wearing to be encouraging when he knew nothing was certain. His restrained reactions had finally depressed even Thomas's high spirits.

And the boy had been more than a bit down pin ever since.

He heard a scratch at the door. "Come!"

It was Roberts, the butler, holding a tray piled with correspondence.

"From the London house, Your Grace."

Jakes, the London butler, sent a footman down to Grainger every so often, once enough letters and other papers had accumulated to make the trip worthwhile.

"Thank you, Roberts," Edward said, going back to his figures. He'd tallied this one column three times and had got three different sums. He was bloody well going to get it right this time, even if it killed him. "Just put them down, if you will."

"Yes, Your Grace."

Out of the corner of his eye, Edward saw the letters land on his desk.

He did not see Roberts leave.

Perhaps if he ignored the man, he'd go away.

Roberts cleared his throat.

Recognizing defeat when he heard it, Edward looked up. The butler was regarding him with an odd expression. He couldn't decide if the man was happy, morose, excited, or worried.

"Is there something else, Roberts?"

The butler took what appeared to be a sustaining breath and then launched into speech. "Your Grace, when Oliver—that's the footman who came down from London—took the letters out of his satchel to hand them to me, they spilled all over the floor."

The man paused, giving Edward a searching look, but what the fellow was searching for remained a mystery.

"Yes?" Edward said, hoping to encourage Roberts to get to his point since he clearly had one.

"Which meant we had to pick them up."

"Right." Now *there* was a news bulletin. What else had the man been going to do—leave the letters strewn over the marble tile?

"Which meant I saw them."

There was an odd note of apology in Roberts's voice as well as something that might be anticipation and . . . anxiety?

Well, Edward could understand the anxiety part.

Can I leap up and shake the story out of the man?

No, of course not.

But what could be the problem? Surely the letters had been sealed, but even if they hadn't been, Edward could not imagine Roberts sitting on the floor of the foyer, reading his private correspondence. The staid, proper butler—who, just as Jakes, had served the previous duke and was far more duke-like in demeanor than Edward felt *he* was—would likely have an apoplexy if Edward even hinted at such a thing.

The look Roberts gave him now was bordering on fatherly. "I believe you will wish to examine them at once, Your Grace."

Edward looked at the tidy pile, half expecting a viper to slither out.

Roberts's voice took on a distinct note of superiority. "While I'm quite certain Jakes *means* well . . ."

Ooh, that was a low blow!

". . . being in London, he is not aware of *Matters*."

A cold finger of dread traveled up the length of Edward's spine and settled in the back of his neck. Matters? What *Matters* could Roberts mean?

"Er, right?"

Roberts nodded. "If he *had* been aware, he would have sent the letter on the moment it arrived at your London house."

Edward gave the stack of correspondence another worried look. "R-right. Thank you. I'll attend to it"—whatever *it* was—"at once."

"Very good, Your Grace. I will leave you to it, then." Roberts started for the door, but stopped when he reached it to deliver a few parting words.

"I do hope it is good news, Your Grace. I know I speak for the entire staff when I say we sincerely want the best for you and young Thomas."

Comprehension dawned.

Zeus! It must be the letter from Jo.

No other explanation for Roberts's words, for his expression and tone, sprang to mind.

Not that anything was springing to Edward's mind at the moment. He felt frozen. He was finally going to discover if he could still have hope.

He managed to nod, smile, even say "thank you." He'd had years of experience as a solicitor acting calm when in fact there was a bloody riot going on inside him.

Roberts bowed and left.

Edward watched the door close, and then turned back to stare at the pile of letters. He would have thought Roberts would have put the most important one on top, but no, that was clearly not the case. He recognized Lord Frothingdon's crabbed scrawl. The daft man wrote him every month, trying to get him to invest in one flimflam or another.

He closed the estate ledger and pushed it aside, giving up all hope of addition and subtraction . . .

Addition? Could Jo be increasing?!

His heart beat a tattoo. It was too soon to know for certain, wasn't it? Not that Jo would have given the matter any thought—she'd said she couldn't have children. *He* shouldn't entertain the notion. He'd been down that path before.

But Helen *had* conceived.

Stop it!

It was nerve-racking enough to wonder if Jo would marry him.

Just read the bloody letter.

He sorted through the stack.

Ah, there it was—a small rectangle, the direction penned in Jo's strong, neat hand. It was a far smaller sheet than the letters she sent him about the Home's business.

He pulled it out, set it in the center of his desk, and pushed the rest of his correspondence to the side.

How long had it sat at the London house?

I should have told Jakes to look for it.

Right. And send *all* his servants into a frenzy of speculation.

He snorted. Whom was he fooling? He'd wager a princely sum that they were all, down to and including the stable boys and scullery maids, swimming and splashing in a sea of speculation already. Jakes, at least, must recognize Jo's handwriting. Everyone knew Edward had been at Darrow's estate for the christening, and they likely had surmised Jo had been there, too, as she was Lady Darrow's good friend.

Well, there'd been no need for guessing. Thomas had mentioned Jo on more than one occasion since they'd got back. Something like that would spread from country to Town like wildfire.

Thomas had probably come right out and said Edward and Jo had shared a bed.

He might be having trouble adding numbers today, but he had no doubt Jakes could put two and two together. This missive, so much smaller than Jo's other letters, would have stood out like a robin in a flock of crows.

So why hadn't he sent it on at once?

Jakes was no idiot. He must have concluded Edward would value discretion in this matter. If there had been even the slimmest hope of keeping this topic off everyone's lips, Jakes would have tried to do what he could.

Or perhaps it was simply that the letter *had* just arrived in London.

I should have told Jo to write me here.

But he'd not planned to stay at Grainger. He'd thought initially that he'd go on to Town once he'd brought Thomas here. But then the notion of subjecting himself to hot, crowded ballrooms, reeking of sweat and perfume, of becoming a matrimonial quarry again, a titled fox to the pack of debutante hounds—

Ugh. He couldn't make himself do it. So, he'd decided to stay here in the country while waiting to see if Jo could bring herself to marry him. If she couldn't, well, then he would step back and reassess matters.

You're delaying. Read the blasted letter.

He let out a long breath and then picked up the slim sheet, slit it open—

Dearest Edward,
  You may be happy to know I have been working with Livy. We have many plans. If it is still convenient, we would welcome your visit.

            Faithfully yours,
            Jo

He stared down at the words. Read them over. And then read them over again.

What the hell did they mean? Plans? What sort of plans? And "*we*" would welcome your visit? That did not sound promising.

It sounded very much as if his hopes were dashed.

But it didn't sound *enough* like it for him to be convinced past a reasonable doubt.

He studied the few words again.

There *was* that "Dearest Edward." If Jo had wanted to be cold and distant, she could have made the salutation "Your Grace" as she had in the past. And while "faithfully yours" was indeed formal, she usually closed her letters "respectfully." Did she mean more by this?

And she *had* signed it Jo and not Lady Havenridge.

Perhaps the mention of Livy meant Jo was open to delegating the Home's day-to-day operations. Which could mean she'd decided to wed him, to become his wife and Thomas's mother.

Zeus, it would have been so bloody easy for her to just come out and write what she meant: "Yes, I'll marry you" or "No, I won't."

He'd been staring at the letter, trying to puzzle out its meaning for what seemed like hours when he heard the door open again. He looked up, expecting to see Roberts.

It wasn't Roberts. It was Thomas.

A worried-looking, subdued Thomas.

Edward got to his feet at once and came round the desk to put his hands on his son's shoulders. "What is it?"

Thomas looked up at him, Helen's eyes wide in his now-pale face. "I heard Roberts say Miss Jo had written to you, that he hoped it was good news." Thomas stopped, swallowed. His voice wavered when he continued, "But it's not good news, is it, Papa?"

Putting on a false smile wouldn't fool the boy, but Edward truly didn't know what to say.

Try the truth.

"I don't know." He would feel his way, as he'd been doing ever since the midwife had put his infant son into his trembling arms. "Let's sit down."

He walked with Thomas to the settee by the fire. He sat at one end, expecting Thomas to cuddle up next to him as he usually did, but instead, Thomas sat at the other, stiff and straight-backed, looking down at his hands.

Zeus, the boy is growing up. What do I do now?

It wasn't a large settee, but it felt as if all of England was between them.

Should he close the gap himself?

No. Not yet. His instincts told him to give Thomas room.

What would Jo say?

He froze, shocked, and then almost immediately accepted the notion that his thoughts would turn to her.

He'd had only himself on which to rely in raising

Thomas all these years. For much of that time, he'd not wanted nor had he trusted anyone else's opinion—and many people had been surprisingly free with their opinion. A shocking number of them, men *and* women, seemed to believe that just being male disqualified him from caring for an infant or a young child.

Especially the women, and especially those who were volunteering to marry him and so save him from . . . his son?

He'd sworn to prove them wrong.

Well, to be honest, he'd been too busy trying to do his best with Thomas to give the naysayers much thought, except to know that he didn't want any of them coming into his life and pushing him out of the way, taking charge of *his* child as if he were an incompetent nincompoop.

The women he'd met on the Marriage Mart had been even worse. He could not think of a single one to whom he'd turn for advice. Hell, most of them would be happy if he'd just ship Thomas off to school. Then they'd have to see the boy only at holidays.

No, it was worse than that. Most would be happier if Thomas simply vanished, opening the line of succession to *their* son. Those women wished to be a duchess first and the mother—not the stepmother—of a duke second.

But not Jo. Jo is different.

Thomas was now glaring at him. "You *must* know and you just won't tell me. You weren't smiling when I came in. You looked sad. You *still* look sad."

The words were contentious, but the strained, anxious note in his son's voice made Edward want to gather him close.

Thomas's stiff posture warned him off.

"Miss Jo's not going to be my mama, is she?"

Oh, blast. He'd been afraid Thomas had got too attached to Jo, but what could he have done to prevent that? He'd hoped Jo *would* become Thomas's mama.

"I don't—"

"It's because she can't have babies, isn't it?"

Edward's jaw hit the floor. "W-what?! Where did you get that idea?"

"Harriet said she heard her mama tell her papa that Miss Jo thought she was b-bare-something."

Did no one think before they spoke within children's hearing?

"And then Lady Adrianna said that meant she couldn't have babies even though you were sleeping in her bed."

And if he never saw Lady Adrianna again, it would be too soon.

Thomas was scowling at him, his lower lip sticking out. "Do you not love Miss Jo because she can't have babies?"

"Thomas . . ."

"Will you not love *me* if I can't have babies?"

Edward bit back a surprised laugh. "It's not quite the same thing—"

"Yes, it is. I hear Roberts and Mrs. Roberts and Jakes and Ambrose and John Coachman and *all* the servants talking. I'm supposed to be duke when I grow up. I'm supposed to have babies so there will be another duke someday. Lady Adrianna said it, too. But when I asked Miss Jo, she said that you would love me no matter what. That you knew that if I didn't marry or have babies, the title would go to someone else—just like it went to you when the old duke and his family died. She said not to worry." Thomas stopped, took a deep breath. "But I *am* worried."

"Oh, Thomas." Edward opened his arms then, hoping Thomas would take the invitation.

He did. The boy made a little noise—a gulp or a gasp or a cry cut off—and threw himself across the settee.

Edward wrapped his arms around his son, holding him tight. "I *do* love you, Thomas. Of course, I do. And I will love you no matter what happens in the future. Miss Jo was right about that. She's very wise."

He rubbed Thomas's back as he had from the time Thomas was little more than a baby. It had always calmed the boy.

It calmed him now.

"Do you remember when I became duke?"

Thomas nodded. "I didn't want to leave my bedroom and our chestnut tree." He sighed. "I wish we could go back to our old house. I wish the title had gone to someone else. You're so busy now, gone so much. I *miss* you." He shrugged one thin shoulder. "And there are so many other people here. So many servants. I wish it was just us again." He looked up. "Us and Miss Jo."

Edward's heart clenched as he hugged Thomas close again. "I wish the same thing, Thomas. I love you—and I love Miss Jo."

Thomas sat up straight. "But if you love her, why don't you marry her?"

"She has to love me back."

Thomas frowned. "Is that what the letter said? That she doesn't love you?"

"No. But she didn't say she loved me, either. I-I don't know how she feels."

Thomas frowned. "Then you should go ask her, Papa."

Edward laughed. Trust Thomas to get to the heart of the matter.

"You're right. I'll do that. I'll leave in the morning."

Thomas grinned. "And kiss her, Papa. Everyone says girls like to be kissed."

Chapter Nineteen

Jo sat at her desk, holding a handkerchief, lightly scented with lavender, to her nose, and berated herself yet again for not being plainer in her note to Edward.

"I should have spelled it out in so many words, Freddie," she said through the linen, "but I wanted to tell him in person that I love him and will marry him."

She'd wanted to see his eyes light, see his lips turn up in that wide smile that transformed his face from serious to boyish and made her feel as if the rest of the world had dropped away.

And then she'd wanted to feel his arms go round her, his mouth come down on hers. She'd wanted to fall into bed with him and tell him with her body how *much* she loved him.

Also, she'd balked at writing the word *love*.

All right, she'd admit it. After "Dearest Edward," her courage had deserted her completely, darting away as if it were a squirrel Freddie was chasing.

And, to be honest, it was too much to put on paper. It wasn't just that she loved him—he knew that. She'd told him so at Darrow. It was that she loved him *enough*. She loved him enough to change her life for him, to move away from Little Puddledon and the Home, to become his duchess and Thomas's mother.

"I'm sure saying it will be easier than writing it."

If she ever *got* to say it. What if Edward took her note to mean she wished to see him only to discuss expanding the Home? What if he decided instead of coming himself, he'd send his man of business?

She moaned, dropping her head into her hands. And why had she had the daft idea of mentioning Livy? Of *course*, he must think she meant only to discuss business. He—

Lud! What if he's *only interested in business?*

Her stomach clenched—and her stomach had been extremely delicate of late.

What if Edward had discovered that what he'd thought was love was actually only lust? That had been the main reason for leaving the matter unsettled when they left the house party, hadn't it? To see if time and distance and returning to their real lives cooled their ardor.

It hadn't cooled hers, but it might have cooled his.

Tears began to leak from her eyes, so she used her handkerchief to mop them up. She was so bloody emotional these days.

Freddie gave her a reproachful look from the other side of the room.

"I'm sorry I had to block off your usual spot, but I couldn't have you so close to me. You . . . well, you . . . *stink.*"

Freddie whined.

"Don't take it personally. *Everything* stinks now. I barely made it out of the brewhouse yesterday before I spewed my breakfast." At least she'd managed to dash around to the side of the building and off into bushes so everyone didn't have to observe the chunks of—

Ugh. No. Don't think about it.

"And today I can't even go *near* the brewhouse. The stench fills the air even with the door shut." She closed her eyes. "And I'm *so* tired, Freddie. All I want to do is sleep. I *must* be taking ill."

"No. You're not ill—you're pregnant."

That was, of course, not Freddie's voice. Jo's eyes flew open to see Livy standing in the doorway.

And then Livy strolled into the office—she and her steaming mug of coffee.

The smell hit Jo like a sledgehammer. She pressed her lips together, willed her stomach to relax—

It was hopeless. She dove for the chamber pot that she'd put in what was normally Freddie's place by her feet and cast up her accounts.

She was surprised she had anything left to disgorge. She stared into . . .

No, that was a mistake. She looked up at Livy, a smirking, smug-looking Livy, still holding her mug of olfactory torture.

"Coffee." Another wave of nausea hit, and Jo clutched the chamber pot to her chest. "Out."

Livy laughed and left. When she returned, both the coffee and the mug were gone.

But not the stench. It was much reduced, but nevertheless detectable.

"You still smell."

Livy shrugged. "It can't be helped. Your nose will adjust."

Jo scowled at her. "How do you know?"

Though Livy was right. Jo's stomach was . . . not settled, but it was no longer threatening to heave again.

She put the chamber pot down and her handkerchief back up to her nose.

"Because I've seen this play before," Livy said. "I ran an"—she grinned—"amatory service, remember. Pregnancy is one of the risks of doing that sort of business."

"I'm not pregnant."

And now her nose, recovered from the coffee assault, detected a fainter, but still quite unpleasant odor wafting from the chamber pot. She moaned.

"Let me empty that for you." Livy picked up the offending receptacle. "I'll rinse it out at the pump."

"*Thank* you," Jo said through her handkerchief as Livy headed for the door.

Livy laughed. When she came back, the chamber pot was much improved. Not spic-and-span, but clean enough that, as long as Jo kept her distance, her nose—and thus her stomach—didn't object.

She was *extremely* grateful to Livy—but also extremely wary when she saw Livy's knowing expression.

"As I said, I've had a lot of experience diagnosing pregnancy." Livy sat in Caro's chair, and Freddie came over to lean against Livy's leg. They both looked at Jo.

Jo felt she was being ganged up on. Livy she might understand, but Freddie? *That* felt like a betrayal.

"Whenever I suspected a girl might be increasing, I brought her coffee. Nine times out of ten, if she was indeed breeding, she'd do exactly what you did—puke."

"I'm *not* pregnant. I can't *get* pregnant."

Livy raised an eloquently skeptical brow. "Theodora tells me you haven't had any rags for the laundry since you got back from Darrow."

Jo flushed. Theirs was a houseful of women. Someone was always having her courses. There would be no reason for Theodora, their main laundress, to make a special note of Jo's.

"You've been spying on me!"

Livy scratched Freddie's ears. She didn't look the slightest bit abashed. "Yes, I have."

Jo had not expected the snake to admit it so cheerfully.

"Well, that doesn't mean anything," Jo said. "My courses aren't regular—not that it's any of your business."

Livy grinned. "Oh? Would you like me to get another cup of coffee?"

"No!" Jo's stomach lurched. "I'm just, ah, coming down with something."

Livy snorted. "The *something* you are coming down with is a baby. But don't worry—the nausea will go away in a few weeks."

"*Livy*." It was time to stop beating about the bush. "I *know* I'm not pregnant. I may not have had my courses, but I saw b-blood."

There, I said it. Now Livy will leave me alone.

"Oh?" Livy stopped grinning. Her gaze sharpened. She looked concerned rather than smug. "When? How much?"

Jo shifted in her chair. The Home might be full of females, but she had never been one to discuss such personal matters. "Not much."

"*How* much? How many rags? How often did you need to change them?"

Jo frowned. This was asking for far too much detail. "What are you, a physician now?"

Livy gave her a speaking look. "Jo, I made my livelihood from swiving, one way or the other. Trust me. When it comes to the signs of pregnancy, I really am an expert."

All right, Jo could see Livy's point—and it was clear

she wasn't getting out of here without telling the woman every embarrassing detail.

"It wasn't much," she said grudgingly, her face hot with embarrassment. "Just a few spots. I only used one rag and likely didn't need that."

Livy rolled her eyes and flopped back in her chair theatrically, as if blown back by Jo's shocking ignorance.

"You don't have to be so dramatic about it," Jo said, annoyed. "So, you see I am *not* increasing."

Livy rolled her eyes again. "Claptrap!" She leaned forward, pinning Jo to her seat with a sharp look. "Jo, sometimes there *is* bleeding at the beginning of a pregnancy. When did you notice this?"

Jo frowned back at her. Livy couldn't be right . . . could she?

"I don't know. Maybe a week or two after I got home. But, as I said, my courses aren't regular." Yet when they *did* come, they weren't shy about it.

Uncertainty nipped at her again.

"They were likely disrupted by the unusual, er, activity I engaged in at Darrow." Yes, that must be the explanation.

Livy snorted. "Right. That disruption is called pregnancy."

Jo shook her head. She could *not* believe Livy. She would not get her hopes up only to have them dashed tomorrow or the next day. There had been a time or two during her marriage that she'd fallen into *that* trap. The first time she'd even told Freddie—

Oh, God, that had been awful.

Livy's expression softened as if she understood some of the storm raging inside Jo. She said, more gently, "All right. We'll put aside the question of your courses—and your sensitivity to smells—remember the coffee?"

Jo's stomach shuddered. She did *not* want to remember the coffee.

"There are other clues we can look for."

"There are?" Jo blinked—and realized she'd always let her attention wander when women started discussing pregnancy symptoms. It was easier—and less painful—not to listen to something she'd never need to know.

Livy nodded and raised a finger as if she were going to tick items off a list. "I believe when I came in, you were telling Freddie that you are tired all the time."

Freddie barked, as if confirming Livy's words.

Jo shifted in her chair. "Er . . ."

Livy's right brow cocked up. "Are you so tired that you feel like you can't move, that you have to drag yourself out of bed?" She nodded at the closed ledger. "So tired you can't open that and manage to keep the figures straight?"

"Ahh . . ." Well, yes. Jo *had* been unusually tired.

Livy lifted a second finger. "Do your breasts feel larger, fuller than normal? Are they sore? Do they hurt if you accidentally bump them?"

Jo flushed. "Maybe."

Livy held up her third finger. "Do you need to piss all the time?"

"Livy!"

Livy was not cowed. "Well, do you?"

Jo shifted in her chair again. Now that Livy mentioned it . . .

"Not *all* the time."

Livy grinned and ticked her points off again. "No courses, sensitive to smells, tired, breasts sore, pissing frequently." She waved her open hand at Jo. "Hallo. You're pregnant."

Could *I be?*

"But, Livy, I was married for three years."

"Right. To Baron Havenridge." Livy stroked Freddie's ears. "A man notorious for his inability to impregnate anyone. The girls used to joke that he might be unpleasant in bed, but at least there'd be no unpleasant surprises afterward—no permanent memento of his visit."

"Ohh." That was what Edward had said. Jo closed her eyes. It was too much. It was all too much.

She burst into tears.

Over her muffled sobs, she heard Livy say, "Being very emotional is also a sign of pregnancy."

Edward followed the woman—Rosamund Lewis, she'd said her name was—along the front of Puddledon Manor. Curtains twitched in every window as he passed and the women of the Home peeked out at him.

Miss Lewis kept glancing back at him as well, an expression of barely suppressed glee on her face. Did she anticipate some sort of entertainment when she delivered him to Jo's office?

Entertainment for *her*. It was far less likely he would be amused.

He maintained his most impassive solicitor façade. He couldn't try for ducal disdain—he'd represented himself as merely Mr. Russell, first when he'd arrived at the village inn and then when he'd introduced himself to Miss Lewis.

It wasn't a lie. It was just not the complete truth.

Not that he thought Bess, the Dancing Duck's innkeeper, had been taken in by it. She'd given him a searching look when he'd inquired about a room—and then her eyes had lit up as if she'd solved a puzzle.

And *then* she'd displayed some of the same suppressed glee as his current guide.

He wouldn't be surprised if his entire history was common knowledge here, with Livy in the vicinity. Livy had known him well—*very* well. And gossip was the lifeblood of any small village.

"Have you ridden a long way, then, Mr. Russell?" Miss Lewis asked, batting her lashes at him as they turned the corner and started across the yard of crushed stone.

He was not going to tell this woman—*any* of the women—more than he had to. "I've been on the road several days."

It had taken him three days of hard riding to get here. He'd decided to leave his carriage at Grainger. He could travel faster on horseback, and he wouldn't be advertising his identity to all and sundry—the only carriage he possessed had come with the title. It had the ducal coat of arms emblazoned all over it.

"Do you have special business with Jo—ah, I mean, Lady Havenridge?"

"Yes."

He hoped his abruptness would stop her from quizzing him further.

He'd rather have skipped the inn and come directly to the Manor, but he'd not wanted to present himself to Jo in all his travel dirt.

Not to beat about the bush—in a word, he'd stunk.

But he suspected that, while he was cleaning up and changing his clothes, Bess had sent someone running ahead to alert the women at the Home that he was coming.

Well, he more than suspected. He'd seen the young woman coming down the path from the Manor as he was walking up it. She'd given him a saucy, significant look. And he'd seen someone—likely Miss Lewis—watching through a gap in the curtains, tweaking them back into place right before he'd knocked on the front door.

Had they all been in on Livy's plot? Because he agreed with Jo—he felt quite, quite certain Livy had had some matchmaking in mind when she'd bundled Jo into Darrow's traveling carriage for the christening party.

I'll have to thank her, if all goes well.

He glanced around the yard, at the stables and brewhouse. The grounds and buildings were well maintained. Darrow was right—Jo looked to be running an excellent operation.

One she won't want to leave . . .

His heart twisted.

Had he made some sound? Miss Lewis looked back at him, her expression forcefully reminding him of a cat, readying itself to pounce on some tasty, small, helpless creature.

He was not small or helpless. His heart had broken before, and he'd survived.

He gave Miss Lewis as calm and enigmatic a smile as he could manage.

She emitted a short breath, likely of frustrated curiosity, and stopped in front of a closed door. "Here we are. Lady Havenridge's office."

"Thank you for escorting me, Miss Lewis. I won't take any more of your time."

The woman realized she'd made a strategic error by not opening the door first. "I should announce you."

"No need. I'll announce myself." He'd managed to slide between her and the door, so she'd have to push him out of the way to reach it.

She looked at the door and then back at him before finally admitting defeat, curtseying, and walking away—slowly, very slowly, looking back over her shoulder several times.

He waited until she was out of sight, and then turned and knocked.

"Come in!"

Blast, that was Livy's voice. Well, Jo *had* said they were working together. He took a deep, steadying breath and pushed the door open.

"Edward!"

That was Jo. She'd been sitting at a desk, but stood and took a step toward him—and stopped.

Are those tears on her cheeks?

"It's about time you got here."

And *that* was Livy. Had she made Jo cry?

He scowled at Livy—and Livy smiled back at him, looking very self-satisfied, as if she could see everything he was thinking.

And feeling.

He looked down in a vain attempt to protect some shred of privacy—and saw a brown and white spaniel. A distraction!

"Hey there." He bent down and held out his hand. "You must be Freddie."

Freddie padded over to sniff his fingers and then allowed Edward to scratch his ears, closing his eyes in canine ecstasy.

I felt just this way when your mistress stroked me, Freddie.

And he'd better not allow his thoughts to run in *that* direction, particularly not while Livy was still in the room.

He gave Freddie one last pat, straightened, and—

"What is it?" Both Livy and Jo were staring at him as if he'd grown a second head.

Livy looked at Jo, so he did, too. Surely, she hadn't minded him petting her dog?

"Freddie doesn't like men," Jo said. "He growls at them."

That's right. She'd said as much that first day on the lawn at Darrow.

"I hope he knows I'm a man." Edward looked down at Freddie, who was sitting by his left foot. "You do, don't you, Freddie?"

Freddie looked up at him, barked in apparent confirmation, and then wagged his tail for good measure.

"He probably recognizes your scent from Jo." Livy gave Jo a speaking look, though what it was saying was a mystery to Edward.

But apparently not to Jo. A bright red flush bloomed across her cheeks.

Anger sliced through him. *I won't have Livy teasing Jo.*

Not that it was his place—yet or perhaps ever—to defend Jo, but his gut didn't wait for his better judgment to assert itself.

"Good *God*, Livy, are you suggesting Jo hasn't bathed or changed her clothes since Darrow? That was two months ago."

Livy was still looking at Jo. "No, I'm suggesting she has something of yours."

He hadn't thought Jo's face could get any redder, but he'd been mistaken. She now resembled a very ripe apple.

And he was beginning to think he'd landed in Bedlam. "Are you calling Jo a thief then?"

Livy laughed!

"Oh, no. She didn't steal it—you gave it to her quite, quite freely."

Jo moaned. She'd gone from red to white. She looked like she might faint.

Edward stepped closer so he could catch her if she started to go down. "Stop speaking in riddles, Livy. It is extremely annoying."

The blasted female looked as if she would explode with mirth. A little snigger did manage to escape before she slapped her hand over her mouth. Now all he could see were her laughing eyes—yet they also held some warmer, more charitable emotion, so he didn't snap at her again.

"I'll just take myself off, shall I?" Livy said. "Jo has important things to tell you, Edward, and I can see I'm very much in the way."

"*Very* much," he said, looking back at Jo.

Jo still hadn't said anything. That was making him very anxious indeed. From his experience—admittedly limited, but still, he felt, reliable—she wasn't one to hold her tongue. What could be the problem?

Perhaps she'd speak more freely once Livy left. Though he couldn't imagine Jo being cowed by anyone, Livy included.

"Come on, Freddie," Livy said.

Edward watched them leave. He turned back to Jo once the door closed behind them. She seemed nervous.

Or perhaps he was the nervous one.

"Why did you name your dog Freddie?" he asked—and then wished he could recall the words. He didn't want to talk about Freddie—canine or human.

Jo frowned. "I don't know. The name just seemed to fit. Maybe he looks a little like my late husband—that Freddie had brown eyes, too." She sighed, shook her head. "Or maybe it was because I saved this Freddie from drowning, and I couldn't save my husband. He didn't drown literally, of course, but I think he did drown in debt, drink, and despair."

Edward nodded. He understood that feeling of helplessness, that inability to change life's course. Helen's death had been sudden, the cause clear. He'd known he'd had no chance at all to save her, but he'd still hated the feeling of powerlessness that had gripped him as tightly as if he were in a vise.

"Did you get my letter?" Jo asked.

"Yes." He frowned. Jo had said she was working with Livy, but . . . He searched her face. She looked pale again, almost wan. There were shadows under her eyes. What could be amiss?

"Jo, did Livy make you cry?"

Jo shook her head—and suddenly her eyes brightened. She looked as if she had a secret to share. Could it have something to do with Livy's cryptic remark about Freddie?

"What did she mean when she said you had something of mine?"

Jo grinned. Well, she *glowed*.

"Oh, Edward! I really can't believe it, but Livy says it's true, and she seems to know about these things. Well, it *is* true I've been unusually tired. And out of sorts. But I never in a million years would have thought . . . I mean I know what everyone said, but I still believed it couldn't happen."

This torrent of words was unlike her—and difficult to follow. "*What* couldn't happen, Jo?"

"You'll never guess!"

Could he shake it out of her? "Right, I won't. So please, just tell me."

If it were possible, Jo's smile grew even bigger.

"Livy says I'm *pregnant*!"

He stared at her, his mouth agape, too dumbfounded to process her meaning.

Pregnant? Could Jo really be pregnant?!

"I *thought* my courses had started." She flushed and looked away. "There was evidence—"

"Jo. Remember. I was married. I know how this all works." *Yes, and I know how it can end—in pain and death and—*

He pushed *those* dark thoughts aside. Nothing in life was certain, so he would try to choose hope over despair. Happiness over worry.

And he *was* happy—very, very happy. Another child? Another son—or a daughter?

He grinned. "Now you'll *have* to marry me."

"Yes." She laughed and closed the gap between them. She flung her arms around him, and he finally, *finally* took Thomas's advice and kissed her.

Chapter Twenty

Edward looked out the window of his traveling coach as it bowled along the road to Little Puddledon. He had a special license in his pocket and his son—along with Bear—on the seat across from him. By the end of the day, he and Jo would be married.

He should be ecstatic. It was almost a fairy tale. He had finally found love, *and* he was going to be a father again.

But have *I found love?*

He loved Jo, but did Jo love him?

She'd said she loved him in the temple that last day at Darrow, but she'd also said she didn't know if she loved him enough to change her life for him. She'd said she needed time away from him to see if what she felt for him would last.

She hadn't mentioned love in the letter she'd written him. No, she'd mentioned Livy and the many plans they had. And she'd not mentioned love when he'd seen her just a few days ago and she'd told him she was increasing.

And then I told her she had *to marry me.*

He cringed and shifted on the squabs.

She hadn't argued the point, of course. How could she?

After a few passionate kisses, they'd moved on to talking about the wedding. Jo had wanted to get married at the Home and had said, rightly, that Thomas needed to be there, too. So, Edward had kissed her once more and got back on his horse to ride for Grainger.

Which had given him three days by himself to think. Three days to water any seeds of doubt and have them grow into a dense forest.

Had he misread the situation? Jo had been crying and pale when he'd first stepped into her office. She hadn't come flying across the room and into his arms the moment she'd seen him. She'd stayed by her desk. Had that been only because Livy was there? But she hadn't rushed into his arms the moment the door had closed behind Livy and Freddie, either.

And yes, there had been those kisses, but had it been more a matter of him kissing her? Had her passion matched his?

Surely, I would have noticed any reluctance . . .

He wasn't entirely certain he would have. He'd been so happy at her news and then so very happy to have her in his arms again, her mouth under his that he might well have missed any subtle signs.

Well, he was afraid he might have missed anything more subtle than a slap across the face.

Does she truly want *to marry me? Does she regret having to change her life?*

The answers didn't matter. Jo no longer had a choice. He'd been right in that. They *had* to marry. Harriet might say that being a bastard was not a great burden, but Lady Bianca had the right of it. Bastardy *was* a burden. A heavy, crushing burden.

Zeus! Jo hated to be pressured, forced to do anything

against her will, and this was the greatest pressure of all. And while it was true she'd gone to bed with him willingly, she'd also believed she couldn't conceive. She hadn't fully accepted the risk.

Did she feel like her body had betrayed her again? Trapped her? That *he'd* trapped her?

He wanted a wife who *loved* him, who was eager to share his life with all its ups and downs, joys and sorrows. A partner. A friend as well as a lover.

It made no difference. He no longer had a choice, either.

"Are you sad, Papa?"

Thomas had come over to sit beside him, and was now looking up at him with searching eyes.

Eyes that always saw too much.

Edward forced a smile. "No, Thomas. How can I be sad? We are going to see Miss Jo. She's going to marry me and be your mother. And you're going to have a baby brother or sister."

Thomas was not fooled. "Yes. But you still look sad."

And what was he to say to that? He wasn't certain he could explain the matter even to himself.

"I suppose I'm just a little tired. And perhaps a little nervous. It's not every day a man marries."

Thomas frowned, clearly not convinced. He opened his mouth—

And was interrupted by Bear barking.

Edward had never been so happy for some canine commotion, deafening though it was in the confines of the coach. What had set Bear off?

Ah. There were the first stone houses of the village.

"Look, Thomas. We've reached Little Puddledon."

Thomas pressed his nose to the window. "Where does Miss Jo live?"

"Up the hill. We'll be there in just a few minutes."

Well, more than a few. He'd forgotten that the coach would need to slow to almost a crawl to navigate the narrow village streets.

"People are staring, Papa. And waving. May I wave back?"

"Of course." There did seem to be a festive air among the villagers—which, ironically perhaps, only depressed his spirits further.

"They seem happy to see us, Papa."

"I imagine they are happy for Miss Jo. She's lived here for a long time, Thomas. They all know her."

And now she would have to leave this village and all her friends to come live with him among strangers.

His spirits fell further.

The traveling coach passed by the Dancing Duck, rumbled across the bridge over the stream, and then labored up the hill to the Manor.

They could walk faster than the bloody vehicle was moving.

"Are we almost there, Papa?" Thomas still had his nose pressed to the window.

"Yes."

Part of Edward wanted to urge the coachman to hurry the horses—and the other part wanted to add several lead weights, slowing their progress even more.

"There it is, Papa! Oh! Look at all the ladies!" And then, somewhat less excitedly. "And all the girls."

Word of their arrival must have preceded them, because there was quite the welcoming committee assembled.

"And there's Miss Jo!"

Zeus! Edward's heart leapt at the sight of her.

Perhaps I love her enough for both of us.

And then Jo saw him, and her smile widened—

Or perhaps it was Thomas she saw.

The coach rocked to a stop. Edward didn't wait for his coachman, but opened the door, let the steps down—

Oh, hell. He saw Freddie just as Bear gave a great woof and flew past him, eager to get free of the confining carriage and meet a new friend.

This was not the way she'd pictured Edward's return, Jo thought as she tried to control the chaos. It was quite a cacophony—dogs barking, girls shrieking, horses neighing, coachman shouting.

"Freddie, behave. Esther, please don't scream. Bear is friendly. No, Bathsheba, he's not *really* a bear."

Bess had posted a lookout—Edward had hoped to arrive today, but hadn't been certain he would, the roads being so unreliable. Once he'd been spotted, Tabitha had come running up from the Dancing Duck to spread the word—and then everyone had found a reason to be out in front of the Manor.

And *then* Bear had jumped out of the coach and pandemonium had ensued.

Edward had finally managed to grab Bear's collar and persuade the dog to sit, even though Freddie kept sniffing around him. Livy had gone over to talk to him. Jo would—

"Miss Jo."

She turned around—and grinned. "Thomas! I didn't see you in all the confusion. I'm so glad you're here." She opened her arms and was delighted he came into them for a hug. "I'm so happy I'm going to be your stepmama."

"I'm happy, too, Miss Jo." Then he whispered, "Will you talk to Papa?"

Her smile faltered. Thomas looked worried. "Is something the matter?"

The boy nodded. "I think Papa's sad."

"Oh." Her heart sank. There was only one reason she could think of for that. "Is he sad about getting married?"

Thomas shook his head sharply. "No. I don't *think* that's it. I don't know what it is. Can you take him off by himself? Maybe then he'll tell you."

"Yes, of course." But how was she going to manage that? She looked around. Everyone who lived at the Home was there, milling around—and looking at Edward.

"I think Bear must need a walk," Thomas said. "Maybe your Freddie does, too?"

"Good idea." She straightened and turned to see Edward and Livy and the dogs walking toward them.

"What plot are you two hatching?" Edward asked, smiling.

The smile didn't reach his eyes. Jo's stomach sank as he turned to introduce Livy to his son.

"This is Miss Williams, Thomas. An old friend."

Thomas made a credible bow.

"And this, of course, is Freddie," Jo said, seeing that her dog was sniffing Thomas's shoes.

Thomas squatted down and held his hand out. "Hallo, Freddie. I'm Thomas."

Freddie licked Thomas's face.

Thomas laughed and looked up at her. "Freddie must like boys, Miss Jo." Then he looked at Edward. "And he must like you, too, Papa. He didn't growl at you."

Was Edward's color heightened? He was likely thinking, as Jo was, of what Livy had said when Freddie had first met Edward.

Livy certainly was. Her eyes gleamed with devilment.

She wasn't going to say something inappropriate with Thomas there, was she?

Jo leapt into speech to forestall the possibility. "Thomas was just telling me that Bear needs a walk."

"An excellent idea!" Livy said. "Why don't the two of you attend to that, and I'll take charge of Thomas?" She smiled at the boy. "Would you like to meet Bumblebee, Thomas?"

Thomas's eyes widened. "A bumblebee?"

Jo laughed. "Bumblebee is my horse's name, Thomas. Well, she's hardly more than a pony and getting on in years. She's very gentle."

Thomas looked at Edward. "May I, Papa?"

"Of course."

Jo stood next to Edward as they watched his son go off with Livy to the stables. She felt such a gulf between them, they might just as well be strangers.

What in the world is the matter with the man?

And then she noticed how the other women were eyeing them. Well, eyeing Edward. Rosamund was headed their way.

I'd better make haste if I'm going to take Thomas's advice.

"Let's go to the orchard," Jo said, picking the first goal she saw on the horizon.

Edward nodded and fell into step with her—*silent* step— as the dogs trotted ahead.

Perhaps he would tell her what the problem was once they were away from the house.

"Did you have an uneventful journey?" she asked.

"Yes."

"Is Thomas a good traveler?"

"Yes."

"And Bear? How did he manage?"

"Well enough."

She was going to scream. Getting words out of him today was literally like pulling teeth.

Well, not that she'd ever pulled teeth, thank God.

When they reached the orchard and stepped in under the concealing branches, she put a hand on his arm, stopping him.

The dogs seemed to sense this was going to take a while. They flopped down next to each other on the ground.

"Edward, what *is* the matter?" Thomas had said the problem wasn't their impending nuptials, but did Thomas really know? "Have you changed your mind about marrying me?"

He sighed. "No, of course not, Jo. I *have* to marry you."

Her stomach lurched, and she closed her eyes. *Of course, that's it. He feels trapped.*

Well, he *was* trapped. *He* was too honorable to turn his back on her and his child.

I misled him. I told him I couldn't have children. I wasn't lying. I thought it was the truth. Oh, why in the world would I think Edward could love me?

She felt his hands on her shoulders. She looked up and saw the pain in his eyes.

"I'm sorry, Jo. I know you don't want to leave the Home and come live with me."

But I do *want to live with you!*

She realized with some surprise that, while she wasn't precisely happy to be leaving the Home, she also wasn't dreading it.

All she'd been thinking about was being with Edward.

"I wish I could say you didn't have to marry me, but you do." He looked away. "I should have been more careful. I know you said you couldn't have children, but I knew Havenridge's reputation."

She thought she was going to puke. "Don't . . . don't you want this baby, Edward?"

He looked shocked. "Of course, I want the baby, Jo. I want it more than anything. I'm just sorry that you feel trapped by it."

"Trapped?" He was the one who was trapped.

"I had hoped you would find you loved me . . ." He laughed weakly. "Hell, I thought when I was shopping the Marriage Mart that love didn't matter. That it was never going to be part of the bargain. That I didn't need it. But then I met you and . . ." He shrugged.

"I'm sorry if I sound like a mewling babe, Jo, but I wish you *did* love me. I hope that maybe you'll still come to love me some day, after you get used to all the changes in your life. I will try to earn your love."

He wasn't making any sense.

She caught his face between her hands so he couldn't look away. "Edward, what are you talking about? Of *course*, I love you."

He stared at her. "You do?"

"Yes. Why would you ever doubt it?"

"But you . . . Well, you said you loved me at Darrow, but you also said you weren't sure, that you needed time to know if you loved me enough to change your life for me. And you didn't mention love in your letter nor when you told me about the baby."

Oh. She never *had* said the words, had she? Well, she would fix that omission at once.

"Edward, what I felt for you—what I *feel* for you—was too much to put in a note. I needed to tell you in person. But then, just before you arrived, Livy convinced me I was carrying your child, and everything else flew out of my head."

She'd forgotten how important it was to actually *say* the words—to have him hear them.

"Of *course*, I love you." She saw hope begin to brighten his eyes. "I never imagined I could feel such a love. I . . ."

What else did he need to hear?

"I would marry you if you were still just a solicitor."

She laughed. "Well, I suppose it would have been easier to decide to marry you if you *were* just a solicitor. So, I will say that I'll marry you even though you are a duke and I'll have to face the *ton* again. I love you *that* much!"

He didn't look entirely convinced. "But would you marry me even if you weren't pregnant?"

"Yes! I had already decided that I loved you—that I loved you *enough*—and would marry you before I knew I was carrying our child." She put her hand on his chest, just above his heart. "*You* are my life, now, Edward. You and Thomas"—she moved her hand to her belly, a gesture she'd seen so many pregnant women make and now, for the first time, truly understood—"and our baby."

It was as if the sun had broken out from behind thick clouds. The shadows vanished from Edward's eyes and he grinned, leaned closer . . .

She put a finger to his lips to delay the kiss she knew was coming. "But I still mean to keep an eye on the Home, you know, if only through letters—and visits. We *will* visit, won't we?"

"Of course."

And then he kissed her and she knew that she was truly home.

Epilogue

Ten Months Later, the Duke of Grainger's Country Estate

Jo sat in the Grainger schoolroom, Lord James Michael Henry Russell—all of seven weeks old—at her breast.

Pen and Caro and their families had arrived yesterday for James's christening. This morning, the men had taken Thomas and Harriet—and Freddie and Bear—out for a morning romp while the women stayed behind with the younger children.

Now Pen was at one end of the room, sitting on the floor building towers of blocks for one-year-old Pip—or, more properly, Philip Arthur Edward, Viscount Hurley—to knock down. Caro was at the other end, trying to keep the eight-month-old Honorable David George Randolph St. John from pulling up on anything that would topple over on him.

Jo sat in the middle and smiled, feeling James's strong pull on her nipple. He had a lusty appetite.

As did his father . . .

How much my life has changed in less than a year!

"How is the Benevolent Home for Mothers and Boys

doing, Jo?" Pen asked as Lord Hurley clapped his hands and did a little dance of joy before sending the block tower tumbling.

Pen started building it again.

"It's already full." Jo shook her head. The new Home had been in operation only six months. "I guess I underestimated the need all these years."

Edward had acquired Harvey Miller's failing farm—Jo would have been quite happy to have the miscreant who'd tried to drown Freddie drown in River Tick, but Edward had a kinder soul. Well, and he'd pointed out Harvey was likely to drown himself in Widow's Brew with the money from the sale, a thought she took great—perhaps even fiendish—delight in.

Edward had supplied the funds and legal advice, but Livy had managed everything else—she really did have an excellent head for business. And for managing people. She'd put Rosamund Lewis in charge of the new Home. Jo had been extremely skeptical, but it was working out surprisingly well. Apparently, once Rosamund had a responsible, consuming occupation, she lost all interest in stirring up trouble.

"Oopsy!"

That was Caro. The Honorable Davey had let go of the chair he'd been holding on to and had tried to walk across the room. He'd landed on his rump, a momentary look of surprise on his face, but had recovered quickly and crawled over to grab his prey, a red ball.

"He'll be walking soon," Pen said.

Caro nodded, but, as always, kept her focus on the topic currently under discussion. "It wasn't so much that we underestimated the need, Jo. We didn't have the resources to expand."

"True." They'd been struggling to keep just the one Home going.

The Honorable Davey lost interest in the ball and decided to interfere with Viscount Hurley's fun. He managed to grab one block, which he promptly put in his mouth, before Caro captured him.

The viscount's lower lip pushed out as if he were going to protest the thievery, but Pen distracted him with another tower and a tantrum was averted.

"Now that you're a duchess, Jo," Caro said, plopping her son back down by her chair, "you have influence. You"—Caro looked at Pen—"*we* can work to change matters so there are more places for women in need to go."

Pen nodded as she balanced a round block on a square one. "Harry means to speak in the House of Lords on the matter. If your husbands joined their voices to his"—she looked at Jo—"especially the duke, perhaps matters will improve."

"Yes. Nick has also—blaugh! Give me that!"

The Honorable Davey had found a tasty bit of floor fluff to sample.

While Caro tried to fish the now soggy fluff out of her son's mouth, and Pen built another tower, Jo looked down at James. She hadn't felt any sucking for a few minutes.

Ah. He'd had a hearty meal and had dropped off, eyes closed, milk dribbling down his chin, lips pulling in and out in fleeting little smiles.

Lud, he's such a miracle.

She stroked his fuzzy little head, studying the delicate shell of his ear and each perfect little finger of his tiny hand resting on her breast.

All mothers must think their babies miracles to some degree, but perhaps she could be forgiven for thinking

James a *special* miracle. A year ago, she'd known with the same certainty as she knew the sun would rise in the east and set in the west that she'd never be a mother, and now, here she was—a mother, a stepmother, and a wife.

She smiled at her sleeping baby. A very *happy* wife. That was as much a miracle as the rest.

Her second marriage was nothing like her first. Well, Edward was nothing like Freddie. He—

Crash!

The noise startled James. His eyes flew open and his tiny, faint brows angled down. She put him to her shoulder and patted his back as she turned to see what had happened.

Viscount Hurley was laughing uproariously, blocks scattered on the floor all around him. The Honorable Davey, dirt successfully extracted from his mouth, was crawling briskly over to investigate, his hands and knees slapping against the floor. This time when he grabbed one of the blocks to chew on, the viscount did not object.

"Shall I build *another* tower, Pip?" Pen asked her son.

Viscount Hurley giggled and clapped his hands.

A year ago, Pip had been as tiny and helpless as James—and Davey had not yet been born. In no time at all, her baby would be sitting by himself, crawling, walking. In just a few years he'd be as big as Thomas was now. And then, someday, as big as Edward and perhaps a father himself—

"Bwaaapp!"

Jo looked at her baby, who gave her a big, toothless smile.

"That was quite a burp," she said.

"Sounded like a juicy one, too." Caro came over, a rag

in her hand. "Oh, yes. He's christened your dress." She dabbed at Jo's back.

Jo held her infant son up in her hands and touched her forehead to his. "You're the one who's to be christened, my lord. Not me. Now I'll have to change."

Pen looked up from building another tower and laughed. "Oh, don't bother. He'll just puke on you again, you know."

Sadly, that was too true.

Caro nodded. "Davey was a messy burper. I took to wearing a rag over my shoulder all the time. Not as stylish as a Norwich shawl, but far more practical." She raised a brow. "And I'll wager quite soon his other end will be emitting something."

Jo laughed. "I'll not take your wager as I'm sure I'll lose—"

An extremely alarming sound emanated from James's hindquarters just as the men—along with Thomas, Harriet, Freddie, and Bear—came into the schoolroom.

The fathers all picked up their sons—except Edward.

"Here you go." Jo held James out. "Just the man I most want to see. Your son needs you."

Edward laughed. "I am not a first-time father, madam, to fall for your tricks."

That's right. When Thomas was a baby, Edward had only himself and a nursemaid.

It didn't help that Freddie had come over and was sniffing James's bottom.

Thomas wrinkled his nose. "James smells."

"Yes, he does," Edward said. "Can you go find Agnes?"

"Here I be, Yer Grace." Agnes, their very capable, experienced nursemaid, bustled into the room.

She, er, scented the issue at once.

"Oh, yer a stinky little bug, ain't ye, Jamey-boy? Come

with me. We'll have ye clean and smelling sweet agin in no time." She whisked Lord James away.

Thomas had gone off to show Harriet his soldiers—being certain to keep them away from the babies—and the other parents were busy with their children, so Jo and Edward had a moment of privacy in the busy, crowded room.

Edward looked down at her. "I do love you, Jo," he murmured, "and I would have changed James for you"—he grinned—"except for the fact that I employ the inestimable Agnes MacLarin, who will do a much better job than I could ever hope to."

Jo laughed. "You don't fool me, Edward. I know you are an expert at cleaning up dirty little boys."

Heat flared in his eyes. He waggled his brows. "And at making them."

She grinned. "And how good are you at making girls?"

"I shall be delighted to try to find out"—he bowed—"in the proper time, of course."

"Of course."

"Mama, come see what I've done with my soldiers," Thomas called over—and Jo's heart melted.

"And thank you for being a mother to Helen's son and making us a family," Edward whispered.

She looked up at him and smiled, her heart too full for words, and then she went over to see what her older son wished to show her.

Love the women of Puddledon Manor?
Keep reading for sneak peeks at

WHAT ALES THE EARL
And
THE MERRY VISCOUNT

Available now from
Sally MacKenzie
And
Zebra Books
Wherever books are sold

Chapter One

A Friday evening in August, Duke of Grainger's estate

She's very beautiful.

Harry Graham, Earl of Darrow, stood in the Duke of Grainger's music room and listened to Lady Susan Palmer, the Earl of Langley's daughter, talk about . . . something. Ah. A dress she'd seen at someone's ball—Lady Norton's?—during the Season.

She had a very English sort of beauty that he'd missed in his years on the Continent. Porcelain skin. Blonde hair. Blue eyes.

Dark blue, not the light, clear blue of Pen's . . .

"And then I asked Lady Sackley for the name of her mantua-maker though I already knew the answer. I was just trying to make conversation. And she said . . ."

How *was* Pen? She must be married and a mother several times over by now.

He'd hoped to see her when he'd come home to England—just as old friends, of course—but he'd discovered she'd left Darrow not long after he had.

He hadn't asked any more questions. It might have

looked odd for the new earl to be inquiring about a tenant farmer's daughter. Someone might remember how much time they'd spent together that summer before he'd left to fight Napoleon.

Not that there'd been anything particularly scandalous about their affair. His brother, Walter, had certainly sown his share of wild oats among the local maidens, many of which had taken root. He'd had so many bastards, people had given them a name—"Walter's whelps." It was easy to pick them out—they all had the distinctive Graham streak, a blaze of gray hair among otherwise dark locks.

He frowned. He didn't like to compare himself to Walter on any front, but particularly this one. He wasn't a monk, but he hoped he treated his paramours with more respect than Walter had. At the very least, he was careful not to gift them with a child.

Walter hadn't been the only one frequenting the maidens'—and matrons'—beds. Felix, the blacksmith's son, had given him stiff—ha!—competition. It had been so bad that far too often, no one, including the mother, knew which man was a new baby's father until the Graham streak showed up, if it did.

It had been better for all concerned when Felix was the father. Then, if there was a husband involved, the man might never realize he'd been cuckolded. Harry still remembered all too vividly the time one of the tenants had come, pitchfork in hand, to find his older brother. Usually, the Graham streak appeared by the time a child was two or three years old, but this man's firstborn son's hair hadn't shown its silver blaze until his tenth birthday.

"Exactly! I'm so glad you agree with me, Lord Darrow."

His attention snapped back to Lady Susan. Good Lord, he had no idea what she'd been rattling on about. He was losing his touch. He'd never been so unaware of his surroundings when he'd been working for the Crown.

He had to keep his mind focused on matters at hand. He'd promised Mama he'd propose to the woman, after all. He was planning to pop the question tonight.

Lady Susan laughed. "To tell you the truth, I was amazed Madame Merchant—"

"Marchand," he said, correcting her and giving the name its French pronunciation. Apparently, she was still droning on about dresses.

If I take her into the shrubbery, at least she'll stop talking.

Though, on second thought, he wouldn't bet on that. Even if he attempted a kiss, he'd likely not slow her verbal torrent. "Madame Marchand. She has her shop just off Bond Street."

"Oh, yes. I suppose you are correct." Lady Susan sniffed. "As I was saying . . ."

He kept one ear on Lady Susan's monologue while his thoughts drifted off again, this time to the French dressmaker. He'd visited Bernandine a few times when he was in London. He liked to practice his French—and other skills—with her. But once he married . . .

There was no need for any of his habits to change when he married, especially not if his wife was Lady Susan. She'd likely thank him to take his male lust somewhere beside their marital bed.

And he *was* going to marry Lady Susan—if she would let him edge a word in. He'd never met a woman who could talk so fluently about nothing.

Do I really want to wed such a jabberer?

No, he didn't, but he didn't have much of an alternative. She was the best of a bad lot.

His mother had laid the matter out quite clearly the moment he'd set a foot back in Darrow Hall after almost ten years abroad. He had to marry and get an heir as soon as possible.

He'd been in Paris when he'd got word that Walter had broken his neck going over a jump. Zeus, he'd never forget how he'd felt when he'd read that letter. It had been as if someone had administered a flush hit to his breadbasket and followed it by dumping a load of bricks on his head.

I never expected to be earl. I never wanted *to be.*

He'd liked the life he'd built for himself. He'd spent the last decade in Portugal, Spain, France, Austria, living by his wits, dealing in ideas, in stratagems and politics, *not* in crops and drainage ditches and leaky roofs.

But he *was* the earl now and with that came the duty to continue the succession. And Walter's death had proved all too conclusively that no one was guaranteed another day on this earth.

Which Mama had pointed out most emphatically. He needed an heir, she'd said bluntly. There was no time to delay. Walter had been only thirty-five, and here he was, dead. And, as Walter had also illustrated all too well, Harry couldn't be assured of having a son on his first attempt. Or his second. Or third. His sister-in-law, Letitia, had produced a baby a year: Adrianna, Bianca, Cassandra. Likely she and Walter would have carried on through the alphabet until they'd got a boy if she'd been able, but she'd lost the last three pregnancies and then, if rumor was to be believed, had refused to let Walter back into her bed.

So, Mama had handed Harry a list she'd made of eligible women, young females with the proper pedigree *and* several brothers. All he needed to do was choose one, marry, and get down to swiving his brains out.

Well, Mama hadn't said that last part, at least not in so many words. But her message had been painfully clear: the sooner he got an heir and a spare, the better.

She'd wanted him to make his selection on the spot, picking a name off the list, but he'd insisted on meeting the women first. They'd all still been in the schoolroom when he'd left England. So, they'd compromised. Mama had agreed to let him take a Season to shop the Marriage Mart without constantly badgering him. And he'd agreed to make his choice once the Season was over.

The Season had ended in June. He hadn't encountered a single woman who made his heart—or even his baser organ—long for a closer relationship, but he'd given his word. He had to choose one.

Lady Susan would do as well as any other. Better, perhaps. At least she was in her early twenties, older than most of the others on the list. Mama would have preferred he choose a debutante—she'd argued that he'd get more breeding years from a girl in her late teens—but he couldn't stomach the thought of taking what to him felt like a child to bed. And since, as far as he could discern, Lady Susan harbored no tender feelings for him, she wouldn't be offended by his inability to feel any affection for her.

He only hoped he didn't go deaf from her constant chatter.

At least she was pleasant to look at. And Darrow Hall was a big place. It wouldn't be hard to avoid her there, and when he was in London, he'd spend all his time at his clubs. Except for the obligatory swiving. With luck, he'd get her with child on their wedding night, and their first two children would be male.

Lady Susan's fashion commentary showed no sign of

abating, but time was marching on. He could feel his mother's and his sister-in-law's eyes boring a hole in his back. It was the last day of the house party. He was supposed to invite the woman for a stroll in the vegetation where he would perhaps steal a kiss and discover if she was agreeable to him asking her father for her hand in marriage.

Of course, she was agreeable. She wouldn't be at this infernal party if she wasn't. Her father was likely sitting in a room somewhere, waiting for him to make his appearance.

His stomach twisted, and he took a settling swallow of brandy. He'd faced worse assignments during the war. At least he wouldn't die from their trip to the garden—unless he drowned in her never-ending stream of words.

The sooner he married and got a son, the sooner he could reclaim his life. He wasn't looking for a love match, after all. Hell, he wouldn't know love if it bit him on the arse.

What I'd had with Pen had felt very much like love. . . .

Ha. He'd been eighteen. What had he known of love? Nothing. His feelings had been lust, pure—very pure—and simple.

This union with Lady Susan would be a typical marriage of convenience. A business arrangement: a title, prestige, and wealth in exchange for a son or two. It was a very common sort of thing among the *ton*. Once his wife—once Lady Susan—completed her side of the bargain, she'd be free to go her own way as long as she took sensible precautions.

He just hoped he'd be more efficient than Walter at getting an heir.

He stiffened his spine, metaphorically speaking. There was no point in delaying the inevitable. He opened his mouth to utter the words that would seal his fate—

And then a bolt of lightning lit the room, followed by a great crack of thunder and a torrential downpour.

God had saved him. There would be no stroll in the garden tonight.

The Lord had even managed to stop Lady Susan's chatter. Briefly.

"My, that was a surprise. I don't like storms. Why, last summer I was caught in a terrible one."

Was he now doomed to listen to an accounting of every raindrop that had ever hit Lady Susan's lovely head?

No. The Duke of Grainger came over to finish what the Almighty had begun.

"Good evening, Lady Susan," the duke said into the silence he'd created by his appearance. "I hope you don't mind me stealing Darrow away, but I'm afraid it's getting late and I have an urgent matter I must take up with him in private."

Harry glanced around, surprised to see that almost everyone else—except his mother and sister-in-law and old Lord Pembleton, sipping his sherry in a corner by the potted palm—had left.

"Oh?" Lady Susan looked uncertainly at Harry. "But I thought . . . That is, I expected . . ." She frowned. "Lord Darrow, I was given to understand we had something of particular interest to discuss."

Then why did you drone on about dresses?

Harry opened his mouth, not entirely certain what words would come out, but Grainger clapped him on the back and spoke before he could.

"Well, there's always the morning, isn't there? I'm sure it will keep. Unfortunately, my issue will not. Please excuse us."

And with that he hauled Harry away.

Harry had never been one to allow himself to be led

anywhere, but he also wasn't an idiot. He could see salvation when it was dangled before him. He went meekly—and quickly—along until they were in Grainger's study with the door firmly closed.

"Zounds!" Harry collapsed into one of the leather chairs by the hearth.

Grainger laughed and went over to a cut-glass decanter. "Can I offer you some more brandy?" He grinned. "It's even better than what you have there."

Harry tossed off the last drops in his glass and then held it out for Grainger to refill. "I should have finished my conversation with Lady Susan, you know."

Grainger chuckled as he took the chair across from Harry and put the decanter on the table between them. "Good luck at finishing any conversation with that woman." He cocked a brow. "You weren't about to suggest what I think you were, were you?"

"If you mean was I going to offer for her, yes, I was."

Grainger shook his head, a mixture of disgust and sympathy on his face. "Offer for that magpie? You'd be deaf before the ceremony was over." He snorted. "I wager you'd have to gag the woman so you could say your vows."

Possibly. "She's very beautiful."

"Then commission a painting of her and hang it in your study. Paintings don't talk."

If only that would solve the problem. "I promised my mother I would find a wife this Season."

Grainger's nose wrinkled in distaste. "And you picked Lady Susan?"

Harry shrugged a shoulder as he took another swallow of brandy and stared into the fire. "I wasn't going to marry a child just out of the schoolroom. Lady Susan will do."

"For what? To drive you mad? She'll manage that in short order, I assure you." Grainger pulled a face. "I've had the misfortune to be seated next to her at more than one meal. The lips move and words come out. They even make sense most of the time, but they are so soul-sucking boring, you want to pick up your knife and stab her to make her stop—or slit your own throat to end your misery." He shook his head. "*And* she doesn't listen. Ever. I wouldn't wish her on my worst enemy."

Grainger leaned forward and waggled his index finger at Harry. "Marry her and I'll never invite you here again. I value my sanity too much. Good God, man, I swear I lose a little more intelligence with every word she utters."

Grainger was making rather too much of the matter.

"So then why did you invite her to this house party?" Granted, this had not been the usual *ton* country gathering. The guests were older—none of the just-out-of-the-schoolroom girls here. A few were widows with young children in tow, which would make sense if Grainger was considering remarriage. Grainger's wife had died several years ago, just days after their son was born.

"I was afraid I could see the way the wind was blowing with you. I don't *want* to have to cut your acquaintance. I was hoping extended exposure to her would bring you to your senses." He grinned and said hopefully, "And has it?"

Harry's senses had never been at issue. "You seem to be missing the point here, Grainger. I need an heir. Ergo, I need a wife."

"But perhaps not this particular wife." Grainger poured them both more brandy. "What's the rush? You're not even thirty yet."

"True, but my brother's sudden death—Walter was only

thirty-five, you know—has made me—" Might as well lay it all out on the table. "Well, mostly my mother and sister-in-law acutely aware of the uncertainty of life. I could overturn my carriage leaving here and break my neck."

"Which might be preferable to marrying Lady Susan."

Harry almost snorted brandy out his nose. "I wouldn't say that." Though if he were being brutally honest, he didn't completely disagree with Grainger.

I can't really prefer death to marrying Lady Susan, can I?

No, of course not.

Grainger cocked a skeptical brow, but didn't argue the point. "Don't you have a cousin or some relative who will inherit if you should meet an untimely end?" he asked instead.

Harry nodded. "Yes. A very distant cousin in my great-grandfather's brother's line."

"Ah. Now that would be quite the calamity, wouldn't it?" Grainger said with a perfectly straight face.

Of course, Grainger wouldn't see the problem in letting . . . Harry wasn't even sure of the fellow's name who was next in line to be earl. Searching among the distant leaves of the family tree was precisely how Grainger had succeeded to his title. Until early this spring, he'd been merely Edward Russell, London solicitor—and then the fourth Duke of Grainger, along with his wife and children, had died suddenly and unexpectedly of influenza.

Harry shrugged, acknowledging Grainger's point. "Perhaps it wouldn't, but Mama and Letitia aren't eager to have their comfortable lives upended."

Grainger's other brow rose as well, and then both settled into a frown. Clearly, he was biting his tongue.

Well, Grainger wasn't saddled—er, *blessed*—with female relatives.

"Don't make it bleed," Harry said. Grainger grinned.

"And it's not just them, of course," Harry continued. "I have a responsibility to all the people on the estate." He might not have given a thought to being earl, but his years in the army and working for the Crown had impressed upon him the need to look out for the people who depended on him.

Grainger still looked unconvinced. "I see. Well, then, I am very sorry to have put a spoke in your wheel. I hope—well, I don't actually hope because I think it's a dashed bad idea, but if you're really set on it, then I imagine you can propose to Lady Susan in the morning."

Harry grunted and took another swallow of brandy. He'd never been enthusiastic about offering for Lady Susan, but now suddenly he felt trapped.

Blast Grainger for cracking open the door to his prison. He was very tempted to bolt. It must be the brandy's fault.

He took another swallow. "So, *do* you have an urgent matter of some sort, Grainger, or was that just a ploy to get me away from Lady Susan?"

Grainger poured them more brandy. If Harry were the suspicious sort, he'd suspect the duke was trying to get him drunk enough to disregard the urgings of his better, more responsible self.

"I do, actually," Grainger said, "though it's not really urgent."

Harry might have growled, because Grainger smiled.

"It requires some discretion," Grainger said, "and I know you've done some discreet inquiries for the Crown."

I shouldn't rise to the bait. . . .

He couldn't help himself. "Tell me."

Grainger reeled him right in, though at least the duke permitted himself only the smallest smile as he did so.

"I've been going over the estate books," Grainger said. "They are a bit of a mess."

Harry nodded. Darrow's books hadn't been that bad, but it was always a challenge to jump into the middle of matters with which one had no previous experience.

"As far as I can make out, for over a decade the estate has been supporting someone or something in a village called Little Puddledon."

Harry frowned. "Never heard of the place. And what do you mean, someone or *something?*"

Grainger shrugged. "The entry just lists the recipient as *JSW*. It could stand for Joseph Samuel Withers or the Just Society of Weasels."

Harry snorted. "I'd say that unless the previous duke had an affinity for weasels, JSW must be his bastard."

The duke grimaced. "Yes, that thought had occurred to me."

"What did the old duke's man of business say it was for?"

Grainger ran his hand through his hair. "That's the devil of it. The fellow was at the estate when the influenza hit, and he, too, died of the disease. No one else seems to know anything about the matter."

Harry frowned. "That's odd."

Grainger nodded. "Very. However, it is only a small sum, paid out once a year, so perhaps it's understandable that it was overlooked. I certainly haven't felt it a priority to sort out before now." He shrugged. "This year's payment was to go out two weeks ago, but I stopped it until I could discover the particulars. I was planning to go down to

Little Puddledon as soon as this gathering was over to see what I could find out."

It was Harry's turn to cock an eyebrow. "The Duke of Grainger is going to visit an obscure village? That will get tongues wagging at record pace."

Grainger laughed. "I doubt anyone will recognize me, but I hadn't intended to announce myself. I was going to ride down on horseback and use my family name instead of my title. However"—he gave Harry a hopeful look—"I freely admit I have no experience in skulking about."

"And I do." Harry could see where this was going.

"Precisely. It could get rather awkward, depending on what I find, if my identity *was* discovered. So, I thought, given the fact that you *do* have experience with, er, sneaking about, you might be a better person to investigate." He grinned. "And it would give you a break from Lady Susan and the entreaties of your female relatives."

True.

"Though I've often wondered how you managed not to call attention to yourself on the Continent." Grainger gestured at Harry's temple. "With your silver blaze, you might as well have a placard with your name pasted to your forehead."

His silver strands, contrasting starkly with his dark hair, did make him stand out in a crowd, though he would be surprised if anyone in Little Puddledon knew of the Graham streak. "It's not a problem that a little blacking won't fix."

The thought of getting away from Mama and Letitia—and Lady Susan—and getting back to a semblance of his old life, even for a short time, was extremely appealing.

It will only be for a few days. Lady Susan won't marry someone else that quickly.

It was rather telling that the thought she might came with a jolt of relief.

I'll take this one last frolic and then I'll settle down to be a model earl.

Harry hesitated only a moment longer. "Very well. I'd be happy to see what I can discover." Elated might be a more accurate adjective. "I'll leave in the morning."

Grainger raised his glass. "Splendid. May I suggest departing early, before the women are up? I'll tell them you went off on an urgent matter for me"—he grinned—"and I promise not to reveal your destination."

Turn the page for Chapter One
of
THE MERRY VISCOUNT

Chapter One

Caroline Anderson gave up her attempt to protect her space and shifted closer to the stagecoach wall, away from the beefy thigh pressing up against her.

The owner of the thigh spread his legs wider.

Blast! She glared at the cloth-covered appendage, her fingers itching to pull her knife out of her cloak pocket and prod the encroaching body part back into its own—

No. There was no point in making things more uncomfortable than they already were. She'd been lucky this coach was wider than normal and could squeeze six people inside, because she certainly didn't want to spend another night in London. And the man wasn't dangerous—his wife was seated on his other side, after all. He was just male and oblivious.

She'd be in far worse straits if the weaselly-looking fellow sitting diagonally across from her were in Beefy Thigh's place. The Weasel had been staring at her as if she were a tasty sweetmeat ever since they'd left London. Fortunately, two other men were wedged onto the bench next to him, preventing him from sliding any closer.

She turned her head to stare glumly out the window.

Oh, hell!

Could things get any worse? The snow, which had been lazily dusting the buildings when they'd left Town, was now falling in thick curtains. It covered the grass and decorated the trees. If it kept up at this rate . . .

No, the road *had* to remain passable. She needed to get back to the Benevolent Home for the Maintenance and Support of Spinsters, Widows, and Abandoned Women and their Unfortunate Children today. It was almost Christmas Eve.

She let out a long breath, fogging the window. She could do with a little luck, but luck—or at least the good variety—had not been her companion on this journey.

She'd had *such* high hopes when she'd set off from Little Puddledon yesterday. Mr. Harris, the owner of the Drunken Sheep in Westling, had again increased his order of Widow's Brew, the ale she produced with her fellow residents of the Home. Even better, he'd told her he'd visited his brother in London and had persuaded *him* to give their ale a try. She'd been so thrilled, she'd almost hugged the man. Getting Widow's Brew into the London market had been her dream ever since she'd perfected the recipe. Here, finally, was her chance.

Some chance. She pulled a face at the passing scenery, her stomach knotting in anger and frustration. *Oh, what a* colossal *fool I've been.*

The pasty-faced man seated directly across from her sneezed, a great, wet eruption—and only then pulled out his handkerchief to give his nose a honking blow.

Splendid. That was all she needed—to come down with a horrible head cold. It would quite put the final flourish on this fruitless jaunt.

She frowned. It wasn't as if she'd gone running up to

London only to fulfill her personal ambition. The Home needed the money. The more ale she sold, the less they had to depend on the whims of their noble patron, the Duke of Grainger.

Well, *patrons* now. When Pen Barnes, the Home's former hop grower, had married the Earl of Darrow in August, the earl had promised to lend his support to that of his friend, the duke.

Ha! Caro had learned from sad experience to trust a peer only as far as she could haul a full hogshead of ale— which meant not at all.

Her frown deepened to a scowl. Apparently, she could trust a London tavern keeper even less. The Westling Mr. Harris had very much mistaken the matter. Yes, his London brother had been eager to discuss terms, but the commodity he'd wished to purchase had not been her ale.

Her lips twisted into a humorless smile. She'd made good use of her pocketknife then. The dastard would think twice before putting his hands on the next businesswoman he encountered.

For all the good that does me.

Her shoulders slumped. To be brutally honest, the bounder's bad behavior wasn't the real cause of her dismals. No, her spirits were so low because she'd finally realized that her dream of breaking into the London market was pure self-delusion. Pen and Jo—Lady Havenridge, Baron Havenridge's widow and the founder of the Home— had tried to tell her that, but she'd refused to listen. She'd had to slam her head into the truth before she'd believe it.

She'd last been to London when she was seventeen, thirteen years ago. She'd forgotten how large and busy and overwhelming it was. Even if she could somehow brew ten times—a *hundred* times—the quantity of ale she did now, her output would be only a tiny drop in the enormous vats of the London breweries. And if she *did* get any orders, she'd never be able to deliver reliably. Little Puddledon was too far from Town.

Oh, Lord. How I wish—

The coach lurched, skidding a foot or two.

"Lawk-a-daisy!" That was Beefy Thigh's wife. "We're gonna end in a ditch, Humphrey. See if we don't."

Beefy Thigh—or, rather, Humphrey—put his large hand over his wife's. "Don't fret, Muriel. The coachman knows what he's about."

Caro heard the quaver in his voice if Muriel didn't.

He turned to the somberly garbed man sitting directly across from him. "Ain't that right, Reverend?"

The clergyman looked up from his book—a Bible—opened his mouth and—

Was interrupted by an expressive snort from Pasty Face, who then had to make quick use of his handkerchief.

"I'm getting off at the Crow," Pasty Face said. "*I* don't want to break me neck."

Muriel sucked in her breath and then moaned.

The clergyman gave Pasty Face a reproachful look before smiling at Muriel. "Now, now, madam. Remember what the Good Book says." He patted his Bible. "'Be not afraid, neither be thou dismayed, for the Lord thy God is with thee whithersoever thou goest.' Joshua chapter one, verse nine."

Pasty Face snorted again, this time with handkerchief at the ready. "The Lord can go with me into the Crow."

The reverend scowled. "Sir, you border on blasphemy."

Pasty Face shrugged. "As long as I border on a nice, warm fire with a pint in me hand, I'm good."

Caro's thoughts veered off on a new path. The Crow wasn't London, but it *was* on the main coaching route and closer to Little Puddledon. If she could persuade its tavern keeper to serve Widow's Brew, word would spread. She might find a larger market that wasn't *too* large.

Should I get off and talk to—

No. Mr. London Harris's wandering hands—it was truly shocking how different two brothers could be—and the Weasel's wandering eyes had reminded her of the dangers a woman traveling alone faced. If she stopped, chances were good she'd be stranded at the Crow for several days. Even if the tavern keeper himself wasn't a lecher, she was certain to encounter more than one drunken, lascivious lout on the premises. Her poor pocketknife would be worn to a nub.

Not to mention coaching inns were terribly expensive, and she was short of coin. *And* she was needed back at the Home.

Muriel was still whinging. "Humphrey, maybe we should get off, too."

"But yer sister is expecting us, dumpling. She'll worry. Ye know that."

"Y-yes. But what if we *do* end in a ditch? What if we freeze to death? What then?"

"Zounds, woman! It's just a little snow." The Weasel finally stopped staring at Caro long enough to scowl at Muriel.

Caro looked out the window again to confirm that the "little" snow had now given the stone walls running along the road white caps.

Pasty Face snorted again and dabbed his nose. "Mebbie it's not much if yer a polar bear. I don't have a big white fur coat. I'm gettin' off at the Crow and sittin' in front of the fire, warmin' me coattails."

That *did* sound appealing.

"What is your opinion, madam?" The clergyman suddenly turned to Caro. "Do you think the weather too, er, *uncertain* for further travel, especially for delicate females such as yourself and this lady?" He nodded toward Muriel.

Caro blinked at him. *Delicate* female? She'd wager she could work longer, harder hours than this sermon-writing, Bible-toting parson. And there was nothing uncertain about the weather. But she couldn't afford—on any level— to take shelter at the inn, and if Muriel and Humphrey got off, the Weasel was certain to move over and sit next to her. Ugh!

"I'm not getting off the coach," she said as they rattled into the innyard.

"Well, *I* am," Pasty Face said. And, true to his word, as soon as the coachman unlatched the door and pulled down the steps, Pasty Face was out and heading toward the Crow's light and warmth and liquid refreshment.

Caro looked longingly after him, tugging her cloak's collar closer in a vain attempt to keep out the cold. She'd like to be sitting by the fire—

Remember the lubricious louts.

"If ye need to use the privy, do it straightaway," the coachman said. "We're not stopping long. I want to make it to Marbridge afore the weather worsens."

"Do ye think it's safe to go on?" Humphrey asked, Muriel gripping his arm and peering anxiously around him.

Caro held her breath.

The coachman nodded. "Aye. The road's good—straight and flat—and the horses are steady. The snow's not too bad . . . yet. But the sooner we leave, the better." He scowled at them. "So be quick about yer business. I won't wait fer ye if ye dillydally."

The coachman stepped back, and Humphrey, the clergyman, and the Weasel clambered out, the Weasel managing to "accidentally" brush his hand over Caro's knees as he passed.

"Pardon me," he said, sending a noxious cloud of stale breath her way.

She forced a smile, fingering the knife in her pocket, and decided she could forego the jakes. Braving the cold and, more to the point, the filth of the public outhouse wasn't appealing, but she especially didn't want to risk being caught alone by the Weasel or to open herself to the possibility that he could rearrange the seating while she was gone.

Muriel must have come to the same conclusion, at least about the outhouse.

"So, yer traveling alone, are ye?" she asked after the men left, eyeing Caro with a nervous mixture of curiosity and suspicion.

Mostly suspicion.

Caro was tempted to say, no, she had an imaginary companion by her side, but bit her tongue and forced a smile instead. She was a good saleswoman and selling herself— that is, her skill and dependability as a businesswoman— was often part of convincing skeptical tavern keepers to take a chance on her ale. She'd use those skills now. "Yes. I'm going home for the holidays."

No need to clarify that home meant the Benevolent Home for the Maintenance and Support of Spinsters,

Widows, and Abandoned Women and their Unfortunate Children.

"Did I hear you're visiting your sister?" She'd also found that throwing the conversational ball back to her inquisitor usually worked very well—as it did this time.

Muriel's face lit up, and she rattled on about her sisters Mildred, Mirabel, and Miranda, who all lived just outside Marbridge, and how she went back every Christmas to celebrate the holiday with them.

Caro nodded and made encouraging noises to keep the woman talking, counting the seconds until the men returned and they could resume their journey. One of the things she most hated about Christmas was the way people dug up their old, moldering memories and dressed them up with garlands and candles and nostalgia. The past was best left in the past. Fortunately, most of the women at the Home agreed with her.

Humphrey and the Weasel returned then. Humphrey climbed right in, but the Weasel loitered in the cold.

Oh, Lord. He's going to try to take Pasty Face's place.

Caro gripped her knife, ready to pull it out the moment any part of the Weasel touched her. If he thought she'd bear his insults politely, he was going to be very *painfully* surprised.

Humphrey turned into an unwitting ally. "What are ye doing out there, sir?" he said. "Get in afore ye freeze yer arse off."

The Weasel shrugged—or perhaps shivered. "I'll g-get in when the reverend comes back. No need to s-sit longer than I have to."

"But ye'll catch yer death out there," Muriel said.

"Naw. I'm used to the c-c-cold."

That was definitely a shiver. In any event, the coachman appeared just then to put an end to the Weasel's plot.

"Get in, man." His voice had an edge to it. "We need to be off at once. The coachy coming from Marbridge said the roads are getting worse."

"But what about the reverend? He's not back from the privy."

The coachman put his hands on his hips. "Are ye wanting to keep him company? Because ye shall if ye don't get in the coach *right now*."

There was a momentary standoff, and then the Weasel grumbled and climbed in. He leered at Caro the moment his rump hit the other bench.

"Why don't ye join me?" He patted the spot next to him.

"Good idea," Humphrey said.

"Do move over, dear." That was Muriel. "We'll all be more comfortable."

Ha! Caro would be vastly more *un*comfortable—as everyone else would, too, after she stabbed the Weasel in the leg.

She was saved from violence by the clergyman, who came stumbling up at that moment, still buttoning his fly.

"Just in time, Reverend," the coachman said. "We were going to have to leave ye here."

"Sorry." The clergyman hoisted himself in, forcing the Weasel to slide over. "Balky bowels."

That was more information than Caro wished to have, but she welcomed anything that forced the Weasel away from her.

The coachman started to put up the steps—

"Wait! Oh, please, sir. Wait."

He stopped and looked—they all looked—toward the

inn. A young woman, carrying a small satchel, and a young boy, about six or seven years old, half ran/half slid over the snow-slick cobblestones.

"Sir," the woman said, her voice tight and breathless, "I've a ticket for an inside seat. They said I might have a place here, since the gentleman got off."

The coachman frowned, hesitating.

"There's only one seat and two of you," the clergyman said. "You won't fit. Go back to the inn."

Now *there* was Christian charity.

The coachman scowled. "Now see here, Reverend. This is my coach. I'll be the one making the decision about who rides and who doesn't."

"I'm the one who has to sit next to them."

The coachman's scowl deepened. "Unless ye wish to get out and stay at the Crow—or take a seat on the roof."

"Have her sit on the outside if she needs to travel."

The Weasel and Humphrey began to grumble as well. The matter was clearly getting out of hand.

Caro spoke up when Muriel didn't. "A child can't sit on the roof."

The man of the cloth—and the balky bowels—shrugged.

The young woman didn't waste her time with the clergyman. She addressed the coachman again. "Please, sir. We need to get to Marbridge afore Christmas, and yers might be the last coach to get through."

The coachman looked at her a moment longer and then let out a long breath. "Very well. But the boy will have to sit on yer lap. No crowding the reverend."

The woman nodded and handed the coachman her satchel as the boy scrambled in. Then she followed awkwardly. Her right arm must be injured. It was hidden under her cloak as if in a sling, a lump that she made no attempt to use.

Caro expected the reverend to inch over toward the Weasel; there wasn't much room, but the boy was as thin as a reed. Instead, the fellow gave the woman a sidelong glare and opened his Bible, not budging a hair's breadth.

The atmosphere in the coach dropped to rival the temperature outside—well, that wasn't so surprising as the coachman was still holding the door open, waiting for things to sort themselves out. But it wasn't just the frigid air causing the chill. It was also the icy stares Humphrey and the Weasel gave the newcomers. Muriel sniffed and made a show of pulling her skirts back, not that she was close enough to risk being touched by either of them.

Caro looked back at the woman. The other people in the coach weren't members of the *ton*—far from it. Their clothing wasn't any grander, though the woman's and the boy's were visibly threadbare. But what emboldened her companions to treat the poor mother with disdain must be the air of defeat and desperation that clung to her.

It was the same air that clung to so many women when they first arrived at the Benevolent Home.

The boy pressed against his mother and, once she'd managed to sit, climbed onto her left leg, careful not to jostle her injured arm. She gave him a small smile that did nothing to dispel the dark shadows under her eyes or the tightness of her expression and hugged him close.

Much to Caro's surprise, she felt a flood of compassion.

She frowned. Jo was the tenderhearted one, not her. Caro was the Home's clear-eyed, practical businesswoman. A tender heart could be a liability when striving to make a tidy profit.

The coachman heaved a relieved sigh. "All right, then. We'll be on our way." He started to close the door.

"Wait!"

This time it was two loud, boisterous young men, swathed in multi-caped greatcoats, who pounded across the innyard, skidding to a stop just before they knocked the coachman over. One had to use the coach to break his forward progress, setting the vehicle to rocking.

"Are you going to Marbridge?" the one not leaning on the coach asked, his words slurring slightly.

"Aye." The edge was back in the coachman's voice.

"Splendid," the other man said. "That's where we're going." He reached for the door.

Surely the coachman wasn't going to evict one of them—well, *two* of them? The mother threw Caro a panicked look. The woman guessed, likely correctly, that she would be the first one thrown out. Caro was afraid she'd be the second.

Just let them try.

Fortunately, Caro didn't have to defend her seat. The coachman stood his ground—and held onto the door, keeping it from opening any farther.

"As ye can see, I'm full inside. If ye want to leave today, ye'll have to ride atop."

The men shrugged.

"All right. We've got coats"—the first man lifted a bottle—"and brandy to keep us warm."

Muriel gasped. "Humphrey, say something," she hissed as the coachman finally closed the door. "It can't be safe to have those drunken bucks riding with us."

"Likely they're the ones at risk," the Weasel offered. The coach swayed as the men hauled themselves up to their seats. "Though if they're drunk enough, they won't feel it when they fall off and hit the ground."

Muriel stared at the Weasel, and then elbowed her husband. "*Say* something," she hissed again.

It was too late. The coach had lurched into motion.

And the young mother's cloak started wailing.

The reverend jerked his eyes off his Bible, a mixture of alarm and disbelief in his expression, and scowled down at her. "Good Lord, woman, what have you got there?"

"That's my sister, Grace," the boy said, as his mother uncovered a very small, very young infant. "She's a baby."

The clergyman snorted all too expressively—he obviously thought "Grace" a vastly inappropriate name—and transferred his scowl to the boy, who bravely raised his chin and held his ground unflinching.

Meanwhile, the mother was trying to soothe the baby in the limited space she had. "Shh." She jiggled the infant. "Shh."

"Grace is only four weeks old." The boy's young, clear voice dropped each word like a pebble into a still pond, sending ripples of consternation through the coach's other occupants.

The mother, clearly all too aware of the disapproval building in the confined space, leaned closer to whisper to her son. "Hush, Edward. Don't bother the people." Then she shifted her arm with the infant closer to the stagecoach wall, trying to make more room for her son on her lap.

The poor woman. It was bad enough she was traveling in a snowstorm, on the public stagecoach, with a young boy and a baby only a month after giving birth. She didn't need to feel alone and judged by everyone around her.

"Here, let me hold the baby for you," Caro said.

The woman hesitated, clearly nervous about entrusting her precious child to a stranger.

"Don't worry. I've lots of experience."

Caro was the fifth of eleven children and the only daughter. Her poor, beleaguered mother had put her to work tending her siblings as soon as she was old enough to rock a cradle. And then when she was seventeen, she'd gone to London to work as a nursemaid—

No. She shoved those memories back into the box she'd made for them and slammed down the lid.

Baby Grace let out a thin wail, and her mother gave in.

"Thank you," she said softly. She leaned forward, and Caro scooped the small bundle out of the crook of her arm. "Careful with her head."

Caro nodded, wondering again what would force a new mother out into the snow just before Christmas.

Ah. The moment she felt the baby's warm weight—the mite couldn't be even as heavy as a tankard of ale—Caro's hands remembered how to hold such a young child. She settled the baby against her shoulder, patting her and humming, feeling a surprising calm flow through her as she soothed little Grace back to sleep.

Women needed to band together to support one another. That's what they did—most of the time—at the Home. Caro looked at Grace's mother. Did she need the Home's refuge? Caro could—

No, unfortunately she wouldn't. Space at the Home was very limited. There wasn't room for two separate dormitories for boys and girls. Jo had made the decision early on that they couldn't take in mothers with sons past babyhood.

If there were only Grace, the Home's doors would be wide open. But there was also Edward.

An uneasy silence had settled over the coach—no one wanted to be trapped in a small space with a howling infant—but once it became clear Grace was going back to sleep, everyone seemed to relax. The clergyman went back to his Bible; the Weasel and Muriel looked out the window on their side of the coach. Humphrey—perhaps afraid he'd jostle the baby awake—slid his bulk away from Caro as best he could. The young mother and her son fell into what must have been an exhausted sleep.

Caro shifted the baby slightly, patting her bottom when she whimpered. The snow was still coming down, but so far, the coach was moving along, thank God. Perhaps she *would* reach Marbridge in time to catch the one coach that would take her on to Little Puddledon.

And then Grace started making little snuffling, hungry noises.

Oh, blast. How could Grace's mother nurse a baby in this cramped carriage of disapproving men? But there was no arguing with a hungry infant. Grace was going to start screaming soon unless . . .

Perhaps a trick Caro had learned tending her siblings could buy them some time.

She gave Grace the knuckle of her pinkie to suck on.

Ah. She'd forgotten how surprisingly strong and rhythmic an infant's sucking was. The sensation made her feel . . . odd. Almost as if she wished she had a baby herself.

Nonsense! What she really wished for was a miracle, that she could keep Grace content until they got to Marb—

"*Tallyho!*"

The coach suddenly picked up speed amid a storm of shouting and cursing from the roof.

Oh, hell. The drunken bucks must have taken the coachman's reins.

Caro tightened her hold on the baby.

"Humphrey!" Muriel screamed. "Make them stop."

"Good God, woman, how am I supposed to do that? I'm stuck in here with you."

The Weasel was swearing quite creatively, and even the reverend addressed the Lord in less than polite terms as they careened down the road.

"Wh-what's happening, Mama?"

The young mother hugged her son. "I think the men riding on top have taken over driving the c-coach, Edward." She tried to speak calmly, but Caro heard the slight quaver in her voice.

Muriel didn't even try to mask her alarm. She grabbed her husband's arm and screeched, "Lord help us, we *are* going to end in a ditch!"

"H-hold on to me, Edward." The mother's eyes, tight with desperation and entreaty, went to Caro.

"I've got Grace." Caro gripped the baby as securely as she could and braced herself against the coach wall. She was not much for praying—she'd found relying on herself rather than a distant and inscrutable Deity usually served her best—but nevertheless she sent a quick, sincere entreaty to the Almighty in case He was listening.

She'd no sooner formed a mental "amen" than the coach started to slide. Everyone except Caro and, blessedly, the baby screamed. Caro was too busy trying to curl her body around Grace's. If the coach landed on its side, it was going to be very hard to keep the baby safe.

The slide seemed to go on forever, and then finally there was a jolt, a shudder, and the coach stopped, still upright.

And then the floor dropped a foot, eliciting more screams and curses.

"What was that, Humphrey?" Muriel squeaked.

The Weasel answered instead. "Feels like the axle broke. Looks like we ain't getting to Marbridge today." He glanced at the clergyman and nodded at his Bible. "But at least we needn't be afeard since the Lord is traveling with us, eh, Reverend?"

The clergyman scowled. "You are offensive, sirrah!"

"I'm cold and hungry, and now I'm stranded in the snow who knows where." The Weasel shrugged. "I'll probably freeze to death, so I suppose I can lodge a complaint with yer God all too soon."

Muriel shrieked.

"Hold yer tongue," Humphrey told the Weasel sharply.

Yes, indeed. Didn't any of these idiots give a thought to the boy? He was looking up at his mother, eyes wide, face pale. "We'll be all right, won't we, Mama?"

His mother forced a tense smile and smoothed back his hair. "Aye, Edward. As long as we're together, we'll be all r-right."

That was all very well, but the truth was they had to get out of this cold, particularly poor little Grace. Sitting around moaning and arguing wasn't going to accomplish that goal. Someone needed to have a word with the coachman.

Obviously, that someone was Caro.

Caro pushed the carriage door open and looked out. The axle had indeed broken; the ground was well within reach. "I'll be right back," she told Grace's mother. "Don't worry. I'll keep Grace warm."

The mother, holding her son tightly and looking wan and defeated, nodded weakly.

Caro climbed out, pulled her cloak snugly around the baby, and approached the coachman, who was trying, along with the two bucks, to unhitch the horses. They were not having a great deal of success.

"Sir, I need a word with you, if you please."

The coachman glanced at her and then went back to his work. "Get back inside the coach, madam. One of these men"—he glared at the miscreants who had put them in this position—"is going to ride on to the next stop and bring back help as soon as we can get a horse free."

She eyed the blackguards. At least the accident seemed to have sobered them up. "And how long will that take?"

The coachman scowled at her. "Likely an hour or more."

She shook her head. "Too long. It's far too cold for the children to wait here. The baby, especially, needs to get inside by a fire immediately."

The coachman's brows shot up. "*Baby?!* Where the bloody—that is, pardon me language, madam, but . . . a baby?"

"She was under her mother's cloak when they got on at the Crow. She's only a few weeks old and needs to be warm by a fire immediately."

The coachman looked annoyed—and desperate and helpless, too. "How are ye going to manage that, may I ask? These idiots can't sprout wings and fly, ye know."

"I know that." What *was* she going to do?

She looked around at the snow-covered landscape, the fat flakes falling thickly around her. There was a break in the stone wall nearby and what appeared to be a snow-covered drive leading to a faint glow. . . .

"What's that light over there?"

The coachman looked in the direction she was pointing. "Oh, Lord Devil must be at home. Ye don't want to go anywhere near him."

Lord Devil?

An odd jolt of nervous excitement shot through her, a mix of dread and eagerness akin to what she felt when she was getting ready to meet a tavern keeper for the first time in the hopes of selling him some Widow's Brew. *That must be Nick. . . .*

No! What was the matter with her? She'd thought herself cured of any sort of romantic foolishness. She'd not seen Nick—if this was indeed Nick—for . . . She did a rapid calculation.

For seventeen years. She'd been thirteen, a naïve child, the last time he'd come home from school with her brother Henry. Her feelings for Nick then had been puppy love. He'd been the only one of her brothers' friends who hadn't ignored or teased her.

That was all this odd feeling was—a faint echo of her old hero worship.

"You mean the new Lord Oakland?"

"Aye."

She wasn't afraid of Nick. "Well, if he has a warm fire, I most certainly do wish to go near him. Even a devil wouldn't turn away a tiny baby." And certainly not the Nick she'd known.

It's been seventeen years. People change.

Yes, they did. But Nick couldn't have changed *that* much.

"I wouldn't be so certain," the coachman said, but she'd already turned away. There was no time to waste.

She stuck her head back into the coach briefly to address Grace's mother. "There's a house nearby. I'm taking Grace there and will send back help."

The woman frowned but must have concluded that the

sooner Grace got inside, the better, because she nodded. "All right. Do hurry."

"And close the blasted door," the clergyman snapped. "Do you want us all to freeze?"

Muriel moaned, Humphrey glared at her, and even the Weasel's look was annoyed rather than amorous.

"Right." Caro pushed the door closed and started through the snow toward the house.

Connect with Us

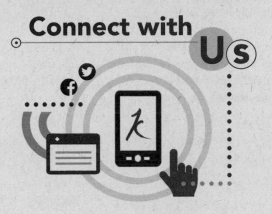

Visit us online at
KensingtonBooks.com
to read more from your favorite authors, see books
by series, view reading group guides, and more.

for sneak peeks, chances to win books and prize packs,
and to share your thoughts with other readers.

facebook.com/kensingtonpublishing
twitter.com/kensingtonbooks

Tell us what you think!

To share your thoughts, submit a review,
or sign up for our eNewsletters, please visit:
KensingtonBooks.com/TellUs.

Books by Bestselling Author
Fern Michaels